AND HE WAS
A STRANGER . . .

not of any of the tribes of the far North. And even across so great a distance, Gen-Karn could see his dark eyes greenly glittering.

Behind the stranger another man appeared. He, with the help of two others, was dragging a large, heavy burden from a weary pony. When they had got it down, they cut away the ropes binding it and tore off the concealing pelts, and a cry of wonderment rose from the crowds. For beneath the pelts was an enormous head still stained with flowing black blood.

It was the severed head of an enormous Darkbeast.

"Alone he hunted it!" cried Kuln-Holn above the hubbub. "And alone slew it! Only I watched, and I did no more than help him bear it up the cliffs. With fire he blinded it, with fire slew it! Three score strokes it took to sever it from the body!

"Men of the far North, behold the man who has done it, the man sent us from the gods—Behold, Ara-Karn!"

In the awed silence which followed, the stranger spoke. And his low tones somehow were heard even above the roar of the flames.

He said, "Wherever he is, let Gen-Karn step forward. I challenge him the right to lead the tribes."

THE
FORMER KING

Canto One of
The Doom-Quest of Ara-Karn
a dark romance

by

ADAM CORBY

A TIMESCAPE BOOK
PUBLISHED BY POCKET BOOKS NEW YORK

Another *Original* publication of TIMESCAPE BOOKS

A Timescape Book published by
POCKET BOOKS, a Simon & Schuster division of
GULF & WESTERN CORPORATION
1230 Avenue of the Americas, New York, N.Y. 10020

ISBN: 0-671-41770-3

First Timescape Books printing September, 1981

10 9 8 7 6 5 4 3 2 1

POCKET and colophon are trademarks of Simon & Schuster.

Use of the TIMESCAPE trademark under exclusive license
from trademark owner.

Printed in the U.S.A.

THE
FORMER KING

I

And through the skies rides God, never stopping, ever roving in His chariot of Jade, called by some, Moon. He rises out of the Ocean of the Dead, soaring ever higher, until He begins to fall. He falls toward the dark horizon, swifter and brighter coming to His home; and in the end He passes once more into blackness, driven ever by the darkness of His Desire.

And He had laughed, and would have destroyed the first man and woman, but that His hand was stayed. Thereat He grew surly and jealous, and went to the darkness at the other end of the world, there to build a Fortress of Black Rock.

II

And above all lands shines Goddess. She never moves, but sits in Her throne of Golden Fire, called by some, Sun. And that is the reason men have light eternal and changeless, to grow their crops and warm their hearts.

And She had stayed His hand, because She loved the first man and woman. And She went to build Her throne of Golden Fire that men might have light and warmth.

III

Once the gods dwelt not in the skies, but laughingly upon the lands of earth in the forms of mortal man and maid. *There were no folk then, and the lands were undivided and lush with ripening fruit. And then they held contest: and God created man, and Goddess woman, each after His or Her own form. And each looked on the creation of the other and desired it, though neither would admit the creation of the other was as good, for pride's sake.*

So they separated. But still does He desire Her, and so goes round in His chariot of Jade. Yet She loves men and will not go. And then is He consumed utterly by the darkness of His Desire, and invades the throne of Golden Fire, and ravishes Her. Then does Darkness fall across the lands of men. And She weakens and might go, surrendering pride for passion's sake. And that is the moment most needful for prayers from Her worshipers on the wide bright shores to redeem Her and call Her back to us.

And woe to all men, if ever She should not heed!

—What they believe in
the lands where men dwell.

CHAPTER ONE

The Chief's Refusal

They were a simple and a warlike people. Also they were proud, for were they not one of the original eighteen tribes? And were they not, as well, the largest tribe yet independent of Gen-Karn, the Warlord of the far North?

It was in the far North that they dwelled, on the shore of the Sea of Goddess, or, as some call it, the Ocean of the Dead; and Her throne of Golden Fire stood five fists above the bright horizon. Related clans had their dwelling-places farther up and down the coastline, but the original village was in the best of places, for it was on a small hill sheltered by the coolness of the forest and overlooking a deep bay of clear blue waters abundant in shellfish.

And the fishermen sailed in their small boats out of the deep bay and cast their nets into the clear blue waters; and the hunters slipped silently into the shadowed depths of the forests and laid their traps. The women grew corn and grain and herbs and vegetables in the small fields, and the men did some killing for food. And traders visited the village, from the civilized lands of the faraway South, from Gerso beyond the Pass of Gerso in the mountains called the Spine of Civilization, or from Arpane on the Sea, the only city on the Ocean of the Dead. The traders came bearing fine-woven garments, tools and implements, blades that would not soon shatter or dull; and they departed with some gold dust or nuggets of silver, but mostly with the vivid green bandar pelts, much prized in the faraway South.

And the women of the tribe wove brightly colored coarse tunics, and the men did some killing to get goods. But mostly the men only killed for sport, or in blood-feud, or tribal raids. One thing that could be said well of them was that there was little blood shed within the tribe. Gundoen the chief saw to that. If men were angry, he would have them wrestle, a skill the chief dearly loved. And if their anger was too great to be appeased by wrestling, Gundoen would send them outside the tribe. It was a saying of his: "If you are so angry that only blood will satisfy you, go and kill a Korla. Then your anger will be put to good use."

The Korlas were their neighbors and hereditary enemies. They dwelt deeper into the forest, close to where the bandar were thickest in the Forest of Bandar. A mean and petty-hearted tribe were they, with little honor among them; moreover, they were the dogs of Gen-Karn, and annoyed Gundoen's people on the Warlord's orders. The Korlas claimed for themselves all the lands on which the bandar roamed, but that was a lie. Bandar were sport for all the tribes, especially when the merchants from the faraway South would trade so much for their pelts.

When the warriors made war upon the Korlas, and that was more often now than before, they took the Korlas' bandar pelts and their weapons. Sometimes they burned their huts, and sometimes they took their women, but that was rare. There is no profit in burning another man's hut, and Korla women were never renowned for their beauty.

And it was a little too hot in the summer, and far too cold in the winter, and the rains did seem to come at the wrong times for the crops. Yet, all in all, it was a good life for the people of Gundoen's tribe, if a little too contented. But then the stranger came among them, and their lives were never the same again. Even before the dark man came there were omens of his power. But at the time none recognized them for what they were, except perhaps for Kuln-Holn the Pious One.

Kuln-Holn the Pious One came up from the sea to chief Gundoen's hall, which was the largest hall in the village, built of stout logs thicker than a woman's hips, cemented together with mud and wattle. Before Gundoen sat here, there had been In-Hall, Gundoen's uncle, and before In-Hall there had been Gornoth, Ru-Anth, and Oro-Born. And before them all had been the builder of the hall, the great chief Tont-Ornoth. He had come from the last stand of the tribes, from Urnostardil on the Edge of Darkness, and he had settled the tribe here, and built the hall. Other structures had been burned, broken, and torn down, but not the hall of Tont-Ornoth.

Here entered Kuln-Holn, blinking his eyes against the smoky, acrid darkness and feeling very out of place. Rarely before in his life had Kuln-Holn been inside the chief's hall, and never during a feast. He was a simple fellow, neither a great hunter or warrior, and the chief disliked him and scorned all his preachings. Now he tried to pierce the darkness with his eyes, uncertain of himself in the din of the feasting.

Upon the walls of the hall were the trophies left by all the past chiefs in commemoration of their lives and victories. Here was the battle-shield of a Korla chief, taken in combat by Gornoth; and there was the great sharp tooth of a Darkbeast slain by Oro-Born in a hunt still sung of. And above them all was the hilt of Tont-Ornoth's sword, which had tasted the blood of Elna the god, and first Emperor of the South. And to mark Gundoen's reign there were hung the bones of great foreign champions, strong-boned, mighty-chested men, the bones broken, the ribs stove in by Gundoen's arms in wrestling match. There was no wrestler greater than Gundoen Strong-In-Girth in all the far North.

Below the trophies, around the great central cook-fires, were set the long tables of polished wood and the carved chairs of honor at the end of long benches. The benches were filled with men, the greatest warriors and hunters of the tribe; the tables were covered with wooden plates, bowls, and much food; and on the grass-strewn earthen floor the dogs gnawed at bones. For it was the time of the second meal; and the welcoming-feast of those who sat in the chairs of honor: merchants from the civilized lands of the faraway South, dining so daintily and taking care to keep their scented robes and perfumed coiffures in immaculate array. They were here because the spring was newly come, and soon would be the time of the great Hunt for bandar.

To serve them all came and went the concubines and

handmaidens of the chief, seven wenches of great beauty and skill. And the loveliest of these, and highest favored, was Alli, the chief's favorite. Kuln-Holn gathered his courage and touched one of the serving wenches on the shoulder. And when she turned he saw that it was Alli herself.

She looked into his face with her dark slanting eyes and smiled boldly. "Yes, Pious One?" she asked. He blushed under that gaze, but kept his head about him, and told her that he had come to see the chief, adding that it was important. Her smile broadened, and she went up to the carved high seat where sat the chief, her figure growing dim as it receded behind the walls of smoke billowing from the cook-fires, which the opened wooden vents did little to dispel. She bent down over Gundoen the chief's shoulder and said something to him, and gestured at Kuln-Holn. Kuln-Holn could see the chief look up and fix his eye in his direction. Then Alli added something else, and the chief laughed, a rumbling, powerful laugh.

He waved Kuln-Holn forward. "Come, come, O Pious One!" he shouted. "You visit my hall too little! What news of doom or visions in the clouds do you bring us now?"

Kuln-Holn the Pious One then stepped up amidst the laughter and faced the chief. Gundoen was not a tall man, but he was half as broad as he was tall. His body was as hard and solid as the ancient logs of his hall, and his arms were corded and scarred like rough-barked branches; his short bowed thighs were knotted like great roots gripping at the earth. The chief wore his sandy hair and beard short, so as to afford no hold in a wrestling match. Below the hair were the broad face like roughened leather, the twisted broken nose, and the eyes bright with humorous mockery as they viewed Kuln-Holn.

"Come, come," the chief shouted over the laughter and the barking of the dogs. "Speak up, man: have you lost your tongue?"

Kuln-Holn drew deep breath and spoke—rather loudly, he thought; but his voice was like the peeping of a mouse after the rumble of Gundoen's.

"O Chief," said Kuln-Holn. "It is important that I speak to you. We need you. Oron is ready."

Gundoen lifted his bowl of ale in one callused hand and quaffed a brimming mouthful of the brown ale, letting the foam trickle down his lips and short beard to drip upon his great chest. "Well, what is that to me?" he mocked through the mouthful. "He was never any friend of mine."

Truly, thought Kuln-Holn, he has had too much of ale, else he would understand my words. Aloud he tried to explain, speaking slowly so that the chief in his drunkenness would comprehend. "Chief Gundoen, Oron is ready. I have prepared his body and filled his barge with all that is needful. He is ready to set forth on his final voyage to the Happy Shores. We only wait upon you, the chief of the tribe. It is your duty to see him off."

Gundoen frowned and set the bowl down loudly. "Duty! Who tells Gundoen his duty?"

"But, chief, Oron is ready. You must see him off to the Happy Shores—"

"Be silent, Little Prophet!" roared the chief. "And speak no more of the Happy Shores, lest I send you off with Oron!" Across the hall the two civilized merchants smiled behind their soft hands. The chief rose from the carved seat, gripping the great sword slung over the chair-arm and brandishing it with one thick hand.

"Gundoen, if we do not send the dead to peace, they will return to give us war."

Kuln-Holn said no more than an old saying of the North; but Gundoen swore, stepped over the low table, knocking off plates and bowls, and thrust the naked blade against Kuln-Holn's bare throat. The Pious One could feel the sharpness of the point and the heat of drawn blood.

"Now"—the chief grinned drunkenly—"say it again."

Kuln-Holn looked fearfully about the hall for support. Never before had the chief refused his sacred duty of seeing off the dead. Yet there was no voice raised in support of Kuln-Holn. The merchants had lost their smiles now. The hunters were angry, and frowned and grumbled, because this blasphemy of the chief was a luckless, ill-omened thing; but they feared the chief's wrath more than any ill-luck. Their eyes played over the bones of the seventeen foreign champions that hung about the hall, crushed and broken; and though they murmured, they did so only to their bowls.

"Truly, Gundoen, it is but your duty Kuln-Holn asks."

It was Hertha-Toll who spoke, Gundoen's wife, whom some called the Wise and others the Sorrowful. She stood midway down the tables on Kuln-Holn's right, the wis-

dom of her eyes belying the stoutness of her middle-aged
body.

She fixed her deep eyes upon Gundoen until he was
forced to look away. There was no woman in all the North
wiser than Hertha-Toll; she was visited with the Sight, and
could cast a luckless fear into the strongest-hearted of
men.

"It is but your duty, Gundoen," she repeated.

But the chief snorted, "To the Darklands with your
duty! Do I rule here, or do you? Go back to your cooking and weaving, woman, and leave the rule of the tribe to
me." But he did take back the sharp-pointed sword and
return to his seat.

Hertha-Toll shrugged and bowed low. "As you wish,
lord," she uttered with dignity, and left the hall.

"Bravely spoken, lord," said one of the foreign merchants, his ringed fingers playing with his smoothly shaved
chin. "I can see that you are above these petty supersti-
tions, as indeed befits a great lord. In the South these
matters are not thought much of. The Empress Allissál
herself, when her revered parents died some ten-and-five
years ago, did no more than entomb them in structures
resembling death-barges. I have visited the great city and
seen them myself. No one bothers actually to set his dead
out upon the sea anymore, except for a few fanatics like
this man here. The playwright Tolpomenes wrote a very
witty play about such people some years ago. It really is
quite amusing."

"Oh?" scowled Gundoen. "And who are you to laugh at
the dead, Southron? I see nothing funny about it— But
then I suppose I am only an ignorant barbarian, eh? Maybe
if we killed you and imprisoned your body under a stone in
the ground we would see the humor better. I've half a
mind to try it. Who will join in?"

At this sally the people's frowns turned again to laughter,
and cries of encouragement rose from all sides. The merchants, blanching even paler than usual, rose from the
carved chairs and bowed.

"Your lordship," said the other, "we beg pardon. My
fellow meant no harm. He only—That is, if you will grant
us leave, we must be—well—going."

And they slunk from the hall amidst loud peals of jeer-
ing laughter. One man thought to throw a half-eaten meat
pie after them; it hit the rear merchant squarely on the

shoulder, leaving a dark stain on his elegant robes. At this the laughter grew even louder.

Kuln-Holn the Pious One waited, shifting his weight from one foot to the other. He did not know whether to stay and ask the chief once again or leave. To come back again when Gundoen might be in a better mood was impossible: Oron was ready now.

The laughter at last died down, and the normal sounds of jests, clanking plates, and barking dogs resumed. But Kuln-Holn was completely ignored. He stood in the middle of the hall, about to try to speak again, when a hand touched him in the back.

"Still here?" Alli laughingly asked. "If you want to eat something, why do you not sit down? Even the most pious can have empty bellies."

He shook his head and left the smoky hall. Behind him followed the rumbling sounds of the chief's laughter. Coming again into the light of Goddess he blinked, half-blinded by the brilliance. "Truly, Gundoen meant nothing," he muttered to the shimmering orb. "It was the foreign merchants, and the ale, and nothing more."

But as he walked down the steep sandy path to the bay, Goddess looked down on him from Her throne of Golden Fire, and there was a tension in the air, a great abiding anger in Her look. And Kuln-Holn, who had known the power of Her anger once before, was afraid.

CHAPTER TWO

Sea Storm

He went down to the bay and walked among the fishing boats. They were pulled up onto the sandy beach now, because it was the time of the second meal. He came to two small boats lying alone, far away from the others.

One boat was a small fishing boat, much battered and worn; but the other was new, and low and broad, and little longer than the height of a man. Draped and painted black was the low barge, with the visage of Goddess carved crudely upon its prow. Inside it were piled weapons and accoutrements, drinking-bowls, clothes, and casks of food and drink. Among these was a figure wrapped in linen, with only the face showing in the stern. Such was the corpse of Oron, and the death-barge of Oron.

Kuln-Holn sighed, and readied the two boats. No one else had come to see Oron off, because the man had left no kin and had been a poor and unpopular fellow. But the chief should have been there, because he was the chief.

Kuln-Holn shoved the boats into the lapping shallows and climbed into the fishing boat, lifting the small sail. Alone he sailed past the long shelving arms of green land and out into the Ocean of the Dead with the death-barge of Oron trailing behind.

To the South, five fists above the bright horizon, Goddess sat in Her throne of Golden Fire. And below Her stretched the vast unending Desert, scorched and baked from the heat of Her throne. There in the desert no plants grew, no streams flowed, and no clouds passed overhead. There were only the sands, dancing in whirlwinds, maddened by the nearness of Her awful beauty.

And beyond the desert, round the other side of the circling globe, were the lush Happy Shores, lands always green with ripening fruit; and thither the dead were guided by Goddess through the turbulent northern Ocean of the Dead in their small black death-barges. And She guided them to those lands they deserved, and when the barges struck the shore the spirits awakened, and rose, and stepped forth to new lives. And there they lived, like young chieftains and hunt-maidens in joy.

Some thousands out into the ocean the green lip of land fell away below the dark horizon, and Kuln-Holn sailed alone in the bowl of swelling waters. Soon he encountered the currents of the Dead, which lead up to the farther North, and thus circle around to the Happy Shores. Here Kuln-Holn slipped the line, holding to the tiller; and in no more than the space of seven heartbeats the death-barge had nosed about and was sliding away on the current.

"Farewell, Oron," called the Pious One. "May She guide your voyage well, and may you find the blessed life beyond the Happy Shores. And may no barge-robbers find you; and may She not turn you back upon the shores of the living to curse your death; and may She hear my words!" For sometimes robbers stole the dead spirit's belongings; and other times She would turn the barge back in anger at the man's crimes in life; and then the spirit would leap forth upon the shores of the living. And then the spirit would grow mad in its grief and haunt and possess those who dwelt on the shores where he had landed.

The swell pitched the black death-barge as it departed on its voyage. The form of those barges was unlike that of any other ship, so that Goddess might see it from on high and guide it well. And the form was ancient beyond the deeps of time; and some said that Goddess Herself had made it back when the world and man were young and the lands still undivided.

When the small barge dipped and vanished over the crest of a swell, Kuln-Holn breathed a second prayer to Goddess and turned the fishing boat back toward the dark horizon.

There, far above the dark horizon, shining brighter

coming in to home, fell the green orb of God in His chariot of Jade. The Pious One did not like God, for He was a proud and angry god, a god of death, destruction, and vengeance unending; and Kuln-Holn was a peaceful, gentle soul. Those who worshiped God were mainly the hunters and the warriors of the tribe, and they did so only for fear, in the hope that His evil might pass them by a little. Before warfare they sacrificed to Him and offered Him much blood, which is said to please Him. Yet He would aid one man only to destroy others; and when that was done He would turn on His favorites and slay them in turn, even at the height of their triumph.

For God hated all men and all the works of men, wherefore Kuln-Holn feared Him, and clove to the gentle worship of kindly Goddess. Only the Madpriests loved God, and they were His people, and fully as hateful as He. They lived in His Kingdom in the Darklands, where only the Madpriests might live, for the perpetual darkness. And even farther into the darkness His Fortress of Black Rock stood far out above the surging dark seas. There in the darkness was no land, only rare islands of sharp rock: for the water that dried on Her side fell in torrential rains on His. And all that could exist there were the monstrous reptilian fishes with long jagged teeth and no eyes bulging in the black depths of those sunless seas.

Kuln-Holn the Pious One averted his eyes from the sight of God and looked for Goddess to invoke Her blessing. Yet now the throne of Golden Fire was robed in dusky purple clouds, which swept on the winds out of the lands of the dead. The seas rose and pitched, and the stiffening winds blew foamy caps upon the swells. A storm was coming—one of the last great storms of the winter.

Kuln-Holn shuddered and drew his cloak more tightly about his arms, praying again to Goddess. "Truly, Gundoen meant it not," he muttered, "It was only the merchants and the ale." But Kuln-Holn should have known that his words would prove of no avail.

With the roar of a wounded thorsa in the hollow mountains of the Spine, the Storm broke over the village of Gundoen's tribe.

It was horrible. It was a message, a punishment, a threatening of doom. It came with sudden violence, but it was not quick to leave. It was such a storm as had not been known in the memory of men. It was such a storm that it could only have been sent by dark God; and it could only have come if She had turned Her face from the people of Gundoen's tribe.

The people huddled in the darkness of their battened huts, trembling. Every window opening had been covered with the stout winter-boards; and even the smoke-holes in the roofs were shut tight. So the folk sat in darkness around their dampened cook-fires, with only the light of a few ill-smelling tallow candles flickering.

Outside the winds blew moaningly, ripping down leaf and branch alike, lifting the waves to twice the height of a man. And the rain fell as if from upturned buckets; and the rain and the louring clouds so slew the light of Goddess that it was as if the village were now beyond the dusky border at the rim of the world, where only the Madpriests live. Those who dared to venture out of doors had to lean against the gusts and, if they went against the wind, struggle for every step gained. Several huts collapsed under the gale, the rain washing away the dried mud and the wind rending even large logs out of their places. Old Elin Dark-Tooth was killed when a great beam of his hut came crashing down on his head; but no one heard his death-cries over the thunder of the Storm.

The village streets were become rushing muddy streams, emptying into the bay. One woman, poor Lista the Weaver, ventured out-of-doors just for a moment—and the wind pushed her away from her hut, and the rain blinded her, and in the end (it did not last very long) she fell heavily in the mud, unable to rise. And she drowned in the middle of the street, in the place now called Lista's Bath. Some folk even claimed the rain was so hard it washed her body down the length of the village and out to sea and that as she passed the corpse of her called out to everyone by name, inviting them to join her.

Of all the folk in the village, only Gundoen seemed not afraid. "This is a storm and nothing more," he said, as they ate their fifth meal in the darkness. "Will the tribe that does not fear all of Gen-Karn's warriors tremble at a little rain and wind?"

But the fishermen knew that such storms as this came only in the winter, and now it was early spring. And not even the oldest woman in the tribe could remember a storm of such ferocity. This was a storm sent from the gods in their terrible wrath, and in their hearts all blamed Gundoen for it. For had he not refused to see Oron on his final voyage?

Arn-Bin, cowering behind a thick wooden bench with his ears close to the wall of the chief's hall, swore that he heard a name repeated in the howlings of the wind. "Oron," it seemed to shriek. "Ooooron." Arn-Bin murmured this to others, who also heard it and cursed the chief under their breaths. But they dared do nothing for fear of the chief's wrath.

And Gundoen saw their fear and anger in their eyes and grew sullen and wrothful. He drank ale and stormed around the hall ranting, drunkenly challenging anyone to come and wrestle with him. Not even Alli could seem to please him. In the end Hertha-Toll the Sorrowful gave him a potion in his ale, and he fell into a deep sleep before he could kill anyone.

And outside the terrible Storm raged on.

The people slept and ate and slept many times in the darkness, knowing that God passed overhead many times as well. And at last the log walls ceased to shudder, and the rafters left off their tremblings. And the moan of the winds fell away, so that only the hissing of the rain went on; and at last that too sighed and was spent. Then the people crouching in the darkness waited; yet nor the winds nor the rains returned. So at last the bolder men, the spear-hunters of the tribe, dared peep their heads out-of-doors and carefully step out of the darkness of their huts.

Above them the sky was a deep greenish blue, shimmering and bright; and the last of the clouds were scurrying away toward the dark horizon. And Goddess, naked and cleansed, smiled down upon them. They stepped into the warm light, the fresh air, the brightness and the space. Kuln-Holn was the first among them to fall to his knees in the mud and thank Her for their deliverance; but not the last.

But when they looked about them their spirits fell, and the women cried out grievously. The huts were crushed, the outbuildings blown away. In the fields where the crops had been planted now stood brown muddy lakes strewn with leaves and branches. And the sand of the beach had become stony, and many of the fishing boats were washed away. Even the single log pier had been torn down and swept out into the abyss. Now they would have to barter away their last ornaments and even some weapons to gather food and seed. And then they could have no hope of standing against Gen-Karn; and even then many would perish from lack of food in the winter, unless some great miracle come to pass.

In the midst of the women's wailings another voice arose, and it belonged to Kuln-Holn.

"Look!" he cried. "Look at the sky!"

They lifted their heads and stared out over the waters of the bright horizon, where Goddess ever was. And at the sight even the women, even proud broad Gundoen, fell into silence, awed at this final portent of doom.

Already, even as they looked, the light had faded somewhat. Already the throne of Golden Fire no longer appeared perfectly round. Already a small dark crescent had been eaten away from Her underbelly. And the crescent was growing larger.

"Come to the beaches!" cried Kuln-Holn. "Come to the beaches, to redeem Her and call Her back to us!"

He ran down toward the beach. The others stood or kneeled and looked after him stupidly, while awareness grew in their eyes. Then, with a convulsive rush, they rose and fled down the steep path to the shores of the sea.

God had assaulted Goddess. Consumed by Desire, He had invaded Her throne of Golden Fire and begun to ravish Her. And Darkness was falling across the lands of men.

All of this had occurred in the past, and the people of the tribe knew what they had to do. They gathered about the bay and fell with their knees on the wet stones. And they bowed and scraped, and cried their prayers with arms lifted to heaven.

Always before had this ritual accomplished its aim; yet this was an ominous time. For She was angered with the tribe. Not yet had they appeased Her displeasure at Gundoen's blasphemy—this the Storm had proven. In Her anger She might well forget the love She bore men and surrender pride for passion's sake, and depart with God, leaving the lands where men dwell cold, dark, and lifeless.

Now were all their cries and prayers needed, from the mighty to the weak; and this none knew better than Kuln-Holn the Pious One. Yet it was Kuln-Holn who looked up during the period of greatest darkness, when the shadows were borderless and weird and the light no brighter than the shadows.

And Kuln-Holn broke off his prayers, and rose suddenly to his feet, and gazed out across the waves.

CHAPTER THREE

Ara-Karn

Throughout all the long and dismal terror of the Storm, only two men in the village had remained calm and unafraid. These men were not to be terrified by wind and weather, which they knew to be natural happenings and no more. And although Gundoen in his drunkenness may have had the boldness to voice such a notion, these men knew it in their hearts. They were as sodden and miserable as any others in the village, but when the rafters creaked ominously, as if with the weight of some prowling body, and the wind shrieked as if with the last cries of the slain, only the foreign merchants of the Southlands could smile and jest above their cups of ale.

And when the tribespeople fell on their knees to bless the sun and rushed down to the sea to cry prayers at the eclipse, the merchants could scarce restrain their smiles.

"Come," said one when the last of the villagers had gone. "They will be at it for some time. Let us see what food and ale there is in the chief's hall."

They had come from Gerso, the most northerly of all cities, which sat guarding the Pass of Gerso, the only easy pathway connecting the lands of the barbarians with the lush Southlands of civilized peoples. The city had been founded after great Elna, first Emperor of the world, had chased the barbarians into the North and almost slain them all in the siege of Urnostardil. In returning to the South Elna built a fortress guarding the Pass and charged its keepers with the duty of waiting against that time when the barbarians might rise again.

Then there had been no real need for the fortress, since the barbarians numbered no more than a few score and were like whipped dogs; and they had never risen or troubled the South in all the centuries since.

In the meantime Gerso had grown into a city; and as the barbarians had spread out and flourished in their new homelands, new industries arose, and commerce grew between North and South. So Gerso had likewise flourished, becoming a city of merchants and traders and establishing her independence from the Empire, which was not now what it had been under Elna. The Gerso merchants gave the barbarians weapons and silks and worked goods in exchange for precious metals and skins—most of all, for the prized bandar pelts.

In such trading there were few men more knowledgeable than Zelatar Bonvis. He was a gray-bearded man of sharp eyes and a sourly humorous turn of lip. His father before him had been a trader, and his father before him; and he could tell at a glance and to the penny just how much a good bandar pelt might bring in the bazaars of Gerso, Carftain, or even Tarendahardil, the City Over the World.

The younger man with Zelatar was Mergo Donato, whose father had purchased him an apprenticeship under Bonvis. This was his first journey to the wilds of the North, and he was liking it not at all.

"Now we will be starved here," he complained as they entered the chief's empty hall. "And I had thought their fare wretched enough before."

The older merchant took out some cuts of meat and ale and settled himself in the large carved high seat. "Mergo, what a foolish man you are. Why do you complain when you have every reason to rejoice?"

"And how rejoice?"

"Well, your education has been placed in my hands, so attend me: this storm has utterly impoverished these people. Their boats are gone, their huts broken, and their crops are washed away. They are desperate lest they be left at the mercy of their enemies. We can command our own price for pelts now—why, we might even pay only half of Gundoen's usual rate!"

The younger man considered this. "You are the expert here," he conceded. "But still I wish we might have done business with Gen-Karn's tribe. I've heard that he at least treats men with the proper courtesy and respect. That is where Telran Welsar goes each year."

"Yes, and pays well for it. Mergo, Gen-Karn spent years of his youth south of Gerso. He knows the true worth of what he sells and charges accordingly. Yet even if he charged less than we could get here, there is another reason why we should deal with Gundoen: the two are bitter enemies. Gundoen is chief of the largest tribe yet independent of Gen-Karn. Despite his temper and ill manners, he is the leader of those tribes wishing to oppose Gen-Karn."

"I do not understand," said the younger man.

"Affairs of state are not here what they are in the South, Mergo. Here there are no titles, no landed estates, no noble families. There are no written codes of law suspended above the marketplaces, no licenses, no prisons. Each man holds respect only according to his personal worth and talents. Offenses are punished summarily by the chiefs or by the kin of the injured men. Even Gundoen—or for that matter Gen-Karn himself—could lose his position if his people thought him unlucky, or another man challenged him successfully. And they despise us, as you have seen. Against a man like Gen-Karn we can only hope to pit another man such as Gundoen."

"Yet why should we concern ourselves in such political matters?" Mergo asked. "We are merchants, not diplomats."

Zelatar looked at the younger man with ill-concealed annoyance. He slurped at his ale. "And if the North were to unite again, where would our trade be?"

Mergo spat upon the earthen floor with amusement. "Zelatar Bonvis, wizard of merchants, with the right to be the first let into the North for each year so long as you hold breath! Do not tell me that you believe those fools who fear that the barbarians will rise again? Such legends are of old date indeed; yet not once have the tribes dared oppose us."

Zelatar slowly shook his head. "When I was younger, Mergo, and came with my father for the first time to the

North, there was never any talk of civil war among the tribes. And in my grandfather's time there were so few tribesmen that he could not support himself solely on this northern trade, but had to make other journeys to the South and the bright horizon. Now the tribes have grown, and begin to elbow one another over territorial rights. They grow restless; they can scarcely grow and catch enough to feed themselves. Hunger is a great goad, Mergo: do not underestimate what it may drive men to. And I have seen Gen-Karn, and know the man. There is much you do not understand as yet, Mergo."

The younger man was about to respond when suddenly he cocked his head in a listening attitude. From below the village rose the faint shouts of the barbarians, suddenly louder and sharper. Mergo frowned. "What are they saying?"

Zelatar rose and walked to the veranda at the front of the hall. "They're calling to us from the bay," he said with surprise. He looked up at the sky, now bright as ever. "The eclipse has passed; I wonder what they want of us? Come along—and mind your words, or I will sell your apprenticeship to Berdelna Tovis."

"Goddess spare me such a fate," said Mergo, chuckling.

Kuln-Holn the Pious One broke off his supplications, and rose to his feet, and gazed out across the waves. He shut his eyes, hoping it was but another of his visions; but when he opened his eyes again he saw it still. He looked up and down the ranks of his fellow tribesmen in the weird half-darkness. He sought to find one who had also seen, one who would tell him what to do and take the awful burden from his shoulders.

But the others rose and fell, continuing their prayers without pause. The sight had been given to the Pious One alone. He took that for an omen. It was for him alone to decide what to do. He looked out to sea again.

Although the thing bobbing on the water was a good deal larger than those of the tribe, there was no mistaking its shape. Kuln-Holn had known it immediately for what it was: a death-barge, being slowly driven by the wind and the tide into the waters of the wide-mouth bay directly toward the shores of Gundoen's tribe.

A death-barge was returning to the land of men.

A death-barge that could only be driven by Her hands

—one which soon, unless some miracle intervened, would come to rest upon the beach among the tribe. And when it landed, its spirit, turned back from the Happy Shores for its crimes, would go mad with grief and haunt and possess the tribe. It would cause women to miscarry and men to fall on one another with drawn swords. Many and terrible were the tales told about such happenings.

Kuln-Holn looked up and down the beach in the darkness. He stepped forward a bit into the water and stopped. He knew what he must do, but he was afraid. He must go into the water and turn the barge from the shore. He could not turn it back to the Happy Shores—that had been forbidden by Her—but at least he could see that it landed on some distant shore.

Yet when his hand touched the side of the barge, he would bring the wrath of the spirit upon himself. It would think him a barge-robber. It would enter his body and consume his soul. He would go mad and perish in the sea. And there were other tales of the terrible fates of barge-robbers. If Kuln-Holn did nothing, he would only be allowing Her punishment to follow its course. And perhaps She would realize that he, Kuln-Holn, had been no party to the chief's refusal and spare him.

He looked up to the skies. Already the circle of blinding fire was reappearing below Goddess. God had had His way, and She was His. Now had come the moment of decision. And perhaps Her decision would rest with what Kuln-Holn would do.

He stepped into the water. He did not want to think of it any longer. The waves, high because of the Storm, slapped coldly at his legs. He waded into the surf, feeling the sea devour him.

It was much closer now, sliding rapidly toward the land. The absence of any sail or tiller, or sight of human occupant, lent it an eerie aspect of silence and of death.

He came up beside it when the water lapped at his chest. He brushed his wet hair from his eyes. The barge swept past him. For one brief moment it was suddenly revealed to him: the barge, the artifacts, the body lying at rest.

The barge itself was of black, as was custom; but on its prow was a sunburst design of beaten gold, now half eaten away by the sea, and along its sides were carved ornate designs, some of strange and mystic charactery, others of half-buried figures writhing in odd postures. The rim was all of gold—an amazing extravagance that could only have been permitted on the barge of some great king.

And the man within, even in death, gave the look of a king. The rags upon his limbs were of the costliest fabrics, dirtied and rent but shining for all that. The artifacts laid about him were of the finest materials and workmanship. Kuln-Holn saw the glint of gold, the shimmer of silver.

The man was a tall, slim man, with dark skin browned by the sun, the arms muscular but unscarred, the hands whole and without calluses. A short beard of only a few weeks' length grew from the handsome gaunt face. About the brow was a simple circlet of pure gold and much jewelry adorned his neck, arms, and fingers. In his right hand he clutched a ceremonial dagger of jade with a strange ornate design.

All of this Kuln-Holn saw in that brief moment the barge swept past him. Out of fear or fascination he did nothing; then the darting light of Goddess suddenly gleamed upon the blade of the dagger into his eyes, he started, and his arms shot out and clutched the stern of the barge.

It pulled him from his feet; he found the sea bottom again and pulled back. With a sudden jerk the barge came to a stop. He could hear the clatter of jewels and artifacts pitching forward. He gripped the stern of the barge firmly, senses prickling. He began to draw the barge back.

A moan sounded in his ears.

Kuln-Holn's heart pounded. Sweat mixed with the salt on his brow. The moan had come from within the barge.

There was another moan and the sound of movement from within. Kuln-Holn could not look. He had to look—he could not help himself. He turned his head to the barge.

An arm was being raised—the right arm, jewels flashing, the naked dagger clutched in the fist—then the arm fell. A shoulder rose. Then the head. The corpse of the dead king turned, and shuddered, and rose. It sat up in its own death-barge and looked at the shore. Then, slowly, it turned around. Kuln-Holn wanted to let go of the barge and dive below the surface of the water, but his fingers were shut tight and he could not make them move.

With strange, unblinking eyes, the corpse regarded the fear-stricken tribesman.

"What is he about?" swore Gundoen, shading his eyes with his thickly muscled hand. "What is he playing at?"

The people of the tribe had watched with joy the crescent of fire grow larger and larger, while the dark oval shrank. Light, golden and warm, flooded back into the world. And She did not move, but hung five fists above the bright horizon as always. Goddess had not yielded or betrayed Her great love; and God had fled.

Yet no sooner had their cries of thanks died down and the tribe come to their feet than they looked seaward and saw the death-barge in the bay and Kuln-Holn standing in the water beside it.

There had been many cries of woe and fear, but these Gundoen silenced with a curt bark.

He looked out at the barge. It was plain now that Kuln-Holn was drawing it in toward the shore. But why?

The people were still under the power of the Storm and the fear of the eclipse. Such an accumulation of menacing omens made each fresh event a harbinger of disaster. Even in happy times the return of a strange death-barge would have been a bringer of woe; now it filled them with horror. Several of the women and not a few of the men ran up from the beach back to their huts. Others followed as Kuln-Holn drew the barge up even closer, until most of the people of the tribe had fled.

Left on the beach were Gundoen and the braver of the hunters and a few of the women, including Hertha-Toll and Turin Tim, Kuln-Holn's grown daughter. These few awaited the incoming barge in an expectant silence.

Gundoen's hand clenched at his side, as if feeling for the sword that was not there.

Kuln-Holn labored through the waves. He pulled the barge heavily halfway up on the pebbles of the beach. Then he collapsed, breathing heavily. The labor, combined with the terror in his heart, had made him faint and dizzy. A shadow crossed him, and he felt his daughter's cool hand on his forehead. He almost fell into a faint, but shook his head, determined to remain wakeful. What had possessed him to draw the barge in to the shore he did not know. He looked up. Dark against the brightness of the sky, the dead man in the barge rose slowly to his feet.

The nearly naked man, bearing the golden circlet of a king about his brow and carrying the jade ceremonial dagger in his hand, stepped forth from the barge upon the shore. The people murmured in awe at the sight of him and drew back—even Hertha-Toll and the chief. Several of them made the sign with their fingers to ward off evil.

The man took a few steps forward and stopped. His gait was unsteady, as if he had been at sea for a long time. He looked about him from man to man. And each man, every woman turned away her face. His eyes were dark, flecked with strange green lights, and set deeply in his face. His hollowed, half-starved cheeks made his eyes seem even more terrible. Though he was a mere shrunken sack of bones among a strange, perhaps hostile people, it was not he who was afraid.

Hertha-Toll was the first to step forward. "We welcome you here among us, stranger," she said courteously. "We offer you all hospitality, yet would ask you first who you may be, and whence you have come, and whether you mean us harm."

The stranger stared at Hertha-Toll. He said nothing.

"Why does he not answer?" complained one of the men nervously. "Can he not speak?"

"Answer her!" shouted Gundoen with all the power of his voice.

The stranger took his gaze from Hertha-Toll and directed it at Gundoen. After a few moments, he shrugged.

Kuln-Holn struggled to rise to his feet, aided by Turin Tim. "Do not anger him," he croaked. "He has been sent by the gods. Can you not see? He is Her messenger. Be wary of him." He said this, but he knew not why. The words had spoken, not he.

The chief snorted. "More like a thief than a messenger. Tell me, fellow, how did you come to be in that barge? And what did you do to the corpse that belonged there?" This time, instead of the tongue of the North, the chief used the trading dialect they used with foreign merchants.

Still the stranger did not answer.

Some of the women fidgeted nervously. The silence of the stranger was ominous, his eyes unbearable. They were eyes that had seen horrors, and looking at them made others see those horrors too, reflected in the flashes of green fire.

Three men and two women turned suddenly and left the beach. The stranger watched them go with no reaction.

The chief's wife called after them. "Summon the merchants. Perhaps they will know this man's tongue."

"Yes, the merchants!" cried Gundoen. A shout arose,

calling the Southrons to the beach. Soon they could be seen walking down the muddy path with quickening strides.

"Speak with this man," commanded the chief. "Ask him his name, what his country is, and what he wants of us."

The merchants looked at the man and the strange death-barge rocking at the water's edge. The younger merchant gaped in surprise, but the older, Zelatar Bonvis, who had been among the tribe many times in years past, set about questioning the stranger.

"Do not fear, chief Gundoen," he said. "I have traveled far, alone and with others, and also under my father. There is not a major tongue in all the round world of which I have not a few words. I will be able to speak with this man."

"Then be about it," snapped the chief.

Yet try as he might, the merchant could gain no response. A dozen tongues he tried, and then a score of dialects—yet all to no avail. From time to time he would pause, looking questioningly at the stranger. The stranger only shrugged.

In the end the merchants ran out of dialects. Zelatar finally gave up. Shaking his head, he turned to the chief.

"Gundoen, I have tried all the tongues I know. It is not possible that this man would not know at least one of them. How could he have come so far North otherwise? He is either deaf and dumb or else a liar."

At this point the stranger, seeing that Zelatar had run out of tongues to try, spoke himself. He spoke a phrase in an unknown, foreign tongue; and his voice was scornful and contemptuous. His words were impossibly strange: so alien, they raised the hackles on Kuln-Holn's neck.

"He is no mute at any rate," Gundoen commented after a pause. "You recognized the tongue?"

"Chief, it is obvious what this man is. Could he be anything other than a barge-robber? Look at him: how could such a man have come by such a barge? Look at all the gold! There is a fortune there—enough to tempt the stoutest man's heart. More than likely he and some others tried to rob the barge. Perhaps there was a fight, or else the other thieves took fright for some reason and fled. This one was lost at sea in the Storm. Now that he has come among you he feigns not to understand us. He knows he cannot explain his presence. See how he clutches the dagger; he knows you will put him to death the moment you know he is a barge-robber."

Gundoen smiled slowly, scornfully. "You could not understand his words."

"Because they were gibberish! There is no such tongue in all the lands of the living. Put him to death and divide the gold among you. Think of the weapons you might buy with it!"

"No!" cried Kuln-Holn. While the others had been trying to question the stranger, Kuln-Holn had merely been looking at him. The terror in his breast had passed, succeeded by a deep religious awe. And now he knew who and what the stranger was, beyond all doubts. The moment for which he had waited for so many years had at last come to pass: the dream stood on their doorstep.

"Do not kill him," he pleaded with the chief. "Can you not see his quality? He has been sent from the gods. Perhaps he is their offspring. Did he not appear when they lay abed together? Else he is some former king, sent back from the Happy Shores by Goddess for some purpose. Have I not foretold such a thing? This I know: you cannot kill him, not a former king. The sight of him was given to me alone. I should have the decision."

The chief laughed suddenly, a deep rumbling laugh. "A former king? This? O Pious One, you surprise even me. The merchant was right; the man deserves only death, lest he bring his curse among us. As for the gold, it has the same curse. Let it be sent back on the currents of the dead."

He picked up a large sharp stone, instructing the others to do likewise. "Stone him to death in the water and send him back with his barge."

"No, I will not let you!" Kuln-Holn leaped in front of the man in rags. The ferocity in his voice was astounding; never before had the like of it been heard from little Kuln-Holn.

Gundoen looked at the short, soft man in the dirty tunic, rage mounting to his brows. The chief had ever laughed at and scorned the poor prophet. He was not used to being defied by such a man. He took half a step forward, as if he would have liked to hurl the stone at Kuln-Holn and kill him with the stranger. But Hertha-Toll restrained him.

"It may be that the Pious One is right, my husband," she said softly. "There have been stranger things come to pass.

Kuln-Holn is willing to shelter the man and undertake whatever curse he may have. That is none of our concern, is it? Listen to my words: I sense danger from this man. Do not provoke him. We can take him in for now; if he is a barge-robber, we will be given a sign and may decide later. Please heed my words, husband."

The chief rocked his massive body back and forth on the balls of his feet. Then the rage broke from his face, and he laughed. It was a hearty laugh. It was also the laugh he gave in a wrestling match, just as he was about to crush the bones of his opponent. Zelatar Bonvis shuddered to hear it.

"It is well," Gundoen said at last. "He shall be Kuln-Holn's pet for now. Let the Pious One give him food and shelter out of his own hut's stores. No one else is to give him any aid. The stranger shall be watched. If he attempts to escape, or if we are given a sign, we will know what to do. Also, of course, Pious One, you understand that if the man does turn out to be only a robber of the dead you will have to be condemned alongside him?"

Kuln-Holn bit the gray hairs of his beard, looking from the chief to the stranger, who stood calmly by while his fate was being decided. Gundoen's ruling, while harsh, was still fair. To aid a barge-robber was to accept his guilt.

"I understand," Kuln-Holn said resolutely.

"Good." The chief grinned, then suddenly laughed again. "Now I will give your pet a name, Pious One. You have called him a former king, so 'Former King'—Ara-Karn—it will be. How does that please you?"

Kuln-Holn was compelled to submit. He nodded. "It is well, O chief," he murmured.

"Now take him away," commanded the chief. "Hertha-Toll, open the smoke-holes and begin baking! We will put aside our troubles for the moment and think of them later. Goddess has remained! Let us feast!"

A cheer acclaimed the idea and the people scurried off to spread the good news, glad to escape the sight of the strange death-barge and the man who had ridden in it. The thick-chested chief, as quick to humor as he was to rage, gave a last mocking glance at Kuln-Holn and the stranger, then led the warriors up from the shore. They spoke hungrily of the feast, of ale and sweetmeats and thick juicy pasties; and they left Kuln-Holn and his daughter and the stranger alone on the rocky beach.

Hertha-Toll was the last to leave them. She gave a final, pitying look to Kuln-Holn, and a troubled one at the stranger. Then she turned beyond the bluff and vanished from the shore.

Turin Tim looked her father in the eye and sighed. "Father," she said, "what have you brought upon us now?" Then she too turned and walked from the shore.

"You do not understand," began Kuln-Holn, but already his daughter was gone. He sighed, his shoulders low; then he straightened them and turned back to the stranger.

He stooped at the water's edge and pulled the barge completely up onto the pebbles of the beach, above the mark of high water. The stranger watched him calmly.

"Come," he said, touching the stranger on the arm. He beckoned him to follow. The stranger nodded. They walked up from the storm-ravaged beach, now empty and desolate except for a few shattered fishing boats and the low, black death-barge with the sunburst design of beaten gold half eaten away, and the intricate carvings of strange charactery and weirdly writhing figures, telling a tale no one but the stranger could have read.

And though many conjectures were thrown about concerning the origins of the stranger, not one of them came even close to the truth. And there was not a one in the village—not the worldly Zelatar Bonvis nor Hertha-Toll the Wise, nor even Kuln-Holn the Dreamer—who could have guessed that the nearly naked man in rags, wearing the golden circlet of a king about his brow and clutching an ornate dagger in his hand still, would in years to come ride in triumphant conquest across the face of the globe— yes, even unto the gilded halls of Tarendahardil, the City Over the World.

CHAPTER FOUR

The Dream of the Wise and the Sorrowful

The stranger ate in the small hut Kuln-Holn shared with his daughter. He ate ravenously, like one who has been long weeks with little or no food; and he drank as deeply. He ate more than Kuln-Holn, who was a poor man supported mainly by Turin Tim, could afford to give him. Once, long ago, Kuln-Holn had been a fisherman, but that had been before he gave his life to his visions.

The Pious One did not think to complain of the stranger's appetite. Instead he sat and watched the stranger eating with as much relish as if the food were going into his own mouth.

"What will you do first?" he asked, unable to restrain his great curiosity. "Where will you lead us? Do not mind chief Gundoen. He is a hunter; hunters never believed as much as we fishermen. He does not recognize you yet. But I do."

The stranger paused and looked into Kuln-Holn's eyes. Kuln-Holn saw the darkness of those eyes, relieved only by the dim green flashes, like jade lightning against distant storm clouds. Kuln-Holn felt the power in those eyes. He swallowed and could say no more.

The stranger returned to his eating. He ate like a god, or a wild beast. If he understood what Kuln-Holn had asked him, he gave no sign.

35

The crumbs of Turin Tim's last baked forsla cake revealed the nakedness of the wooden plate. Kuln-Holn went to the storage-hole of the hut and peered within. It was empty save for a bit of dried meat they had been saving for the feast before the great Hunt. He took out the meat and set it before the stranger.

Kuln-Holn felt the eyes of his daughter upon the back of his head. They were angry eyes; he could feel the heat of them. This was the last of the food that Turin Tim had worked so hard to provide. Kuln-Holn loved his daughter —she was strong and dutiful, a good provider. But still he had to admit that she could not know what he knew, nor see visions in smoke and hearth-ash and dusky clouds.

Kuln-Holn sighed and did not look at his daughter. He pushed the meat in front of the stranger. "Eat, eat," he said. "All infants entering life are greedy for food, nor are the gods different in this than men. Later you will sleep."

He heard Turin Tim snort angrily and leave their hut. Kuln-Holn sighed once more. He pitied his daughter because she was growing old with no men chasing after her, and also because she could not see the dreams in smoke and hearth-ash and dusky clouds. She had only work, and that was never enough. May this man's coming bless her too, prayed Kuln-Holn.

When the stranger had finished the last of the meat and mare's milk, Kuln-Holn showed him the dimchamber, the small room without windows where he slept on the little bed of grass. Kuln-Holn pointed beyond the stitched-skin hangings.

The stranger shook his head. He rose to his feet, the golden circlet shining against the shadows of the shabby hut. Somehow the man seemed even taller here. He went to the low doorway, stooped, and left the hut.

Kuln-Holn hurried after him. Outside the hut he looked about, dazzled by the brightness of Her light. The stranger was walking down the steep path that led back to shore. Kuln-Holn followed at a distance. He did not know what to expect. Could he have insulted the messenger of the gods already?

Behind him he heard footsteps. He turned. Following were Urin-Baln and Ka Al-Drim, two strong young warriors, their weapons glinting in the sun. These were the men Gundoen had chosen to watch the stranger.

"Do not follow too closely," Kuln-Holn warned them. "If you offend him, he may blast you with a look."

They laughed. "Go and tell your stories to the children, Pious One," they said. "We do not fear the barge-robber."

"I have warned you." Kuln-Holn shrugged. "Your deaths will not be upon my hands." The two warriors laughed again, but thereafter kept their distance.

No others were in sight, the rest of the tribe being gathered in and around the chief's great hall, feasting their salvation from the Storm. The breeze brought the sounds of their revelry and the delicious smells of roasting foods.

The stranger went down to the beach, where lay his death-barge, a few paces out of the water. He began to gather the things within it into a large bundle. Kuln-Holn came down to the stones of the beach and stopped, watching him. The two guards stayed on the grasses above the beach. "Tell him not to try to sail away," they said. The stranger ignored both them and Kuln-Holn.

He gathered together the bundle in his arms and walked down the beach. In the bundle Kuln-Holn could see the glimmer of gold, the shimmer of silver. Kuln-Holn followed, unquestioning, uncomprehending.

They walked around the bay to one of the long arms of land thrusting out into the sea. The sea birds wheeled over them, screeching when they passed too near the hidden nests. When he had come to the end of the land, where the coarse long grasses bent over the jagged rocks falling to white foam and waves, the stranger set his burden down. He looked out across the sea, shimmering with the brilliant visage of Her.

Kuln-Holn squatted in the grass behind him, watching. He did not know what the stranger would do next, but when it happened he was not surprised.

One after another, the fine and beautifully crafted objects of the bundle were hurled into the waves. Ornaments and vessels that had been placed in the barge with loving mournful care, which had survived by Her grace the rough and stormy seas, the stranger now threw to the winds. There were many things of great value among them. Their wealth might have fed the entire tribe for more than a year.

Kuln-Holn could hear Urin-Baln and Ka Al-Drim swearing softly behind him. "Look what he does, by the dark God!" they muttered to each other. "Is he mad, this barge-robber?" Kuln-Holn smiled to himself. The sight of so much wealth being thrown away convinced him more than ever that he was right. Only gods could have contempt for gold.

The stranger, oblivious to those behind him, pulled off his rings and jewelry and threw them after the rest. Then he stripped off his clothes, the ragged remains of elegant fineries, and threw them in the sea as well. He stood naked on the rocks, with only the dagger of strange design, staring into the foam. He stood thus for a long time. A fisherman, sailing out of the bay in a repaired boat, looked at him in fear and wonder, and loudly swore.

The words seemed to break the stranger's revery. He reached up to his brow and took off the golden circlet. He regarded it almost lovingly for a moment. But then his hand jerked, and the golden circlet too flashed for a brief instant and vanished into the abyss.

He raised his head and called a word into the waves.

Kuln-Holn could not recognize the word, but thought it sounded like a name. And he felt fear in his belly, for he could not tell if the word had been spoken out of the depths of love or hatred. And he thought, What sort of man can he be whose hatred could be confused with his love?

The stranger turned, holding the jade dagger easily in one hand. He stooped and picked up out of the rank grasses the only other artifacts he had saved: a long, curving instrument of polished wood and a pouch of slender sticks. He approached Kuln-Holn and looked into his eyes. The gaze seemed to pierce Kuln-Holn's very soul; he squirmed in the grass under it, uncertain what he should do. Then, as if it were a voice speaking in his brain, he realized that mortals were not meant to be comfortable in the face of the immortals. For what was awe if not exalted terror?

The stranger nodded. He passed on, gesturing for Kuln-Holn to follow. He walked past the guards as if they were no more than the grass about his naked feet. Nor did they laugh or smile when he passed them, but murmured sullenly, looking down at the water of the bay.

Even naked, Kuln-Holn thought to himself, even bedraggled from the storm, even with ragged beard and his feet scarred from the rocks, this one looks more the king, and more than king, than anyone who has ever set foot in the North before. And he felt his chest swelling with new pride.

They went back to Kuln-Holn's hut. Now the stranger went to the dim place and fastened the hanging behind him. Kuln-Holn heard the body collapse on the low-slung bed, a long rending sigh, and the rhythmic breathing of a deep sleep, the sleep of babes, the innocent, or the dead.

Kuln-Holn went out to sit on the log step before his door. It had been long since he himself had slept, and longer since he had eaten. He knew he should be tired and hungry, but he was not. Some strange new fever burned his brow, deep into his brain. He felt as if he would never again need food or rest: only to follow this man on his holy quest. He looked out on the village he had known since birth and saw that it was as it had ever been. The feast at the chief's hall had ended, and the folk, full and satisfied, were coming back to their huts for the short sleep. They laughed and joked to one another, and some pointed here and there at the damage of the Storm, commenting on how it was best to be repaired.

Turin Tim appeared, bearing armfuls of food. "Leftovers from the feast," she said. "Hertha-Toll took pity on us."

"Did I not tell you it would be well?" he asked. "He will bless us, Turin Tim."

Turin Tim sighed and went into the hut. He heard her angrily storing the food and muttering to herself.

He looked back on the village. And he realized that the place where he had been born was not as it had ever been, even though none of the others knew it. It was changed only because of one naked man sleeping in the dim place of Kuln-Holn's hut; but that would make a very great difference. The tribe would never again be what it was, because of him; and never again would Kuln-Holn be able to go back to being that man who, long ago, had gone to see chief Gundoen for the rites of Oron's final voyage.

Once again the chill of fear came to Kuln-Holn's heart.

And in the chief's great hall, when all the feasters had gone their ways and the serving wenches were cleaning up the mess, chief Gundoen rose and stretched his broad-muscled frame, and sought his own dim place, and fell into a deep, restful sleep.

Sometime later Hertha-Toll entered and woke him. "What do you think of the stranger?" she asked him.

He looked at her for several moments, and she looked away, glad of the dimness. Even there—there of all places —she could feel the reproach he felt toward her. She almost wept, though he saw it not.

"He is nothing," said Gundoen. "Much wreckage washes to our shores. This one happened to be alive, that is all. A thief or blasphemer, likely. Certainly from the civilized lands," he added with disgust. "He'll bring us no ill-luck, if that's what you fear. And if he does, why then his death will end it."

She shook her head. "That is not what I feared." She hesitated, choosing her words. "He will bring us no ill-luck. That I can sense. Rather he will be lucky." She wondered how much of her dream she should tell him, and how much was true.

"What then?"

She sighed. "He is . . . of death."

Gundoen chuckled harshly. "Do not tell me you believe with the Pious One!"

"No. He is no more than mortal, certainly. But there is a strangeness about this man. Great pain, much death. Death—surely very much of it. And there is something else."

"What?" His voice grew concerned. "Hertha-Toll, what have you seen?"

She looked about, leaned closer.

"His eyes," she whispered. "They are like the eyes of a Madpriest."

The last word was breathed so softly, not even Gundoen could hear it. But even without hearing he knew what it was. Only those dark souls could inspire such terror in the heart of Hertha-Toll.

"Do not even think it!" he commanded. "It is not true. You are upset because of the storm. He is some barge-robber, I tell you—nothing more. Truly, nothing more."

"Let Her hear you," she said softly. She rose to leave him and returned to her own dim place. The tears trembled at the wrinkled corners of her eyes, but she fought them back. She prayed that her dream would not be truth, and that her husband would not some pass lie screaming in agony as the stranger Ara-Karn looked calmly on.

* * *

For the next weeks, as the jade orb of God passed relentlessly overhead ten times each week, Kuln-Holn fed his charge, clothed him in the rough tunic of the tribe, and taught him the words of the language of men. After that first breaking of his fast the stranger ate little, slept less, and was very moody. Often he would go to the shore and sit above the waves, rocking back and forth on his haunches under the gaze of his guards, looking out across the Ocean of the Dead. Other times he would slip away into the forests in the direction of the great mountain of Goddess. What he did there Kuln-Holn could not guess; but that the others knew no more he was sure.

Once they came to him angrily, Urin-Baln and Ka Al-Drim, and took him up to the chief's hall. The stranger had escaped them in the wood, they said; now Kuln-Holn's life was forfeit for it. They found the chief had gone hunting, and waited. But Hertha-Toll approached them and, when she discovered what they were about, gave them a worried look. "Why," she said, "the newcomer is not gone. I saw him myself, just now, sitting out at the edge of the bay." The guards brought Kuln-Holn roughly down to the water. There he was, just as the wise-woman had said. Urin-Baln and Ka Al-Drim swore savagely at him, but the stranger merely looked calmly over his shoulder and smiled. And afterward the guards did not complain when he went into the wood, not wishing to admit that two such great woodsmen were unable to keep the track of one mere man.

Each waking Kuln-Holn sat in the sand of the central clearing of the village, preaching the worship of his new-arrived god. Some of the women and a few of the men gathered around him with doubt and laughter in their eyes; but whenever they saw the figure of the stranger at the edge of the bay, dark like a carved pillar of wood against the brilliance of the sky, their laughter lost some of its assurance. Of course, they all knew he was no more than some civilized man, probably from Arpane on the Sea: what else could he be? But when he passed among them, silent always but with those eyes of his casting about like sharpened bandar-spears, they looked down and away, and went around, out of his path. The impudent naked children had cast pebbles and rotten fruit at Kuln-Holn the little prophet, deriding him from behind dirty noses; but they shunned the stranger with an instinctive fear.

Yet he was quick to learn their tongue. One of the first

questions Kuln-Holn asked him was, "What is your mission? What would you have us do for you?" But the stranger shook his head. Whether this meant that he did not understand or that the mystery was not yet to be revealed, Kuln-Holn could not say. But he knew that, when the time finally came for the stranger to enlighten him fully, then Kuln-Holn would know happiness and peace for the first time in his new life.

Once a woman whose husband was away fishing too often drank two bowls of beer and offered herself shamelessly to the stranger; but he only laughed and walked past her, leaving her blushing angrily in the street while the other women smiled behind their hands. She went to tell her husband a lie, and he confronted the stranger. This frightened Kuln-Holn, because the fisherman, Ob-Kal-Ti, was a strong, ugly man whose dealings were little trusted. Kuln-Holn warned his guest, but Ara-Karn only shook his head, as if he did not understand. One time Kuln-Holn went down to the beach to find the stranger washing his arms in the waves, smiling, staring far out to sea. And the next time the warriors went to the grove of dark God to make offerings, they found the rotting head of Ob-Kal-Ti stuck on a post before the idol. And afterward Kuln-Holn found that more men attended to his preachings and that they listened with greater respect.

Only once did Kuln-Holn ask the stranger of his origins. It happened one time when they had been laughing over some small matter, and the strange new sound of his guest's laughter emboldened Kuln-Holn.

"And you," he asked, "where is it you come from? Can you remember anything of your past life—what country gave you birth, who your kin were, and who were those you most loved?" For Kuln-Holn was not yet unconvinced that Ara-Karn was the reincarnated spirit of some great king of ages past.

But Ara-Karn did not smile, and his laughter faded as if it had never been. He looked at Kuln-Holn with such eyes that the prophet quailed within himself, so that unthinkingly he cried,

"Forgive me, forgive me!"

Then Ara-Karn left the hut, and Kuln-Holn was a little reassured. Later he wondered why he should have been so fearful of gentle Goddess's messenger, and just what it was that had made him cry out so. But he put it from his mind with his dreams. He did not see the stranger for quite a while after that.

When they did meet again, Ara-Karn took Kuln-Holn up to a nearby hill and pointed to the great mountain rising to the South, which because of its shape and the color of its snowy peak was known as the Breast of Goddess, Kaari-Moldole. Kuln-Holn nodded, explaining as best he could. The mountain was the site of the women's worship. There lovers went to pray to Goddess and others to seek Her aid in all things from childbirth to the fertility of the fields. It was the holiest place for many weeks' journey around, a place shrouded in mystery and holiness. The stranger looked up at it strangely, then gestured to Kuln-Holn.

They journeyed to the slopes of Kaari-Moldole, taking two passes to reach her base. For food they ate berries and nuts and trapped small game; they lapped at the banks of hill-fed streams for drink. At the base of the mountain, where the sacred woods began, Ara-Karn made Kuln-Holn stop while he went on alone. Kuln-Holn should have warned him about the prohibitions and curses laid upon trespassers, but he did not dare. This man was Her servant.

He made camp in the wild, hearing in the dense green about him animals prowling, branches snapping, and the calls of the clustering birds. Many birds nested on these sheltering slopes. He went up the base of the mountain until he came to a clearing, where he felt safer. He could see the expanse of the sea below, and serene Goddess beyond, and he knelt to Her, gave prayer, and slept. When he awoke the sky was dark and She had disappeared. The winds were rising, and the clouds, dark gray and greenly foul, they were falling. The air grew close and angry, and Kuln-Holn was alarmed. The clouds settled about the crown of the mountain, where the Holy River was rumored to have its source. Then the dark cloud obscured the peak and the winds rose, violent, scattering dead leaves in the air. Kuln-Holn shivered, waiting under an overhanging rock for the lightning and the downpour to begin. He heard the rustle of the many birds flying down off the mountain, fleeing to the woods below. Suddenly a great black cloud rose from off the sea, and rose swiftly toward the mountain —then he saw it was not a cloud but a flock of great black evil birds—thousands of them—flying too closely together, their deadly beaks aimed this way and that. They flew around the mountain, screeching as if in call or answer; then they vanished, and Kuln-Holn saw no more of them. The earth beneath shook once, in reply to one tremendous clap of lightning; he cried out to Goddess to let this storm break and be done; but the storm never broke. Instead the air was somehow lightened, and the clouds broke here and there. Kuln-Holn climbed up on the rock, nervously looking about him; but of the dense green cloud and the deadly birds there was no sign. At the end of the sea the clouds parted, and gold-bearing Goddess shed Her light upon the mountain once again.

Shortly thereafter the stranger came back down the mountain. In his hands he held the thick bundle of pointed sticks with black feathers on their ends and the curved wooden instrument. Without a gesture Ara-Karn passed the rock and went on down the path. Kuln-Holn hastened his abasements and followed, daring to ask no questions. So they came down out of Kaari-Moldole and were not even stricken. Again Kuln-Holn wondered greatly that the storm had not broken, and he wondered if it would be safe to add this to his preachings. But for then he thought it best to speak no word of this.

When they returned to the village, not even the guards awaited them. All was bustle there, for it was the time of the great feast, to bid the hunters good luck before they departed on the great Hunt for bandars.

CHAPTER FIVE

The Warriors' Departure

When Gundoen awoke from the thanksgiving feast, he forgot all about his wife's ill-omened words and sought out Estar, Foron, and Garin, the best trackers and most skilled woodsmen of the tribe.

"It is time," said Gundoen the chief. "After this storm we will need a good Hunt. Are you readied?"

"Since the feast, chief," laughed Garin, who was a handsome young brave with curling hair the color of the bark of the coslin tree. "We will cast a weird upon all the bandar we see, that none but us may bring them down!"

Then Gundoen laughed, and the trackers slung their packs over swift ponies and took the path past Outpost Rock into the territories of the Korlas. As they passed the brown fields, they laughed, and waved to the men and women toiling, then plunged into the forest's shadowed depths. Gundoen went back to the village, smiling; but when he saw his wife standing bleakly on the porch of his great hall, his smile washed from his face, and he passed without a word. In the village below he helped repair the ruined huts, lifting great logs unaided and laughing as his muscles bulged and cracked like iron fired red hot.

Later the women prepared hardbreads that would not soon go stale, dried smoked meats that would be eaten from horseback, and skins of ale and mare's milk. And the men sharpened their swords and skinning knives, and polished their heavy hunting spears. They worked their wooden shields with new leather, embossed with red symbols of protection. They tended to their ponies, fattening them more than many people of the tribe. There would be little food for the ponies on the long trail to the Forest of the Bandar.

In the great chief's hall the warriors gathered. They were the pride of the village, mighty spearmen, agile trackers. Warmed by the smoke of the blue cook-fires, they tested their weapons, argued strategies, and swore great curses on the Korlas' heads.

In all the world, bandar roamed only in these wild lands north of Gerso, only in certain deep woods, the Forest of the Bandar. High up were these cold forests, and far from the sea—many passes' ride from the village of Gundoen's folk. And only once in all the year were the skins of the bandars the bright-shining green so prized in the faraway South. And that time was now, for the springtime mating season was upon them, bull and cow. Yet this too was the time of their greatest ferocity and unpredictability. The bulls were savage in their rut, the cows most dangerous protecting their newborn. Every year they chose different mating grounds in the hidden depths of the cold, high forest; and this was why the work of the scouts would be so vital.

Too, other tribes would hunt the beasts. Korlas would be there, and Buzrahs, and stout Durbars, and hunters from Gen-Karn's Orn tribe. Most of the tribes sent expeditions, because selling bandar skins was the only way many of the tribes could obtain the valued things from the civilized lands of the faraway South: costly cloths and silks, spices, fine weapons with a lasting sharpness on their edges.

Some years, especially after a long, harsh winter, the bandar would be few and the hunters many. And recently there had been hunts on which no bandar pelts were taken at all. Instead the hunters had warred upon one another, starting harsh blood-feuds. So Gundoen thought to hunt earlier this year than was customary and steal the finest pelts before the other tribes' hunters even reached the hunting grounds.

In all this time of waiting, Gundoen never saw the

barge-robber; but the guards who watched him reported all that he did. They told him the man's beard grew longer and that he wore the tunic of the tribe—also that he learned the tongue of the North, though his words were few. At the first, Gundoen showed great interest in the stranger's doings, and he laughed when he heard of the randy woman left standing; and he shrugged when he heard of the finding of the head of Ob-Kal-Ti. But when they spoke of how the folk had begun to pay a greater heed to Kuln-Holn's hourly preachings, Gundoen quickly lost his interest. He had been quick to ask for anything that might give him an excuse to kill the stranger; when it became clear this would not come to pass, he grew bored and no longer asked the watchers of the man's doings. In time and amid the flurry of preparations for the great Hunt, the guards themselves lost interest, and the watch upon the stranger ceased.

Gundoen saw the Pious One only once, and then he saw that the little prophet had cut his beard neater and mended his tunics so that they were not quite so ragged as before. Also Kuln-Holn seemed to walk with a more upright bearing, as if he were a hunter with kills to his credit. The chief frowned, but did not ask what these changes might portend. He did notice that the Pious One was looking noticeably thinner, as if he were not eating enough; this made Gundoen laugh. The barge-robber was eating the man out of his hut, he thought. It was good to see him paying the price of his foolishness.

When the weeks of ten passes of jade God overhead had lapsed, and they began to look from Outpost Rock for the return of the scouts, the foreign merchants came to see the chief. They were as usual all smiles, bows, and flowery gestures, now that they knew that the tribe was about to embark upon the Hunt. Gundoen only looked at them with ill-concealed disgust.

"Greetings, O Chief," bowed the older merchant Zelatar Bonvis. "We trust that all goes well with the preparations? Is there anything we can do to aid your people?"

Gundoen shrugged. "Well enough. We need no help."

"Your hunters look forward to the Hunt with great eagerness, and that is well. Each man hopes to be celebrated as the Hero of the Hunt."

"The Hero of the Hunt?" asked the younger merchant, whose chin was smooth as some woman's.

"Yes," responded Zelatar smoothly. "In every great Hunt there is one hunter who is most responsible for its success. This man is named the Hero of the Hunt and is awarded the greater share of the gold—more even than what the chief receives. Of course, those years when the chief's share and the Hero's share go to different men are rare indeed. For usually it is Gundoen who is the Hero of the Hunt. What hunter is greater than Gundoen?"

Gundoen shrugged and turned back to the tending of his ponies. They were sleek, plump creatures—especially the brown mare, a wild and amorous creature who had foaled several of the finest ponies in the tribe and was one of the chief's most prized possessions. "That is one of the reasons I am chief," he muttered.

Behind the chief's back the two merchants exchanged knowing smiles.

"Not the only reason, I am sure," resumed Zelatar. "There are many reasons why Gundoen is chief—each better than the others. He is a great fighter, a wise leader, and the most skilled battle commander in all the North. Yet most important of all is the chief's skill at wrestling."

"Yes." The younger merchant nodded. "Even I had heard of that before I ever came to the North. They speak of his skills at the gates of Gerso. They say he has never yet lost a wrestling match, and that the bones of all his many adversaries, crushed by the main strength of his arms, decorate the walls of his great hall."

"All foreigners are liars," growled the chief. "I have only a few of the bones, and those of men from other lands. Otherwise the spirits of my tribesmen would haunt me. But it is true when they say I have not yet been vanquished. Do they really speak my name before the gates of Gerso?"

"Often, great chief. And now that I have met you, I find no cause for wonder in it."

Gundoen looked down at his massive torso, his great long arms and short legs like tree trunks upside down, growing thicker and more knotted as they rose.

"Tall men make poor wrestlers," he said simply. "Also, it is more important that a man need to win in his heart than that his arms have power."

"This will be the greatest Hunt of your career, O Chief," said the bearded merchant. "What else were the storm and the eclipse if not omens for the good? They foretell great deeds done by strong men. You will gather more pelts this year than you have ever done, more than three ordinary hunts. I prophesy it."

"Mighty is Gundoen," chimed the merchant newly come. "So, therefore, mighty is the tribe of Gundoen."

"While we, on the dark side, are but poor, impoverished merchants. The nations of the South grow surfeited with bandar skins, and will pay us no more than a third of the prices that once we got. Every year that passes leaves us less and less money. Yet even so we will not pass our miseries on to Gundoen. We have known him long, and dare call him friend. However, great chief, so that we are not driven penniless in our efforts to bring you the finest of Southern goods, we must ask that this year the price of pelts be halved."

The chief frowned. "Only half?" he cried.

"For our own protection only, O Chief!" uttered Zelatar. "Truly, we would not do this unless we were forced to it. And perhaps next year things will be better. And think—this will be the greatest Hunt in all the history of the tribe. Even at the lower price you will gather more gold than you did last year."

"You think to cheat me," growled Gundoen, pulling out his great bright sword. "You would only give us half of your gold for that for which we risk our lives! What do you say to half a head to do your business with?"

"Mercy, great chief, mercy!" The merchants fell to their knees before him, groveling shamelessly. "If you slay poor merchants, how will others come to trade with you? And perhaps next year will be better!" The wily Zelatar knew that this was the moment of greatest risk, upon which all his gamble depended. The chief would either slay them out of hand or concede to their price.

For a terrifying moment the chief looked down at them, and it seemed that his anger would get the better of his need. But then he spat with disgust. "You are not worth dirtying my blade. You foreigners are no more than robbers even at your best. Get you gone, bandits! You know well enough I have no choice but to accept your price."

Zelatar and Mergo bowed fearfully and slunk out of the chief's sight. They walked through the village streets with heads and shoulders bowed, as if the chief had utterly abashed them. But when they returned to the guest hall, they caught each other's eyes and laughed aloud.

At last, Estar, Foron, and Garin returned, bursting with news. On a crude map etched on hide, they showed the areas where the signs of bandar had been most plentiful and where the Korla lookouts had been. The Korlas, knowing the spears of Gundoen's men, watched the paths whenever they were clear. The hunters met again, in earnest now, and determined which paths were best to follow and at which points the Korlas would most likely set their spies.

The women packed up the last of the foodstuffs, and the hunters put a final rubbing of animal fat upon their blades. The ponies were packed with supplies and brushed down. And when all was finally made ready, the feast was set forth.

This was the good-fortune feast, and to it all members of the tribe, even outcasts like Kuln-Holn, were invited. A large clearing in the middle of the village, just before the chief's hall, was swept clean, and pits were dug in the ground and filled with branches and logs for open cook-fires. Fresh straw was strewn about over the hard sandy ground. The largest tables from the halls were brought forth and placed in a great hollow square. Then the chief poured out the ceremonial cup, the God's cup: brown ale spilled into the fire, whose steam, they prayed, would find pleasure in the nostrils of dark God and stave from them His envy and His evil. This Gundoen did in the custom of their grandfathers before them; then they all cheered and cried for feasting. Out came the finest foods and baked goods; out came kegs of ale; and out came goats and mares and pigs, butchered and thrown, roasting, over the blazing red cook-fires. The stores of the village were being exhausted in this feast, but that did not matter.

"If we have a good Hunt, we'll have all the food we want," the chief said. "If the Hunt is bad, why feed dead men?"

The people were glad enough to put aside the troubles of the past and rejoice in the promise of future luck. The young men and women danced together in the square to the beat of the wooden drums, and there was much singing. Hertha-Toll invoked the blessing of the Goddess, and

Alli passed out the first round of brimming dark ale. The feast began.

After the feast came the entertainments. Especially popular was Alli, favorite of the chief's concubines. She danced an enticing roundabout, then brought out her young son, a strapping big fellow for his four years. Everyone cheered at this, loudest of all the chief; and it was as if the Storm had never washed away the crops.

Then Hertha-Toll, the Wise and the Sorrowful, came to the center of the tables. It was her custom to speak on what she had seen or dreamed concerning the Hunt. Everyone quieted at seeing the look that was on her face.

"I have had a dream," announced Hertha-Toll. "I have seen swift feet and red spears, the flow of much black blood. The spears of our people were drenched in it, yet in hunting our men had little success. Even so, the pile of pelts I saw was large—larger than I have even seen before. This is to be a great Hunt, the most successful in the generations of our tribe—this I prophesy!"

Boisterous cheers roared at her words. The two foreign merchants from the civilized lands nudged one another and smiled. They too had reason to be glad at this news, for Zelatar had had enough experience of the woman's wisdom to know that many things forecast by Hertha-Toll came to pass.

"And the Hero, wife!" called Gundoen, holding out his ale-bowl so that Alli might refill it. "Who is to be the Hero of the Hunt?"

Hertha-Toll's glad face vanished, and she was silent. She looked about the square of long tables and gazed at each man. Last of all she looked at the stranger, the barge-robber, sitting next to Kuln-Holn.

She turned back to the chief. "His face was in the shadow," she said at last. "I could not recognize it. It was a strange face."

Gundoen frowned darkly. The people's murmurings fell lower. Hertha-Toll walked back to her place at the chief's side in silence.

Gundoen rose suddenly.

"The final offering for Him who is without name," he said, growling. He poured the dregs of his bowl of ale into the coal-lit fires. A cloud of hissing steam arose from the spot. "I call upon the Dark Lord to grant us luck and witness our Hunt!"

"O Chief, a boon!"

Broad-chested Gundoen turned. Standing forth was the gray-bearded little prophet, Kuln-Holn. His voice sounded thin after Gundoen's bellowings and the strange power of Hertha-Toll's voice. Uncertainly, the Pious One stepped forward.

"What is it?" growled Gundoen. By custom, at this moment he could not refuse a boon formally asked. To do so would have been to cast ill-luck upon the Hunt.

"Chief, I do not ask it for myself, but for Ara-Karn. You have placed him in my charge, so I thought it my duty to speak."

"Well?"

"Chief Gundoen, Ara-Karn wishes to join the Hunt."

There was a brief silence. Then the chief threw back his great broad head and began to laugh. It was a hearty laugh, rather like the one he had given vent to on the beach, when the stranger had first come among them. The people looked to one another and then, uncertainly, joined in the laughter. Soon everyone was laughing, laughing drunken peals of great laughter, and they did not notice it when the chief suddenly ceased and looked sternly across at Kuln-Holn.

The laughter gradually faded.

The chief gave Kuln-Holn a grim wolf's-smile.

"O Pious One, never before have you been on a hunt for bandar. Never have you used any other weapon than a pronged fish-spear; and never have you fought a man to death. Will a fisherman's net hold a bandar, do you think? What kind of bait will you use to draw out Korla spies?"

Kuln-Holn reddened at the barbs and the laughter they drew forth. But he did not draw back as he had done in the chief's hall when he had asked about Oron; nor did he look at all abashed. He said bravely, "I did not ask this for myself, chief, but for my guest. He wishes to go on the Hunt, not I. I dislike bloodletting. I will stay here in the village as always."

"What foolishness is this?" snapped Gundoen. "They tell me you have been teaching the barge-robber our tongue, Kuln-Holn. Can he speak it yet?"

Kuln-Holn looked to the table where the stranger sat. The man nodded, rose, and came into the middle of the square.

His hair and beard were longer, combed and cut square.

His rags were gone, replaced by a simple tunic of soft leather, such as most of the fishermen of the tribe wore. There were no jewels on his fingers, no golden band around his brow; yet he still wore the ornate ceremonial dagger of jade. Save for that, he looked like many another tribesman of the far north, until one looked at his face. There the features were too refined, almost cruel—and the depths of those dark eyes were not the wide light blue-green of a Northman's. And he held himself as if it were he who ruled the tribe, or ought to. Hertha-Toll, standing beside the chief, looked closely at the stranger; yet when he looked at her, she cast down her eyes.

The last of the laughter died down when the stranger looked around.

"I speak."

His voice was deep, compelling. It was not so deep or booming as Gundoen's; but the words were pronounced with a strange accent that commanded attention. Hearing that accent recalled the time when he had first spoken those alien words on the beach.

Gundoen frowned. "And you understand me? You wish to join our hunt even though you will probably be killed?"

"Yes."

"Why?"

The stranger smiled. The chief lifted his ale-bowl to his lips, frowning.

"You will be slain, barge-robber." Gundoen wiped his lips with the back of his hand. "Do not think you can escape on the journey. Where would you go? There are only bandar and Korlas in these parts, and they have not the generosity or the hospitality of our tribe. Do you wish to be found dead a second time?"

The stranger did not answer.

"Let him come," said Hertha-Toll. She had been staring at the stranger as if this were the first time she had seen him; as if he were an enemy. Almost against her will she counseled the chief. "Let him come. He will bring the Hunt luck."

Gundoen looked at his wife fiercely. "Woman of ill fortune," he murmured savagely to her, "this is the second time you have interceded on this man's behalf. Do you love him so much then? Do you wish to belittle me before all the tribe?"

"Not so much, no." She shook her head, trying not to

gaze in the stranger's direction. "I have never interfered
with the rule of the tribe, husband, except to do you good.
This you know well. I have no reason to love the stranger.
Just the opposite. Yet what I have seen I say. This man
will bring luck to the Hunt." It was almost as if she re-
gretted her own words. And Gundoen heard the truth in
those words.

He shrugged, spat. "Well. So be it. I cannot refuse this
boon, if Kuln-Holn is so foolhardy as to ask it still.
Stranger, do you wish to be buried with the carcasses of the
bandar or shall we send you off again in your own barge?"

Later in the feast there were the wrestling matches. The
chief went against Kul-Dro, Garin's father, a great strong
man and the second best spearman in the entire tribe, a
man who would be needed in the Hunt. Gundoen threw
him twice, his eyes like fire reflected off dark red ale. He
crushed Kul-Dro's ribs and almost tore his right arm from
the shoulder, so savagely that Kul-Dro lay abed for three
weeks and completely missed the Hunt.

When he rose from Kul-Dro's broken body, the chief
looked about, turning like a wild beast rising from the kill.
The hair stood out from his head and a bit of blood oozed
from his broken lower lip. When he saw the stranger, he
raised his lips, curling them away from his strong white
teeth in a horrible grin.

The stranger returned the smile and politely inclined his
head.

The hunters departed down the path by Outpost Rock.
Many wives and children bade them touching farewell—
they knew that not all who set out would return. Kuln-
Holn looked to say farewell to Ara-Karn, but the stranger
had already gone on and was well down the path with the
leading hunters. The Pious One turned back, saddened.
For all his faith, he did not know if he would ever again
see the man who was to him more than man.

Hertha-Toll looked on the hunters, giving them each the
sign of Her blessing with a face like chipped stone. She
had taken leave of the chief during the longsleep after the
feast; yet what words of secret advice or warning she had
offered him, none could say. Some, however, hinted that
there had been loud and angry words exchanged.

Soon the lines of riding hunters were wholly swallowed
up in the leafy darkness leading into the territory of the

Korlas. The wives and children began to disperse and return to their customary pursuits. The fields must be resown with what grain they had been able to barter; the damages of the Storm were still not fully repaired. Only two of all the people lingered by the rock: Kuln-Holn and Hertha-Toll.

At last they too turned and trudged back up the hill through the broad brown fields toward the village. Neither one would look at or speak to the other, which was strange, for they had been friends of old. Yet now the stranger's shadow lay between them.

The hunters rode through the paths of the forest, rumbling dust marking their trail. The light of Goddess fell dappled through the branches; the high canopy of young spring leaves cast a light green glow upon the muffled floor of the deep forest. In the distance could be heard young birds' mating calls and the snap-and-tassel of the sharp-eared wornors.

Ahead and to the sides of the main columns rode the scouts. They rode lazily now, as there was little chance of encountering any Korlas this side of Darkbole Forest. Yet Gundoen took no chances. At the tactics of intertribal warfare, at warfare subtlety and combat surprises there were few to equal Gundoen in all the far North. That was why the other independent tribes looked to him for leadership against the crafty Gen-Karn.

They rode for two meals' time. The first meal was eaten in the saddle. For the second they stopped to water the ponies at a low-banked brown stream. Sometime later they came to the outskirts of Darkbole Forest. A few great giants of the woods, their trunks a shining black mottled by the spread of green lichen, marked the border.

"Here we go with greater caution," announced Gundoen. "Be alert, you scouts: death comes swiftly here."

He signaled for them to proceed; properly subdued, they did so. The chief watched as the first few ranks rode in, then he rode on ahead.

In all this time the chief gave not a glance or word to the stranger. He was Gundoen, chief of his tribe, leading his hunters upon the most important hunt of his career. It was as if the stranger no longer existed to him. Yet the stranger rode, whenever he could, close by to the chief, watching him, paying close attention to all he did. It seemed almost to those who noticed as if the stranger was studying the chief for some future purpose.

The columns went slowly through Darkbole Forest. There had been no need for the chief's admonition to silence. Naturally and of its own accord, the jubilance of the men faded. They spoke only when they must, and then in hushed tones. This was not done out of fear of any Korla spies: the Forest commanded its own respect.

The barbarians feared the Forest. It was primeval, dark, oppressive. A man on horseback could have concealed himself, horse and all, behind some of those massive boles. High, high above, the light of Goddess flickered in dim jewellike flashes through the leaves. Below, all was shadow.

The darkness and closeness were why Gundoen had chosen this forest for their route. The Korlas would have to stumble within twenty paces of the column to have been aware of its existence. And the superstitious dread felt by the men of Gundoen's tribe would affect Korlas no less.

Gundoen rode now not at the head of the column, but up and down its entire length, giving low words of encouragement to those he passed. He was one of only two men who seemed to feel no fear in the Forest's silent darkness. His presence lent support to men who needed it badly; they even smiled wanly when he passed and spoke of the victories they would gain when they finally reached the hunting ground. Gundoen smiled and rode on.

The other man who seemed to feel no fear was the stranger, Ara-Karn. He rode at ease and in complete serenity. Not even the chief could match him for apparent indifference. And there was also this difference: the chief felt his fear but conquered it. Ara-Karn seemed actually to enjoy the thick darkness, the oppressive, stultifying air wet with dripping leaf and fear, the prospect of imminent, sudden, savage death. Once, in fact, he seemed to forget himself and rode out in front of the column, being lost from sight for several moments.

The men who saw him fell in awe of the stranger. They sensed his eagerness and knew there was something foreign and luckless in it. They began almost to fear him. For the last two marches through Darkbole Forest, Ara-Karn rode alone, a barrier of emptiness between him and the nearest tribesmen.

At last they emerged from Darkbole Forest. They came again into the sun, and sighed their great relief. Many were the thanks breathed to Goddess as the men rode up into the hills beyond.

Five more passes they traveled, still seeing no sign of the Korlas, though they knew their sneaking spies must be about. They passed up into the hills along an ancient dried riverbed, making excellent progress now. They crossed over the lip of the low mountains along the southern edge of the Forest of Bandar, which now lay spread below them. Here they made one last camp in the concealing rocks to rest their ponies and sent the scouts on ahead.

Foron was the first of the scouts to return. Many were the signs and tracks of bandar, and of those beasts he had glimpsed he was sure their skins were brightly green indeed. Some short time later Estar rode back, reporting much the same news. The hunters grinned and took out their skinning knives, testing the sharpness with their horned thumbs.

Garin, last of the scouts, returned, riding swiftly up the slope of the hill.

"Korlas!" he gasped, out of breath. "More than a score of them heading this way."

"Conceal yourselves," Gundoen warned. The green tents were pulled down and strewn with grass and dirt. The ponies were tethered in a thick brake of bushes over the crest of the hill. The hunters scattered themselves over the dark side of the hill. They lay behind rocks and the scroungy bushes that tenaciously clung to life even here where the sun never shone.

"If it is only a patrol and they do not see us, they will ride on, reporting nothing," said the chief. "If not, perhaps we can conceal our true strength and get them to attack."

The hillside quieted. At first only the faint chirrupings from the forest below could be heard in the hunters' ears. Then the sound of approaching ponies sounded slightly, borne upon the spring breezes. The sound grew louder. Rising dust could be seen on the left, along the base of the hills that skirted the forest's edge. A man on a pony appeared, followed by another. Soon a full score-and-five could be seen, riding toward the hidden hunters. They looked from side to side routinely, obviously bored with their duty. They rode below and passed the hidden hunters, who breathed soft sighs of relief—though several tightened their fingers on the bone handles of their knives, their faces contorted with hatred.

Suddenly one of the Korlas at the rear reined in his pony and looked at the ground. He called out to the leader, and the column halted, wheeled about, and surrounded him. They dismounted and walked about the earth, examining it carefully. They gestured rapidly with their hands. The sound of their excited voices floated up to the ears of the hunters, but too faintly to make out what they were saying.

Gundoen swore under his breath. It was clear the Korlas had discovered something—probably the tracks of the scouts leading into the forest. It was also clear that they had no idea they were presently being watched by Gundoen's hunters. If they had guessed that, they would have already taken horse back for their village. Korlas were cowards at heart.

Gundoen made his decision.

He raised his fist with the thumb at right angles, the sign of attack. The hunters who could see him nodded, and in turn repeated the sign to those whose positions were concealed from Gundoen's eyes.

The hunters wormed forward, carefully, silently. Below, the Korlas were still arguing over the meaning of what they had seen.

When they could creep forward no closer, the hunters rose silently and ran headlong down the darkened slope.

"Let none escape to tell the tale!" roared the chief. He grabbed a stone and flung it down at the Korlas' ponies. Other hunters followed his example, until a rain of stones pelted men and horses, making the men lift up their shields and cower in fear and the ponies bolt for cover.

One man was knocked unconscious by a stone. He fell with a cry, blood spouting from his head. Then the hunters fell upon them, swords redly threshing.

The Korlas, now that they saw who their foes were, fought back. Their desperation lent their efforts a savage ferocity that at first was able to repulse the attackers. They formed themselves into a crude square, shields locked together and swords flashing out from all sides.

They began to back into the forest.

Among the trees and heavy foliage, the greater numbers of the attackers would not be so effective. And as soon as they reached the forest the Korlas would dash apart in all directions. In the dense forest at least one of them would reach the Korla village to give the alarm. When Gundoen's men, tired from the hunt and loaded with pelts, tried to return to their home, they would be met by large parties of Korla warriors in ambush.

The chief rushed the shield-wall. His great strength shattered the Korlas; he fell into the middle of the square, Korlas to all sides of him. He killed two of them right off; then the others closed about him.

There were only a few Korlas left now. The chief's rush had shattered their formation, allowing the other hunters to slay Korlas right and left. In a few moments it would all be done, but that would not save Gundoen. Not even the broad-chested chief could strike out on all sides at once.

Two Korlas were behind him, swords already reaching back to give the death-stroke. A shout of warning alerted the chief; he turned and thrust his sword in the naked throat of one of his attackers. The man fell, crying out not sounds but blood.

Yet the other was already sending his blade at the bowels of the chief. Nor could Gundoen do aught about it. There was no time to wrench his sword loose to fend off the blow, and his shield was behind him protecting his back. The other hunters were out of sword's reach. Gundoen could only watch as the Korla sword drank deep his blood.

He saw the triumph in the Korla's eyes, saw the thirsty blade flashing. Then the triumph turned to agony in the eyes, and the sword quavered and fell harmless to the ground. A gasp came from the Korla's mouth.

He fell dead without another sound.

Gundoen grunted. He wrenched his sword free from the bloody throat, and hacked off the sword arm of a Korla whose back was to him. It was not the chief's nature to question gifts of the gods.

There was not much to the fighting after that. Not a single Korla escaped; every one fell dead to the ground. Only two of the hunters had been injured: Es-Tarn had got a cut high on his sword arm, and Turn-Ton was gashed on his upper thigh. The wounds would impair their hunting abilities somewhat, but would heal cleanly. Not a single one of Gundoen's hunters had been slain.

The other hunters were amazed when they saw Gundoen, unhurt save for a few cuts, stepping from the pile of hacked red bodies. Casually the chief wiped his bloody blade clean on the back of one of the dead, then sheathed it.

"Gundoen!" cried Arnoth in joy. "We thought you dead for sure!"

"It was close enough." The chief shrugged. "But no Korla has yet been born who bears my death on his blade."

"I was sure you had died," said Garin, puzzled. "I saw two Korlas at your back readying your death-stroke. How is it you escaped?"

"I do not know. I slew one of them but had no time for the second. I saw death in his hand, but then he fell. I never saw what struck him down."

"Let us examine the body," Garin suggested. So they hunted through the butchered bodies until they came upon the one they sought. Gundoen recognized him immediately. But when they turned the body over, they found not the mark of a single sword or rock, nor wound nor bruise—only a slight feathered stick protruding from the man's back.

Round where the shaft had entered there was a great stain of drying blood.

CHAPTER SIX
The Great Hunt

They camped deep in the Forest of the Bandar near where the scouts had seen the most recent signs of bandar. Here they fed their ponies and themselves, and examined their weapons a final time. They clustered together in small groups here and there, gossiping at ease, excited now that the great Hunt was about to begin in earnest. They spoke a good deal of the mystery of the dead Korla, but since no one could explain it, the matter was dropped at last. They had concealed the remains of the Korlas in a pit dug in the dark earth, where their spirits would never reach the Happy Shores; and they had gathered the Korla ponies for their own use. Their tracks they had carefully obscured, so that no other patrols might see where they had entered the forest.

There was almost no danger of encountering Korlas in the forest. There were laws against fighting within the hunting grounds, and those laws were broken only under the greatest provocation. The Korlas might wonder what had happened to the patrol, but by the time they got around to investigating, Gundoen hoped to be long gone. They had come early this year for that very purpose.

When all the ponies were fed and the hunters rested, they gathered around the chief. Now came the time for the hunters to separate into smaller bands of three or four hunters each in order to get the most kills. Every hunters' band would have one tracker, and the other members would be spearmen. Some bands, formed of close friends or kin who had been together for years, joined together first and stood somewhat apart from the others.

The remaining bands would be chosen by lots. Every man put his mark upon a leaf or piece of bark and put it in a bag—one bag for the spearmen, another for the trackers. The chief would draw forth first a mark from the bag of trackers, then two or three from the bag of spearmen. If any two men who had strong feelings against each other were chosen for the same band, their lots were put back in the bags and drawn again in different order.

First, however, came the time for Gundoen, as chief and as the hero of the last year's Hunt, to pick out his band personally. There was always clamor at this, for members of the band with the most pelts were all given prizes in addition to the award for the Hero of the Hunt. And Gundoen was such a mighty hunter that it was almost certain that his band would gain the most kills. So all the hunters wished to hunt with Gundoen and follow his spear home, as the saying went.

The great-chested chief went up and down the lines, eyeing every hunter. Merely to be chosen was an honor. Men looked at him hopefully or confidently, according to their beliefs in their own abilities.

"For my tracker," said the chief—and all the clamor hushed—"I choose Garin."

Garin stepped forward. The others clapped him on the back and gave him words of encouragement. Garin was the best tracker in the tribe and a very popular young man. There had been no surprise in this choice.

"And for my fellow spearman," Gundoen announced, "I pick—Ara-Karn."

A silence fell upon the hunters. The stranger stepped forward as calmly as if he had expected to be chosen all along. One man grumbled, "What has the barge-robber done to deserve this?"

Gundoen stared at the stranger's face with the harsh grin of a man who has his enemy under the point of his spear, as if to say to him, Now I will show you how great is Gundoen.

But Ara-Karn only looked calmly back, a slight smile about his lips, as if to reply, We shall see.

The bands were drawn from the lots in the bags and grouped about the green glen. They separated, each following the lead of the band's tracker along the paths of the forest. They would not see one another, save for the occasional chance greetings at the crossings of trails, for twenty passes of God overhead—two weeks' time. Then they would gather on the dark side of the mountain they had last camped on, according to custom and the chief's command.

Garin led Gundoen and the stranger along a well-worn game trail. They led their ponies behind them: the forest was too close for riding, and the horses would make too much noise. The wet leaves brushed against the hunters' thighs. The damp dark earth of the trail smelled of decaying vegetation and the droppings of many animals. Gundoen breathed the scent in noisily, sighing for pleasure. The Hunt begun at last!

They came to a small stream where the trails crossed. Signs of bandar were plentiful all about; Garin pointed them out to the stranger in hushed tones. He stooped, examining the leaves of a bush overhanging the stream. He straightened.

"A large bull has passed this way recently," he whispered. "He leaves the sheddings of his last brown furs on the branches here. Follow." He plunged into the thicket with no more sound than a slight breeze would leave, and Gundoen followed him. Ara-Karn hesitated for a moment, then plunged after the others.

Garin followed the trail for some time in silence. Suddenly he halted, head held high in the air. Silently Gundoen and Ara-Karn came and squatted beside him.

"He is near," Garin whispered. He parted the leaves surrounding them. Through the gap could be seen a small clearing. "Is this acceptable?" he asked.

Gundoen nodded. "How will you bring him around?"

"Through the far side."

The chief nodded again, and Garin slipped away noiselessly, leaving his pony behind with the spearmen. Gundoen and Ara-Karn were now alone.

The chief nudged the stranger. "We must tether the ponies down the trail. Tie the cords well: ponies are frightened at the smell of bandar blood." He grinned mirthlessly. "Don't you be like the ponies."

When they returned to the clearing, they squatted down

in the bushes just beyond the opening. The scent of opening blossoms was heavy in the still air. A bee buzzed by
their ears.

"Do you know what he will do?" Gundoen asked. The
foreigner nodded, but Gundoen looked his doubts. "This
is only your first kill," he warned. "Leave it to me, but be
ready to assist in case there is trouble. I don't think you'll
be needed. Gundoen alone is usually as good as any two
other spearmen." He looked the stranger over suddenly.
"Why have you no spear?" he asked sharply.

Ara-Karn smiled.

"Well, take one of mine. This is a fine spear; treat it with
respect. Maybe later we can make one for you. If you still
live."

Ara-Karn took the spear and hefted it. It was of the
usual spear length, coming to the nipple of a standing man.
The wooden shaft was thick, polished, heavy; it had seemed
smaller in Gundoen's mighty fist. Along one face were
etched many runes of good fortune.

"He comes," Gundoen commented, rising to his feet and
stepping into the clearing. "Stand a dozen paces to my right,
but stay concealed until I call."

The stranger nodded and crept away.

The faint noise grew louder. There was a dull thudding
of great hooves, an angry snorting, the rush of a massive
body through the underbrush.

Suddenly Garin brust into the clearing.

He saw Gundoen in a glance and dove off to one side
into leafy secrecy. Then the bandar was upon them.

It burst into the clearing, hoof and claw, tusk and snout.
It was a prime bull, tall as a man, tail lashing, deep-set
eyes blazing redly. Its coat was the resplendent vivid green
of a bull in heat.

It paused for a moment after entering the clearing. It
moved its great head wickedly from side to side. Then it
saw Gundoen with its darting small eyes. Bellowing a harsh
shriek, it charged forward. The massive body of the chief
was like a weakling babe's before that tremendous bulk.

Gundoen laughed, egging the beast on.

At the last moment, when it had seemed the curling yellow tusks had ripped his flesh, the chief dodged to the right
slightly. Immediately the bull shifted its broad head after
him, tusks straining to gore this puny man-thing that dared
challenge its supremacy.

But Gundoen, moving with a quickness that belied his massive frame, twisted back to the left and drove his spear deep into the right shoulder of the bull. The beast's forward motion wrenched the spear, but Gundoen held fast, his great muscles bulging and cracking at the effort. The long spear edge ripped at the point of leverage, working its way deeper into the green neck. Great torrents of blue-black blood burst forth into Gundoen's face.

Gundoen laughed again and wrenched the spear free.

He circled to the bandar's hindquarters. The beast, confused by pain and weakened by the loss of blood, tried to wheel about, but stumbled and lost the footing of its front hooves.

This was the moment the chief had been waiting for. With a great leap he landed squarely on the beast's back, locking knees about the huge barrel chest just behind the forelegs.

At this new outrage the beast bellowed, its head waving in the air. Vainly it attempted to rise and shake off this thing astride its back. It rose up a little of the way, straining to come to its feet.

Ara-Karn and Garin stood to one side. The chief's spear was in the hands of the stranger, who stood fascinated by this violent, barbaric spectacle.

The scene lasted only a moment. Just as the bandar seemed on the point of gaining its feet, Gundoen lifted his spear in both bloody fists and brought the point shatteringly down on the back of the massive head. The point entered the skull just behind the pointed ears. With a soft crunch it pierced through the small brains into the roof of the mouth.

With a final shriek of rage, the beast sank back to its knees. Its belly fell upon the earth and the great head, still transfixed by the waving spear, sank down to touch the sward.

The silence that followed was shattering.

Gundoen shook his head as if to clear it. Slowly he climbed down off the massive, quivering back. He stood on the ground, swaying slightly back and forth. He planted one foot on the snout and gripped the wooden haft of the spear. He gave a grunting wrench and pulled the blood-smeared spear free.

"A wonderful kill," cried Garin, rushing forward to slap the chief's shoulder. "What a victory, and over such a bull!"

Gundoen grunted, looking down at the vanquished bulk. He seemed almost sad that the thing was done.

The tracker turned to Ara-Karn. "Stranger, what a triumph you have seen! Did you mark how he held fast to the haft when the bull rushed forward, so that it ripped the veins of its own neck? That is called Gundoen's Rend, for only he has the strength to accomplish it. It weakens the beast in one stroke and does not damage the pelt.

"Oh, this is a fine pelt," he went on, examining it. "Do you see how few brown marks are on it? In the winter the bandar are all brown: they lose that fur and become green only now that they rut. This pelt will bring much from the traders! I only hope your first kill will be half as fine."

Gundoen grunted. "We shall see soon enough. The next bandar we spot, I will assist you, barge-robber. Then we'll see of what stuff is Ara-Karn made."

For the next several hours they camped by the body of the slain bandar. Gundoen and Garin stripped off the pelt in one great piece and set about scraping the guts and blood off the inner side. The stranger made a small fire and cooked several steaks. Bandar meat had a bitter taste, but Gundoen wolfed down his steaks almost raw, the bloody juice running down his beard and chest.

"No meat finer than the first kill of the season," he growled contentedly, gulping mouthfuls of stream water.

Ara-Karn cooked his steak longer than the others, and ate but sparingly. The chief saw this and laughed rather scornfully.

"Not delicate enough for a former king, eh? Never mind. Wait until your first kill, if you can manage it. You'll gobble that meat greedily enough."

With that he stretched out, drawing his tent-dim-place over his head to take his short sleep. Garin too, after he had packed several pieces of well-cooked meat for eating on the trail, settled down for sleep. Soon the regular movements of their chests indicated that both men were sleeping soundly.

Ara-Karn rose and slipped silently into the dense forest. Gundoen snorted and half-rolled over, but did not awaken.

The stranger was gone for some time. When he returned, he held a small bag filled with fresh-picked roots and leaves of a ruby color. He dumped them into a small pan over the fire. Immediately a pungent odor issued from the pan; Garin coughed, but did not wake.

Ara-Karn fried the leaves until a thick liquid had collected in the bottom of the pan. He took out his pouch of slender straight sticks, which he had saved from his own death-barge. He dipped the iron tip of each stick into the brown syrup. He took the greatest care lest any of the syrup drip upon his hands or clothing.

When they had broken camp, the hunters sought the watering pools once again. Bandar, as Garin explained to the foreigner, are huge beasts, eaters of flesh, leaf, and worm, endlessly thirsting. They go to lakes, pools, and streams both to quench their own thirst and in search of prey.

Garin had no trouble finding the trail of another bandar and tracking it to the beast's lair. They halted outside a huge brake of thorny bush.

"A bandar nest," Garin muttered. "They build these themselves during the mating season. They root out bushes with their great tusks and drag the thorny brambles together to shelter their newborn young. Within that barrier there are dozens of them—bulls and cows and calves—a fortune in pelts."

"When do we begin?"

"Fool, we do not enter there," sneered Gundoen. "Nowhere are they more dangerous than in their nests. Not even all the hunters of the tribe could hope to kill all the beasts of one lair."

Gundoen squatted down behind the bole of a large tree. "No, stranger, we must wait," he said. "When one comes out, we will follow it a way from the lair, and then attack.

"Then it will be your turn, barge-robber. Do not feel too nervous or fearful: Gundoen will be beside you." The stranger only smiled, and the chief grew angry, but could think of nothing further to say.

"A bull is leaving," said Garin.

They looked down at the thorny wall. A great bull, almost as huge as the one Gundoen had slain, was pushing its way out of an opening in the brake that seemed half its size.

The chief grunted. "Not big enough by half. For a former king, only a kingly bull will do."

They waited longer. Breezes came and went, and birds flew and perched overhead. Several bandar left the lair, but they were small, or dark, or had too many patches of brown left. Suddenly Gundoen said, "Here is one that will do well."

The others looked. A huge bull, much larger than the one the chief had slain, was emerging from the barrier. It was a patriarch of bandar, big as a small hut, its pelt bright, bright green. Its yellowed curling tusks were longer than a tall man's thigh.

Garin protested the choice, but Gundoen only laughed. "If my friend here wishes to choose a smaller animal, that is up to him. But if he does choose this one, he need not fear: Gundoen will be close by to save his life."

Ara-Karn smiled. "This one will do very well," he said softly.

Garin looked at him sharply, then shrugged. "If you wish to end your life, it is your own business," he said. "Come then."

They followed him along the dark path. Overhead the faint green orb of God could be seen through the canopy of trees. Gundoen went last now, leading the ponies behind. About a thousand paces down the trail, the bandar paused by a large pool, slurping water noisily. Garin found them a good clearing as before. Only now it was Ara-Karn who stood out in the open, while the chief concealed himself a few paces off to one side.

Calmly, the stranger knelt and unslung his pack. He drew forth the curved instrument of polished wood and a handful of the thin straight sticks. To the pointed tips of the instrument he stretched a taut gut string. He flexed the string a few times, listening to its soft thrumming sound.

"What are you doing, fool?" hissed Gundoen. "Will you play the bandar a tune to kill it? Can you not hear that the beast is coming? Throw away those prayer-things and take your spear like a man!"

"It is your spear, not mine," said Ara-Karn. "Here, take it back."

He tossed the heavy spear over in the dirt by the chief's feet.

"Die then," swore the chief with an oath. "We will be well rid of you, barge-robber!"

Not answering, Ara-Karn rose. The rumble of the approaching bandar was deafening. Garin broke into the clearing, scrambling for cover, the beast hot upon his heels.

Not a moment did the bandar pause, but charged straight forward. He was a bull late in his prime, a magnificent beast much experienced in these games the men-things played. Many were the hunters, and numerous their tribes, who had been gored by his monstrous curling tusks or trampled to a wet mush beneath his cruelly honed hooves. He knew that the twisting, scrambling one would elude him, but he cared not. There would be another one standing across the clearing who would not elude him. He was in a rage and would kill—any death would do.

He charged Ara-Karn with all the strength of his house-like body, watchful for the playful feints hunters in the past had employed in vain.

But Ara-Karn did not attempt to dodge. He nocked an arrow in his bow and drew it back. He released it with a humming sound. The slender shaft shot like lightning, burying itself in the breast of the bandar.

It was a mere pinprick to the beast, only serving to augment its rage. Quick as heartbeats came two more arrows, but now the man-thing was almost within reach of the eager tusks. And suddenly a wave of weakness struck the heart of the patriarch of bandar—with pain such as it had never known. The poison flushed outward like the heat of a good rut and blocked out vision from its eyes.

Gundoen did not flinch when he saw the bull rushing down upon the defenseless stranger. If the man was foolish enough to seek death, then Gundoen would let him gain his journey's end. The barge-robber had crossed him long enough. When Ara-Karn was dead, and the beast triumphing over the broken red remains, then Gundoen would step in and see what he could accomplish.

He was just on the point of leaping forward, spear clutched tightly in his ball-like fists, when he saw—suddenly, miraculously, like something out of the legends of dark God—the bull pause, waver drunkenly, and crash deafeningly to the earth, just at the feet of Ara-Karn.

CHAPTER SEVEN

Red Gold

Kuln-Holn the Pious One was troubled in his heart.

Each pass, in the time between the second and third meals, Kuln-Holn sat in the shade beside the sandy square, preaching the words of his visions; and the women and the old men sat and listened. And each pass, after the fifth meal, Kuln-Holn bestrode Outpost Rock, gazing down the path to where it vanished in the darkness of the wood. And he told all who would listen, how of old he had hoped She would forgive him and send him a sign; and how then the destiny of the tribe would be fulfilled. They would know only food and comfort and the respect of other tribes. They would be the favored of Goddess, and many would come humbly as pilgrims to the village. Yes, even the greatest of monarchs of the civilized lands of the faraway South would come among them as pilgrims and pay homage to their shrines. So preached Kuln-Holn; yet the hunters did not return, and his words of hope rang hollow in the throat of Kuln-Holn; and he closed his eyes in the sickness of the shadow. And yet he knew not what he feared.

Kuln-Holn wandered through the brown fields when the time of sleep lay upon the others, and he went up into the wood. He drifted near the slopes of Kaari-Moldole and gazed upon her peak, dazzling still with snow; yet he dared not pass the sacred limits now as he had done when Ara-Karn had led him there.

From the lower hilltops Kuln-Holn looked toward the dark horizon. There the hills and valleys rolled away, secret beneath the green-leaved trees. The winds passed in flaws over the treetops; and it minded him of the thick seaweeds at the bottom of the bay, where the crabs hid. That was the territory of the Korlas; and beyond that, away out of his vision, lay the Forest of the Bandar. Kuln-Holn tried to envision the Great Hunt, but he had never known one, or even seen a bandar alive. He thought of Korlas, and of the way Gundoen had looked at Ara-Karn when the chief thought none could see. Kuln-Holn thought of the head of Ob-Kal-Ti rolling in the bottom of its empty death-barge; and it was as if a hand had closed about his heart, and he trembled. If only they would obey Ara-Karn in all things, all things would be well. So he told himself many times. Yet this was not the way he had thought Her word should come to pass.

Kuln-Holn went back to fish. It was long years since he had fished—not since the time of his punishment, of which he did not like to think. Now he found his lines rotten and his nets eaten with holes. And now the palms of his hands throbbed as they had not done since his boyhood. But as he sat upon the swelling bowl of waters and played out his lines in the deep lonely spots, a little of peace swam down to the poor fevered mind of Kuln-Holn.

Kuln-Holn caught no fish, as he had known he would not. The magic of the fisherman had been taken from him long ago. When the time was fitting, he slept in his boat and drank water from his skins. He ate little and had no use for food. Then the last of his water was drunk, and he turned his boat back to the land. In the bay he saw that all the other fishing boats were drawn up on the beach; this surprised him, for it was not a time of sleep. He looked toward the arm of land where the stream came down among the rocks and saw no women washing there, though the air was warm for the drying of tunics. None even of the children played there. Then Kuln-Holn knew what this must token, and wished the winds on faster. He drew his boat up aland, bowed to thank Her for Her providence, and hastily went up from the beach.

Among the village huts the hunters rode proudly—big men, strong-armed, their silent faces grimly smiling. In the sandy square before the hall of Tont-Ornoth they gave their ponies into the keeping of the old men who had stayed behind. They took bowls of ale from the women and squatted in the sand. Some of them had wounds the women saw to, salving them with pastes whose secrets were known only to Hertha-Toll. And the word of the hunters' homecoming went outward to the fields and waters and the people crowded back into the village at the call; and among the last of them was Kuln-Holn. He looked anxiously over the faces of the hunters for the face of the stranger. Then he saw him, sitting near the chief, the bowl full of ale lying scorned before his crossed trousered legs. Safe he was and unwounded. Yet even then the fear did not depart Kuln-Holn's heart.

When all the tribe was assembled in the square, the tale of the hunt was told. In addition to the pelts the hunters returned with a score of extra ponies laden down with meat killed on the way back. The hunters had passed the Korla ambushes with only a few dead; they, like the men slain by bandar on the hunt, had been set in crude barges and left floating down the Al-Sin River, which flows out of the mountains and down to the Ocean of the Dead.

And to show for it all, to pay for it all, were such piles of bandar pelts—piles and piles and piles—as had never before been seen together in one place. Not the oldest woman in the tribe could remember when there had ever been such wealth gleaned from a single hunt. The two foreign merchants in their so-clean robes were beside themselves with joy, when they saw the abundance and quality of those pelts.

The tribespeople craned their necks to look at Hertha-Toll, where she stood by her husband. The women whispered to one another in awe: once again had the prophecy of the wise-woman been proved truth. The Hunt had been a great one. Ara-Karn, the stranger, had brought them luck.

Now was the time for the accounting. The hunters lined up in a row before the chief's hall. And their women went to the great piles of pelts and distributed them in heaps before the feet of the hunters as the men directed. Before each man were laid the pelts he himself had taken; and between the spearmen of the bands stood their trackers, with whom some praise must also dwell.

The women and the men who had not gone on the hunt jostled forward now, eager to see the counts. It was largely

on the basis of the counts that the Hero of the Hunt would
be decided; and the close friends and kin of the hunter
named Hero could hope to share in his wealth.

But some women and men hung back, as if they did
not care to see the accounting. "What difference will it
make?" they grumbled. "Everyone knows that Gundoen is
always the Hero of the Hunt because he always gets the
choice of the best trackers." They were envious of their
brash and boastful chief, and there were many such. But
the others crowded eagerly forward to see the counts.

And here was a hunter with five pelts before him, and
that was a goodly number; and here was one with eight,
which was very good. And there were some with but two
or three pelts, which was more common. And there were
many with but one pelt, or only bare sand before their
feet, but that was not shameful, for not all could be great
hunters, and often the year's luck turned against a man.

In the end all the hunters had their pelts before them
except those of the last band, of Garin, Ara-Karn, and
the chief, Gundoen. Yet most of all the many, many pelts
lay untouched.

The people murmured seeing this. "Surely," the women
said, "surely not even Gundoen could have slain so many
bandar? Perhaps Garin has killed some." But the men answered, "Foolish women, little you know of the craft of
the great Hunt. Trackers do not slay bandar, and Garin is
the best tracker of the tribe. Perhaps they stole most of
those pelts from the Korlas."

Hertha-Toll went to the piles of untouched pelts and
drew some forth. Garin was unmarried yet, and Ara-Karn
had no women, so the chief's wife did the service for all
three. She brought the pelts over and laid them down
according to the marks cut on the hides; and well she knew
Gundoen's mark after those many years.

Before the chief she laid seven-and-ten pelts, a great
number indeed, and one more than Gundoen had ever
gained before. It was a great victory for the chief, and
many of the tribe cheered and began to acclaim Gundoen
the Hero of the Hunt. The chief only reddened at this,
and shouted angrily for quiet; and the folk, seeing the
wild light in his eyes, fell suddenly silent.

Hertha-Toll went back to the piles of pelts and dragged
some more around.

Five pelts she laid before Ara-Karn, and that was a

goodly number—an excellent number for a man on his first hunt and for a foreigner from civilized lands at that.

Three more she laid before him, which was very good. And another five, and one further bundle of five; and Ara-Karn now had one more pelt before him than even the chief. And still Hertha-Toll went back and forth between Ara-Karn and the dwindling piles, until all the pelts were gone.

Before the stranger stood a pile of pelts so high the others could not even see his waist. Eight pelts and a score lay there, all of them before the stranger, the barge-robber. That one man, on his first hunt, had slain more bandar than many entire tribes did.

A great silence fell over the tribe. Some gazed in the direction of Kuln-Holn, who beamed happily, as if this were all his doing. Then they looked back and saw the chief, and grew timid at the look on his face.

Hertha-Toll stood in front of the row of hunters. She raised her voice in the silence and said, "There is an end to the accounting. People of our tribe, whom do you acclaim as the Hero of the Hunt?"

The women and the men, children and graybeards, and even some of the hunters, raised their voices and cried as with one tongue:

"Ara-Karn! Ara-Karn! Ara-Karn!"

Gundoen did not cheer these words. He only looked down on the ground before him, where lay his pile of pelts: a large pile of a great Hunt, perhaps the greatest the chief would ever have. And it looked like nothing beside the pile of the stranger's first. Gundoen's face turned dark as blood as he looked, and his brows drew down together heavily.

Alli and the other concubines stopped their cheers, seeing that look on the face of the chief.

The foreign traders came up to the stranger first in the rush, laughing and clapping him on his shoulders, praising his victories. "Such a Hunt!" they exclaimed when the chief had gone into his hall out of hearing. "Young man, you are the finest hunter we have seen in all this wild North—not like these barbarians at all. You do not belong here among them. If you wish, you may accompany us back to Gerso and the civilized lands."

"We will leave as soon as we settle accounts with the

chief. You will be a wealthy man with your share, Ara-Karn. Yet what can a man buy here?"

Ara-Karn smiled, his eyes dark. "When I go to Gerso, it will be in my own fashion," he said. Behind him, the women were bustling about the cook-fires, lighting them in preparation for the great victory feast. The roar of the crackling fires almost drowned out his words. "How will I be wealthy?"

The merchants laughed. "Have they not told you? You are the Hero of the Hunt—the lion's share of the gold will be yours. And you cannot get better prices for pelts than from Zelatar Bonvis!"

The stranger stooped and picked up a pelt from his pile. "And what would you pay for this?"

Zelatar appraised it: a fine huge pelt practically whole, with no rents and very few brown discolorations. It was the great pelt of the monstrous bull that had been the first to suffer the poison of Ara-Karn's arrows.

"A fine pelt indeed," said Zelatar, stroking it appreciatively. "Fit to be a cloak for the Empress Allissál herself. It must be worth at least three denas of silver, at the current low prices; but I will not be tight-fisted with you. Five denas of silver."

Ara-Karn's smile broadened. "I know nothing of your denas or your empress," he said, "but I know a little about merchants. We should not quibble: I will accept fifteen denas of your silver for this pelt."

The people around them laughed or gasped; the merchants let fall their mouths, silent for once. "Surely," they stammered, "surely you cannot be serious! Why, even fitted out as a completed cloak in the imperial bazaars at Tarendahardil it would not bring so much!"

The stranger shrugged. "As you say."

He walked over to the roaring open cook-fires and threw the pelt onto the burning logs. Almost immediately it blazed, sending forth a sickening stench that hung over the entire village and brought the chief suddenly to the veranda of his hall.

"What are you doing?" cried the merchants and tribespeople alike, outraged at the loss of such a beautiful pelt.

"Destroying fifteen denas' worth of silver," shrugged Ara-Karn. "But no, not so much: you said only five, did you not?"

"You threaten us and then destroy your own property! You are a madman. How can we deal with you?"

Ara-Karn smiled mercilessly.

"Well then," he said, "I have no use for the rest of these, if you will not buy them." He took two more pelts, both of premium quality, and hurled them onto the fire after the first. The merchants, outraged, sputtered; the tribe looked on astounded. Never had they witnessed such a spectacle as this. They did not know whether to laugh at the discomfiture of the merchants or be angered at the stranger. They looked to Gundoen for leadership, but he seemed just as bemused as the rest of them.

Ara-Karn paid them no mind. He returned to the pile and picked out three more pelts. They too landed on the fires now billowing with acrid brown smoke. Six fine pelts he had destroyed—a goodly number for any hunter's year and enough wealth to sow all the village crops twice over. He went back to the dwindling pile and picked out three more pelts; but this sight was more than the merchants could abide.

"Stop!" they cried. "You do not know what you are doing!"

Ara-Karn stopped. "You will meet my price?" They did not answer.

He walked back to the fire.

"We will meet it!"

"For all the pelts the tribe has? For us all?"

Their shoulders fell. They nodded, defeated men.

Ara-Karn's eyes glittered in the firelight. "Of course, you must also pay for the pelts that were destroyed through your own stubbornness."

Resentment flared on their faces, but only for a moment. Their faces fell once more as they nodded.

Ara-Karn laughed. But the sound of it was lost in the sudden uproar from the tribesmen, all of them but Gundoen standing in the black square of his own doorway:

"Ara-Karn! Ara-Karn! Ara-Karn!"

"Well, Bonvis?" Mergo asked sneeringly, as they walked dejectedly away from the site of the great victory feast. "You almost had me believing in those fairy airs of great wealth. One half the usual rate! Now we will be lucky to gain back what we spent on the things we have for trade and the gifts to the chief and his hunters! When we come next year they will expect as much from us again!"

Zelatar shrugged, the sour humor in his downturned lips more than evident. "Such are the risks of the trade, Mergo. Yet now Gundoen's tribe may have the wealth to defy Gen-Karn after all. Is that not worth a temporary loss?

"As for that man"—he frowned—"he is a madman who detests us: how can sane men barter with the mad? Whence he comes I know not, but I wish he would return. Do you know, Mergo, what they used to say of the wastes of the far North? Before great Elna chased the barbarians here centuries ago, they said that the wastes could not be inhabited. They said fierce spirits dwelt here that ate the brains of any men foolhardy enough to come hither. And those men were all driven mad by the loneliness and their travails. Looking at that man for the first time on the beach, Mergo, I was minded of those old tales.

"Worry not," concluded the older merchant, straightening his shoulders and looking thoughtfully back. "Next year we will be able to negotiate the old rates. If I know Gundoen, that man will be dead within three passes. I saw how the chief looked at him, when they declared the stranger Hero of the Hunt. Such a man will not last long here or anywhere else. When we come here from Gerso next spring, we shall not see him. Doubtless not even his name will be remembered."

That look the merchant had noticed was not gone from Gundoen's face as he sat in his high seat above the long tables in the square. For across from the chief, sitting in the carved seat of honor reserved for the Hero of the Hunt, was the stranger. And every time the chief raised up his head he could see nothing but the flushed face of the barge-robber, seemingly grinning back at him in triumph. So the chief did not look up from his plates much or join in the festivities more than he had to. He only stared sullenly down and drank his beer in full bowls. But he could not shut his ears to the tales and the laughter flying around the boards.

"It was a feat such as no man ever has done before," Garin was saying loudly. The hunters were seated all around the tables, so that all those who had not gone on the hunt could be near one who had, in order to hear the tales. But Garin spoke the loudest, and all faces were turned to him, because he spoke those tales of the stranger that only the chief had heard before and before that had had to live through.

"An entire bandar-nest he slew all by his own hand with the marvelous weapon that throws death. He had told none of us about this magic, surely provided by none but the gods. So when he stood before the charging bandar and threw aside his only spear—" Here Garin was interrupted by cries of astonishment from his listeners; he grinned, and nodded back at them. "Yes, that is the truth: his only spear, the one the chief had lent him. Ask chief Gundoen himself, if you do not trust my tongue. He stood unmoving while the bandar charged him. We thought that he was mad and sought death, but he was cleverer than we. He raised the little bow, which seemed the plaything of a child, and the great bandar fell dead at his feet."

Garin paused to wet his throat with beer, while the tribespeople turned to one another, evincing much astonishment at the tale. Many called out to the chief for corroboration, but Gundoen only concealed his face with his ale-bowl and did not answer them.

"Then he came to us," continued Garin. "And he said, 'I am going back to their lair. This waiting for them takes too long for me.' He left to us the task of skinning the great beast. Again we thought him mad, for we thought it had only been luck, or an illness of the bull, or else the shadow of God. And such miracles do not happen twice to any man. We followed him, though, to see what he would do.

"First he climbed into a tall tree above the brambles of the bandar-nest and settled himself in the crotch of a large branch. He fitted a death-bird to his bow and sent it down among the bandar. Again and again he fired; and the slim shafts went deep into the bodies of bulls, cows, and calves alike. At first there was no response at all, except that some of the bulls snorted angrily, and some of the calves cried. Then one by one they began to fall. And before you could have counted three score, every single bandar in the lair lay dead!"

Again was he interrupted by shouts of disbelief. "It is all true," he laughed delightedly. "Ask the chief, I tell you: he saw it as well as I.

"But the greatest wonder was when he saved the chief's life. We did not even know it at the time, and he himself said naught. But later we knew that it was true." So he told them of the battle with the Korlas, and of Gundoen's wild charge, and how he had been saved from sure death only by the slim shaft that had entered the Korla's back. "And now we know that the shaft was one of the arrows of Ara-Karn."

Here was a wonder as great as the pelts, and the folk turned to the chief, clamoring to know if this was true, and if indeed he owed his very life to the stranger.

Gundoen looked up from his bowl with red-rimmed eyes. "I did not ask him to save me," he said sullenly. "But it is true enough, I suppose." Across the square of the tables, the stranger smiled very nicely, which was the last thing he should have done if he wished to gain the chief's good favor at that moment. Gundoen took yet another beer and shouted angrily at Alli for the way she had served it.

After the feasting the serving wenches cleared away the long tables, leaving only the stained bowls for the beer, which still flowed freely. Those accomplished at music beat a tune on the wooden drums and blew their flutes, and the rest of the feasters clapped in time to the music. Between the tables went the dancers: Borna with her brown hips flashing, El-Star with his great belly bobbing, and Alli with her slanting eyes shining. The onlookers cheered, clapped, and chanted. They stamped their feet upon the hard sand. The roar grew tremendous.

In the midst of all this revelry and unseen by any save perhaps Hertha-Toll the Sorrowful, the chief rose unsteadily to his feet. His face was flushed with beer, but still his brows were drawn down.

Yet he smiled his lips in an effort to dissemble it.

Drunkenly he made his way around the tables until he came to where the stranger sat. He tapped Ara-Karn on the shoulder, none too gently.

"Stranger, I would have a word with you," the chief said. He had tried to whisper, but the great chest of Gundoen was ill-made for silence, and despite all the noise, those who sat nearby heard him clearly. They stopped their clapping to hear what the chief had in mind.

"Stranger," said Gundoen, "this dancing is well enough, but it does me nothing to watch. Good shows need a good fight. Now I am used to wrestle with someone at such feasts as these. I will not hide it from you that I am a great wrestler—perhaps even almost as good at wrestling as you are at hunting. But I promise I will not hurt you if it can be helped. Well do I know the debt you put upon me when you in your greatness saved the little life of Gundoen. Will you not wrestle with Gundoen?"

The stranger looked upon the chief.

Throughout the entire feast, Ara-Karn had spoken no words. Those about him had showered him with questions, but he had made as if he had not heard them and turned his dark side to them. When one man had not accepted that, and had shaken his shoulder to gain his attention, then Ara-Karn had turned such a sudden look at him that the man's words trailed away, and he was abashed.

Thereafter the stranger had but picked at his food and drunk his beer sparingly. Even here in the midst of joy and revelry, much of it in his own honor, Ara-Karn had become morose and withdrawn; whereas before, when most of the tribe had feared or hated him, he had but smiled. And now the only time he seemed pleased was when the chief had raised his head sourly to look upon his rival. When the food had been cleared and the dancing begun, the stranger had looked upon the joyous scene with dull dark eyes, resting his head upon his fist as if bored.

But now, at the chief's words, the strange green flecks returned to the eyes of Ara-Karn. He smiled again and straightened with interest.

"These things of yours"—he gestured disparagingly at the dancers, among whom was the chief's favorite concubine —"do not impress me much. What can the crude entertainment of so many filthy, drunken savages mean to such as me? I have seen better things done by children. Yet perhaps this wrestling might divert me, a little."

Gundoen bowed, his face the color of blood. "I will try to hold your attention," he said in a low voice.

The men and women sitting near Ara-Karn heard these words and straightaway told them to their neighbors, who spread them in turn around the tables. It was well known than the chief rarely allowed his wrestling foes to live, and then only by a special effort; and most of those who had lived were maimed by the combat. Too, they had all been mighty warriors almost as large in girth and thigh as Gundoen himself. And the stranger had a tracker's build.

By the time the combatants had toasted each other, gazing into each other's eyes over the rims of their bowls, the drums had ceased, the flutes had paused, and the dancers had stopped their feet. And the entire scene was silent with tense expectation, save only for the low murmurings of men already seeking wagers on the chief.

CHAPTER EIGHT
Sinew and Bone

The two combatants stood at opposite corners of the square, being prepared by their attendants.

The long tables had been pulled back, and the sand swept clean. Where the tables had been were now the people of the tribe, squatting on their haunches, legs tucked under buttocks, elbows rubbing elbows. The wealthy men —the greater of the hunters, warriors, and a few fishermen—sat in the first rings, sipping ale, making comments on the fighters' physiques and making bets. Behind them were the rest of the men, weaker or older—those whose limbs had withered with the passing years like grass stalks under Her summer stare. The women sat yet further back, rising now and again to tend to the children or the passing of the ale-kegs. In the farthest background were the children, naked brown babes and scrawny boys with dirt on their hardened limbs. They were back among the huts surrounding the square, and some, too small to see over the heads of their elders, clambered up onto the thatched roofs to get a clear view. A rough square was empty in the center of the sandy clearing. At one side of the square the coal-mounds of the cook-fires gave off dense heat and a dull light, reflecting off the naked bodies of the two combatants.

Many attendants had the chief: friends and old comrades, and men who knew a winner. They rubbed the chief's massive, wooden-hard limbs with fat and oils, and joked with him in low tones. Gundoen chuckled occasionally at their sallies, offering one or two of his own. His gloom had vanished as soon as the stranger had agreed to the wrestling. Alli smiled to see her lord himself again; but Hertha-Toll looked at the stranger with worry on her face.

Ara-Karn had for attendants only the faithful Kuln-Holn, who had never assisted at such a thing before and could only glance at the chief now and again with a look of profound unease, and Garin, who had said he did not like to see any man go into battle without a friend. These two stripped Ara-Karn of his tunic, his rings, and his sandals, and bound his long square mane in a cord fillet, so that it would not fall into his eyes.

"It is too long," said Kul-Dro, Garin's father. He lay propped against a keg, breathing with difficulty. He could eat and drink and walk about now, but still his chest was covered with blue bruises where the chief had broken his ribs. "Gundoen will pull your hair, stranger, so beware. Men's necks have been broken when the chief has snapped back their heads with his hands in their hair."

He looked across at the chief, as if he might wish that he were doing battle again. Then he looked back at Ara-Karn. Garin and Kuln-Holn were rubbing the grease over his limbs now. "The grease will make it harder for him to gain a handhold," he grunted. "It will prevent your skin from being torn, and also hold in your sweat. There are good herbs in the pot. Fight well, stranger, and save your life. Gundoen will get no honor from this. Does he think you are a mere foreign barge-robber now? You are the Hero of the Hunt; and if you live and are whole, you will gain much esteem." The warrior looked at him as if Kul-Dro might have wanted Ara-Karn even to gain the victory; but that he knew was too much to hope.

He counseled the stranger of Gundoen's ways in battle: his favorite tricks, and what to be wary of. Ara-Karn listened, his dark eyes glimmering green. He held his head eagerly, as if his melancholy too had been dispelled at the prospect of this battle.

When all the preparations had been made, they spat on their palms and slapped Ara-Karn on the back for luck. Then the stranger stepped forward into the square.

Gundoen awaited him there.

The chief's body shone in the sunlight on one side and glowed redly from the coal-light on the other. It seemed more massive now than ever, as if he were not a man but some bull bandar. His great muscles swelled, and his chest was like a huge boulder made smooth by the waves. He strutted on his short gnarled legs, which bowed outward about the knees. The long horned toes gripped the sand powerfully.

They came up to each other wordlessly.

Gundoen grinned, drunkenly and maliciously, the glow of triumph already in his eyes. Ara-Karn eyed the chief carefully, solemnly. Their eyes met, locked, flashed. The stranger was the taller by more than a head, but tallness was no edge in wrestling. And his arms seemed almost womanly compared to the chief's.

The drummers beat the hollowed carved logs, once, twice, thrice.

They gripped hands in the customary fashion, Ara-Karn as the challenged gripping with his left hand Gundoen's right. Their fingers strained and interlocked, each striving to crush the bones of the other, to give more pain than he got. Their other hands remained free: these were the weapon-hands.

The drummers beat the hollowed carved logs, once, twice, thrice. Once more they beat—and the wrestlers began to move.

They circled each other, locked hands straining. Now the chief seemed not so drunken as before. His movements were swift, sure, dangerous. He sought to crush the bones of Ara-Karn's hand in his grip; his left forearm swelled and hardened. The long lines of veins and tendons burst forth. More than one opponent of the chief in the past had grown faint under this mighty pressure.

Ara-Karn chuckled softly, sweat beading on his greased forehead.

Along the rings bets were placed and called. Words of encouragement, shouts and jests crossed the sandy square. Kuln-Holn looked away from the combatants, where Ara-Karn seemed so ill-matched to face the chief. But the sight of the crowd, rendered half-mad by glory, ale, and blood-lust, only sickened him the more. He looked about for Hertha-Toll, to see how the wise woman was; but the chief's wife had already gone up into the darkness of the great hall. He began drawing images in the sand before him, trying not to hear that all the odds favored the chief by heavy margins. He drew designs that were like the patterns of hearth-ash, smoke, or dusky clouds. The sight of them filled him with terror; hastily he rubbed them clear.

And in the center of it all, the naked wrestlers danced.

Already the sweat was pouring forth from their shoulders. The sunlight and coal-light shone on it, and the men seemed like living statues poured from liquid metals. They darted toward one another and pulled back. The weapon-hands snaked forth, seeking a hold or striking off an attempted one. Their feet performed complex steps, sometimes on the point of tripping, sometimes firmly anchored in the sand.

Now suddenly Gundoen had got the hold he had been seeking. He reached forth with his weapon-hand and gripped Ara-Karn's leg just above the knee. He pulled, he heaved. By sheer bull-like strength, he lifted Ara-Karn's body.

The crowd gasped.

Ara-Karn did not resist this move, which was the chief's favorite. Instead he gave instantly with the pressure, pushing his body against Gundoen's and pulling sharply with his shield-hand. Their hips struck together, and the chief, instead of falling with his full weight upon the stranger, spun past him, and, turning in midair, flipped onto the ground on his back. He landed with the sound of a tree falling on a stone, and the stranger fell on top of him.

It was such a move as none of the tribesmen had seen before, performed with superb skill. They roared their approval. "Ara-Karn!" some cried: but the most roared out the shout of the chief in anger and encouragement, and that they might not lose their bets: "Gundoen! Gundoen! Gundoen!" And these cries easily swallowed the few for the stranger.

The two men grappled and rolled in the sand, dangerously close to the mounds of embers. Arms, legs, hands, and heads whirled; the dust rose in dank clouds about them, clinging to their sweating, greased bodies.

Gundoen was getting the better of it now: his greater bulk, and more compact limbs, were overcoming the stranger. Yet he looked up moment to moment at the mounds of the dying cook-fires. They were coming very near to them; the heat made the grease on their bodies melt and run, and made their hair wet with sweat.

Ara-Karn turned suddenly toward the fires. They rolled desperately into the coals for a moment, bodies black against red heat. Gundoen screamed in pain and leaped out of the coals, rolling on the sand. Ara-Karn leaped after him, chuckling horribly.

The combatants rose to their feet and faced each other once more. Their bodies were piebald: here painted yellow where the dust had caked, there a crimson or purple where the coals had left their patchwork of burns. The madness was in the chief's eyes, a battle-madness broken only by death—his enemy's or his own. Ara-Karn smiled calmly and spat the dirt from his mouth. They paused thus, panting, their bodies wracked by heaving sighs of near exhaustion. Then they came at each other again, and the earth shook at the meeting of their bodies.

The rule that they must clasp each other's shield-hands was gone, vanished with the first fall; now there were no rules. Scratching, gouging, biting were frowned upon—but not forbidden. It was a hard land of hard people who had no sympathy save for survivors. He who lived won; the loser usually died. The crowd roared, coughed, drank their ale in convulsive gulps.

They hurled each other about the square. From one end to the other they grappled, made stances, threw each other to the earth. Their hands gripped and clawed at the most tender parts, scraping the red weals of the burns, clawing at the underbuttocks. They spat and snarled like beasts of the wood, the stranger no less than the chief. Time and again the chief seemed on the point of victory, but each time Ara-Karn eluded him by some strange unheard-of move.

Then, with screams from the people and a frantic rushing of bodies to either side, the wrestlers burst from the square.

They did not cease battling at this. Their limbs flailed and twisted regardless. They had no thought of a good show, or of combat rules, or of the safety of any spectators. Their only thought was maiming, crushing, bone-bending death—each other's death. They pushed and rolled and fell through the strong hunters, the men, the graybeards, the women. The naked brown babes squealed with delight as they grappled past them. They fought down from the level of the square onto the steep village lane, leading down through the log huts, down unto the bay.

The people scrambled to their feet and followed, clustering in eddying mobs around the rolling, writhing bodies.
The shouts were deafening, incoherent, and now there
were as many screams of "Ara-Karn!" as of "Gundoen!"

Down the street they rolled. Here was not the smoothly
swept sand; their bodies were hurled against flat stones,
sharp rocks, and the wooden ramparts of the huts. Massive bruises of bluish purple formed next to the red open
burn-weals, on their backs, their arms, their thighs. Flesh
was torn like rotten rags, dirt was clotted with human
blood, sweat, and spittle.

Past the last of the huts they went battling. At times
they broke and stood, and hurled each other's bodies about;
more often they rolled, and grappled, and clawed. There
was no intention on the part of either one of them to continue to tumble so, but the path was so steep that they had
no choice but to tumble. They might have given pause for
a rest and drink of water, and they might have returned to
the clean sandy square. But they did not. They would not
stop until the thing was done, and one of them lay broken
and writhing in the dirt.

The crowd followed them. Sometimes one of them
would be caught between the wrestlers and a hut; then he
had best look to his life. Enna-Born was caught thus and
did not move quickly enough. His head slammed into the
side of a hut, and he did not move for two passes. And
when he did wake, he was never the same, being addled in
the skull. The others, seeing him fall, gave no heed; they
followed, screaming, the bodies of the chief and Ara-Karn.

Yet they kept behind the wrestlers thereafter. No one
dared run around in front of them, lest he suffer the fate
of Enna-Born. So when the bodies rolled through the tall
beach grasses, over the crest of the dunes, and disappeared
from view, none knew what it might portend. They ran to
the crest of the dunes, forming a long line parallel to the
shore, just as they had done before, at the time of God's
assault upon queenly Goddess. And they looked down onto
the pebble-strewn sand of the beach; and the hoarse cries
died in their throats, and there was only the sound of the
sea waves lightly lapping as the tribespeople looked down.

The two bodies lay sprawled on the stones, bleeding, be-
grimed, bruised, battered. Neither moved; neither made a
sound. There was not even the movement of breath in
either one. They were like corpses lying mangled in the

welter of their own drying blood. The folk looked down
on them with respectful awe, uncertain whether to cheer
or weep or gather up the bodies.

Kuln-Holn came running up behind. He had been following the crowd at a distance, not wishing to see the
battle, afraid of what he might behold, but neither able to
walk away as Hertha-Toll had done. Now he had heard
the silence, and known that it was done. He ran with a
quickening pace and forced a place on the crest of the
grassy dunes. And he saw his guest, the messenger of the
gods, lying like one dead, the arms and legs twisted into
unnatural positions. The Pious One fell to his knees. He
put his hands over his eyes and wept tears upon his fingers.
The tears were hot and bitter, for to Kuln-Holn more than
a man had died.

On the pebble-strewn sand, a hand moved.

It gripped the sand and relaxed. Then the arm above it
moved; and slowly, painfully, a body rose. It rolled to its
side, got on its knees, and, at last, stood to its feet. It
swayed rather unsteadily in the sea breeze, then shook
itself and stood firmly by an act of sheer determination.
And the body was that of the stranger, the barge-robber,
Ara-Karn.

He gazed upon the faces of the people of the tribe, who
looked at him with almost superstitious awe. Not a one of
them could have believed that this man might wrestle
great-chested Gundoen to death. Now they saw him,
bloodied, bruised, the cord fillet torn from his brow and
his sweat-and-blood-plastered hair ruffling free in the
breeze. The foam had dried about his torn lips, and grime
and blood were his only garments. More a beast he looked
than a man: a grim specter from some dim, primitive past,
unbelievably savage, invested with terrible strength and
ruthlessness. And there was not a man there who could
have dared to challenge him in any combat whatsoever at
that moment. They looked upon him speechless, their eyes
wide with fear.

Kuln-Holn looked up through his wet fingers and saw
his master, still alive, though horribly so. He wiped the
bitter tears from his eyes, and wanted to leap and laugh;
but the sight of the eyes of Ara-Karn stopped him.

Below on the sand, the body of Gundoen issued forth a
ghastly groan and turned a bit. Ara-Karn regarded it, the
vivid green shining in those dark eyes.

Gundoen groaned again through cracked and purple lips. He rolled, feeling the separate agonies of his arms, of his hands, of his back, of his legs, of every part of him. Never before had he been so sorely tried. There was a distant ringing at the back of his skull; some moments passed before he could remember where he was. He wished only to turn upon his side, hold the salt air in his lungs, and painlessly expire.

Instead, he opened his eyes. The light of Goddess was blinding; he blinked against it, but still it filled the sky. Then a dark form intruded, obliterating the light. The shadow of Ara-Karn fell across the chief's face. Gundoen saw him standing first, steady on his feet, his hand extended.

Painfully, Gundoen groped. The outstretched hand covered the sun; he felt and found it. The hand gripped his—gingerly, for both their hands were bent and sore from each other's fierce grip. Gundoen felt the hand pull at his arm, and he responded. With the stranger's help he gained his feet. His skull rang like an anvil, and he felt as if he should retch. And he knew that he would not die, but must live on, beaten by Ara-Karn.

The two stood thus in silence for a space, supporting each other. Then Garin and the other attendants scrambled down to the beach, helping the wracked, grimed men up. Only then did the crowd raise its voice in one tremendous, deafening ululation:

"Ara Karn! Ara-Karn! *Ara-Karn!*"

CHAPTER NINE

The Dead Child

From that moment onward, the chief and the stranger were inseparable. Ara-Karn left Kuln-Holn's small hut and went to stay at the guest hall, the merchants having completed the last of their trading and slunk off to Gerso. Gundoen bade Ara-Karn eat at the chief's hall for every one of the five meals, and at every meal he insisted Ara-Karn take the high seat of honor opposite to his own. One was never seen out-of-doors without the other—usually with the faithful Kuln-Holn following them at some distance. The chief still disliked Kuln-Holn, whom he had dubbed the "Little Prophet," but for the sake of his guest he put up with him.

He even went so far as to offer Ara-Karn the pick of his concubines, the most desirable women in the tribe. The stranger refused. So the chief asked him if he saw any other woman in the tribe he fancied. Again the stranger said no. "Will you have no one to warm your dim place and tend to you then?" asked the chief. "No one," replied the stranger. "Not even the queen of the world." And he was true to his words: for no one ever saw him take any woman of the tribe during all his stay there. Gundoen was amazed at this; it was many passes before he could finally understand that Ara-Karn had meant what he said. "Perhaps Kuln-Holn was right all along," was all he could murmur, shaking his massive head.

The change in the chief's heart amazed the people of the tribe. Never had they seen anything like it; but then, they had seen many new things since the dead man had come among them. Gundoen, who had never before been able to refer to the stranger without using the words "barge-robber," now treated Ara-Karn with such respect that he even consulted him on matters of tribal rule. And the stranger's advice, which he was not slow to give, showed a wisdom far beyond his apparent years.

The chief was now completely sincere in his admiration for the newcomer, just as he had been completely sincere in his former dislike for him. It was no deception, no pattern of deep guile—nor did anyone think of it as such. Such sophisticated falsehood was beyond the capabilities of any of the tribe, let alone Gundoen, who had never been known for such subtlety. Moreover, what would have been the point of such guile? The stranger was fully in the chief's power. Though he would have been censured for doing so, Gundoen could easily have ordered the stranger's death on any pretext. Hero of the Hunt or not, he was not of the tribe, nor did he have any kin to avenge his blood. It would have been a simple matter for Gundoen to have killed him with his own sword.

Instead, he fawned upon the stranger. And the people, who found such a transformation beyond belief, credited it to the magical powers of the stranger. The man who had been washed up on the beach dead and naked had in only a few weeks' time become the Hero of the Hunt, slaying more bandar than any other hunter ever; traded so skillfully with the foreign merchants that the tribe was now one of the most wealthy in all the far North; and crushed Gundoen, the greatest wrestler in all the North, in a battle far beyond all his apparent strength. Was it any wonder, then, that the people took some heed of Kuln-Holn's insistences and began to look now upon Ara-Karn not with the contempt for a foreigner but with instead the awe for a god?

Kuln-Holn was ecstatic over the change. Though now he saw far less of Ara-Karn than he had in the past, he had always grieved that the messenger of the Goddess should have been so alone among those who should be his servants in his divine mission. Now people offered gifts to Kuln-

Holn, asking to be commended in Ara-Karn's eyes; and the Pious One came to be almost an important figure of the tribe. People went to Ara-Karn to ask his advice on all matters, and not a few were those who asked him to bless their babes or their new weapons. It seemed to be the confirmation of all Kuln-Holn's past visions and dreams.

To Hertha-Toll the newfound respect for the stranger was vaguely disturbing. She saw, deeply buried in the people's attitude, a trace of awe bordering on fear. Even in Gundoen she seemed to sense this. When he had drunkenly challenged the stranger, it had unfolded before her eyes exactly as she had seen it happening in her dream. She had gone into the silence of her dim place in her husband's hall sure of how it would all turn out. She had known that her husband would be defeated, even though it was clear that Gundoen's strength of limb was far beyond that of Ara-Karn. That it had ended just as she had seen only served to confirm her in the truth of her other, far more terrifying dreams.

Yet she treated both their terrible wounds in silence. She was quite skilled at the healing arts; yet as she gazed upon the bruised, burned body of her husband, the sight blended with another sight from her dreams until in the end she was forced to look away.

Once she tried to speak to Gundoen of her fears and warn him, but he would not listen. He only grew very angry and thought she meant to say that he was only afraid of the stranger.

"Woman of ill fortune," he swore at her, "was it not you who counseled me to spare this man's life and take him along on the hunt? Your words blow with the winds. You may have the Sight, wife, but not all your predictions have come true. I remember many rosy prophecies concerning our children—and what happened then?"

This hurt Hertha-Toll deeply, so that the tears started to her wrinkled eyes. It was the greatest tragedy of the tribe that the chief had no children to carry on his name and avenge his death. Many times had Hertha-Toll borne for him—two girls and five fat boys. Yet in every instance death had taken them back. One of the girls and one of the boys had died before weaning of cold and disease. This was not unusual, for some years two babes died in the cradle for every three born. The other four boys and girl, however, had given every sign of health and grown past the dangerous age. Yet one of the boys drowned, the girl was slain in a raid by the Korlas, two boys died while daring each other to see how far they could jump from a nearby cliff, and the last boy had gone to fight Korlas to avenge his sister and had never been seen again, though his pony returned with a bloody saddle-blanket.

Now Hertha-Toll was old beyond the childbearing age and had fallen into Gundoen's disdain. So she wept bitter tears. "I know that now you have every right to cast me off as a luckless bedmate and wed another," she said. "And I am always thankful that you have not done so. Once, remember, I was young, and many of the warriors sought my favors, but I submitted to none—not even on the feasttimes, when all is permitted. For I had set my heart on you, the nephew of the chief. I loved you, Gundoen, and love you still for all the years; and when I tell you these things, it is not with any mind to hurt you, but only to warn you and arm you with truth against adversity."

The chief took her in his great hairy arms and comforted her. "I know, wife. Nor do I place all the blame upon you for what happened to our children. Perhaps, after all," he joked, "I am the cursed one—who can see into the minds of the gods? And I value your wisdom greatly. What other great chief so listens to the words of his woman as do I? Yet you only anger me when you speak against Ara-Karn."

She dried her tears and promised to speak to him of Ara-Karn no more. And she kept her promise as best she could, even though, with the dreams she was later to have, it proved a difficult vow to keep.

One of Gundoen's earliest demands upon his new friendship was that Ara-Karn teach the tribe the secrets of the strange weapon he called "bow," and fashion others of them for the hunters of the tribe. Ara-Karn smiled and brought forth an armful of bows, the fruit of his labors on Kaari-Moldole. "Truly, then, you have never seen such a weapon?" he asked them.

"Not we or any of the tribes of the North," they answered. "Nor any of the lands to the South we now deal with. If they had such marvels, the merchants would have sold them to us long ago."

"Incredible," murmured Ara-Karn. So he showed them what woods were best for bows and how to fashion the gut strings for the greatest strength and fewest breaks. Also he instructed them on how to craft good, straight arrows, as he called the darting death-birds, and how to feather the notched ends for sure, straight flights. And finally he showed them how to brew the deadly poison he used to tip the points.

With the wealth of the great Hunt the tribe quickly restored their village and replanted all the crops. The crops were late now, and would not bear as much grain or fruit. But the women planted three more fields of late seeds to make up the differences and still had gold enough to purchase fine clothes of delicate weavery, new, bright-bladed weaponry, and golden ornaments from the merchants who sailed up to the bay from Arpane on the Sea, the only city on the Ocean of the Dead. And Ara-Karn, out of his share as the Hero of the Hunt, bought much iron, with which the village metalworkers formed the iron points for the feathered death-birds. And as God passed overhead, the weather was so fine, with such a good mixture of sunshine and rain, that the crops grew almost as great as if they had been planted on time; and the village was as it had ever been, only richer, fatter, and more powerful.

There was no more trouble with the Korlas. Once indeed the women of the tribe found a Korla spy lurking in the forests about the fields. They stripped him naked and whipped him through the muddy streets, cheering and laughing as if it were a festival; the whole tribe turned out for the event. In the end they painted him red and green and tied him backward on his pony, without weapons, pack, or clothing, and sent him riding back to his own lands. Many were the ribaldries exchanged concerning what would happen if he appeared first among the women of his tribe. Yet beyond this one incident it was as if the Korlas lived beyond the Spine for all they were heard of.

The hunters grew increasingly skillful with their new weapons. At first they had difficulties—most of all, the chief himself. His strength was so great he kept breaking his bow. So Ara-Karn made a special black bow for him, twice as large and three times as powerful as any of the others. "Try your strength upon this," he said, handing Gundoen the bow.

The chief took it in his massive hands. He strained against the string, pulled back the long arrow, and let it fly. It shot forth with the speed of a blinking eye. High it sped, over hut and tree—almost too fast for the eye to follow. And it curved gracefully in the blue-green sky and fell away, so distant it seemed a mere speck falling over the end of the world.

Gundoen looked after it, amazed. "Why," he breathed, "with such a weapon as this, what might I not be capable of? I could sit upon my back step and hunt bandar from here, if only I knew where to aim!"

Thereafter he redoubled his efforts at mastering the fine weapon and at firing arrows with all the speed and smoothness of Ara-Karn himself. And the other hunters, seeing the chief's patience and marveling thereat, ceased their last complaints. Soon they grew so skilled they began holding contests, and with each new contest the marks of all were higher. And they hunted the game of the deeps of stream, air, and wood, and brought to the village so much game that all the storage-holes were soon chock full. Alli jested that it was too much food and that soon everyone in the tribe would be as fat as Southrons.

This became a popular joke, often repeated toward the end of meals.

The hunters went farther afield than was customary, for the game about the village was growing scarce, and they were so excellent with their bows that Ara-Karn praised them as fine marksmen all, for only five arrows were lost of all that were shot. And Gundoen laughed for sheer joyousness; and they went back loaded down with game to a blackened, burned-out village. The triumphant shouts of the hunters vanished when they heard the sobbing of the women and the cries of the children.

They rode the entire length of the village. The crops were cut down, trampled underfoot; the boats of the fishermen were stove in or set adrift on the currents; and many of the huts were burning still.

They got down off their ponies and strove to quench the fires still blazing. Luckily it had rained only recently and the logs had still been damp, so they were successful in saving many of the huts. But only a few fields of the harvest could be saved.

And oftentimes, as the men ran with the heavy buckets of slopping water, they would stumble over something in the earth and, looking down, would see the body of some murdered child. One man found the spear still in the body of an old graybeard who had foolishly tried to combat the raiders. The man pulled the spear free, examining its mark-

ings and the fashion of its make. And he said only one
word: "Korlas."

When the last of the fires had finally been turned to
hissing smoke, Gundoen sought out his wife. The chief's
hall had not been torched, so that it was whole and strong
still. But upon entering the chief could see that the invaders had been there, for many of the valued trophies
were gone and the bones of the foreign champions had
been shattered on the earthen floor. And missing, too, was
the hilt of the sword of Tont-Ornoth, which had tasted the
blood even of Elna, first Emperor of the South.

Gundoen found Hertha-Toll sitting in the dimness of the
hall, bestrewn with ashes from the silent hearth-fire. Barely
could he see her at first, for though without Goddess
shined brightly, within all was darkness. The winter shut-
ters had been battened over the broad portals in the de-
fense of the hall.

When his sight had grown in the darkness, Gundoen
saw that his wife was huddled over some object in her lap,
weeping bitterly. Then Gundoen stopped; he had recognized what the thing in her lap was. It was the body of a
child some four winters old, and it was plain that the body
had been trampled to death. There was little enough to
guess who it had been, but the chief knew it. It was the
body of young Ord-Bal, Alli's son.

Gundoen did not speak to Hertha-Toll. The wise woman
wept on as if she were unaware of his presence. The chief
gazed upon the little body for a while in silence. Then he
turned and left the hall. He walked slowly out of the village and went alone into the woods.

The women and oldsters told the tale to the hunters.
Almost as soon as the dust of the hunters' ponies had
fallen, the Korlas had swept down out of the woods, wild
savage cries upon their lips. They must have been waiting
concealed in the forest, watching for the hunters' de-
parture.

They had swept the streets, killing all who stood in their
way, throwing torches upon huts right and left. They had
smashed the boats upon the shore and trampled the green
crops in the fields. Fortunately not all the boats had been
upon the beach, for many of the fishermen had been, and
were still, out upon the deep. Many of the old men had
buckled on their swords and taken spear against the in-

vaders. The Korlas had only laughed, and struck them down. Some women had been violated in the village streets. Many others had been carried off to the village of the Korlas; among these were Turin Tim and Alli. The raiders had taken all the gold and pelts they could, and even the sacred hilt of the sword of Tont-Ornoth.

Alli's young son had rushed from the chief's hall and defied the invaders. When the Korlas had sacked the hall, the women had hidden themselves and the boy, but in the confusion he had managed to squirm free. He had taken his little toy sword, which Gundoen had carved for him out of wood. He had run into the square crying challenges to the Korlas in his piping voice.

The Korlas had seen him and laughed hatefully. They had kicked the flanks of their ponies and trampled the toddler down. Hertha-Toll had run out into the square in an effort to save the child; she might well have been slain herself, but she gave no heed to that.

She had arrived too late. The hooves of the war-ponies reached the boy first; and when she came up to the spot, all that remained for Hertha-Toll were the mangled little remains that Gundoen had seen her holding.

The hunters were outraged at this tale. This raid of the Korlas had gone far beyond anything else they had ever attempted. Though the hostilities between the tribes were real, both tribes had obeyed certain rules of custom—until now. Loud were the cries for vengeance and the shouts for Gundoen. Yet the chief was not to be found in all the village.

Hertha-Toll went into the woods after him. She sought him out in a place that was a favorite of his: a rock by a wide and lazy stream in a clearing in the forest. He was sitting, staring into his reflection on the water, saying nothing. But the great tears rolled silently down his weather-roughened cheeks and soaked his short sandy beard.

Hertha-Toll approached him, making enough noise so that he would surely hear her. But he did not turn about. She gently put her hands upon his massive shoulder.

"I tried to save him," she said softly. "I ran after him but could not reach him in time. He died like a little warrior, Gundoen."

He covered her hands in one of his, but did not turn around still. "Woman," he said, "I did you wrong. You are not the one Goddess put Her curse upon."

They remained thus for some time, and she gave him what comfort she could. But he told her it was enough, and to leave him. When she turned back at the first bend in the path, she saw him still sitting on the rock, gazing down at his own murky reflection.

Later they took the bodies of the dead down to the side of the sea and set them lovingly into the death-barges. Gundoen himself brought down Alli's young son. Around the shattered little body he spread sweetmeats, candies of dried sugar, milk, and thinned beer in stoppered clay jugs. These were the things the boy had liked best. And in the place where warriors would have had their weapons and armor of war, Gundoen put the little wooden sword, which had been broken in two by the hooves of the Korlas' pony.

Every one of the tribe who could walk went to see the barges off. Even those who had not lost a friend or relative were as touched as if it were their own mother or son lying in the gray state. This had been a raid not on families or individuals but an assault upon the very tribe itself. And it had gone against all custom, for the Korlas had waged war only upon the helpless of the tribe.

So every boat that could hold water was filled with folk. There were not enough boats for all; the others hurried out to the ends of the arms of the bay and waved their last farewells to the dead as they went past the foaming waves.

Gundoen and Ara-Karn rode in Kuln-Holn's fishing boat. It was barely large enough to hold the three of them. The boat had not been touched because it had lain in its customary place far up the beach, away from the other boats. The Pious One sailed now before the others, because he knew best how to reach the side of the currents of the dead.

When they reached that place where none of the fishermen set their nets, no matter how teeming the game might be, Gundoen rose on unsteady land legs and spoke words for all the dead.

He spoke in faltering tones, and his voice broke several times. Everyone could see that he no longer held his shoulders as he was used. He seemed like a man whose spirit had gone on before his body.

They cast off the lines and held to the tillers, and Kuln-Holn invoked the blessing of the Goddess for the dead, even as he had done alone for Oron—Oron whom none had loved. They watched the many death-barges sliding softly away. When the swells had cut off the last of them from sight, the people sighed heavily. And they sailed back to the land where silent, burned, and mournful huts awaited them.

The warriors held war-council in the chief's hall shortly after the voyaging. They were all there, from the lowliest youth to Gundoen himself. They filled the hall, elbow to elbow and back to back. The air of the hall was close and tense even with the sea breezes coming through the long open portals. The warriors were distraught and expectant. They looked to Gundoen for leadership; he was their chief.

But the broad-chested hunter was subdued and silent. He ate no food and supped no ale. He had spoken hardly a word, outside of the oration for the dead, since they had returned from their hunting. Some of his concubines went up and down the tables, serving bowls of ale cooled in the underground storage-holes. Yet Alli was not there to lead them.

"We must strike swiftly!" said one of the younger warriors. "Our women are among them and we must take them back. When they decide the shares of the raid, they'll parcel out the women. We must attack before then lest we find our wives bearing Korla brats!"

"The Korlas never could stand up against us in an equal encounter," said another, older man. "Did they not wait until we were all out of the village before they attacked? They fear us with good cause. We should attack them with all our forces and teach them a lesson."

"More than a lesson," said another warrior. "This was no ordinary raid, but butchery of babes and women. The Korlas should be attacked and slain wholesale, and their huts burned as ours were!" Many others cheered this idea.

At the sound, the chief roused himself. He looked from man to man with bloodshot eyes until they were silent once more.

"Korlas," he said sadly. "Do you think the Korlas would have the courage to do this thing? If Korlas were all we had to face, we should be able to slay them all easily, even to the last warrior. But Korlas are not our foe."

"But the spear!" they shouted. "It was a Korla spear!"

Gundoen spat upon the earth beside his chair. "So they are clever," he shrugged. "All the more reason to be wary.

Mark you now, I do not say there were no Korlas on that raid. Perhaps, indeed, they were *all* Korlas. But if so, the ones who stirred them up, and the ones who planned this, were anything but Korlas. Do you not think the Korlas would realize that such an attack would only bring destruction on many of them?"

"Who then?" they cried as with a single voice. "Who has done it?"

Gundoen looked down at the table. "Men of the Orn tribe," he muttered. "Gen-Karn."

They fell silent again. As soon as the chief had said them, the truth of his words became evident. The Korlas were at best poor fighters, not brutal madmen. To destroy the village yet leave the warriors unharmed was only to incur the death of every Korla who had participated in the raid; and the Korlas were not such fools that they would not realize it. No Korla would have enough of the rutting-madness to do this. But the Orns would, and Gen-Karn would—especially if they were clever enough to dress as Korlas or incite the Korlas to enough madness to do the thing for them. And Gen-Karn, Warlord of the far North, was indeed clever enough for that. Yet why had he done it?

"To trap us," said Gundoen sadly. "And he has done so. Now we are caught just where he desired. The destruction of our tribe is now unavoidable. In another year, after the next Assembly of the Tribes, Gen-Karn will rule the chief of every tribe in the North."

Shouts were hurled at the chief denying his words, especially from those who were young or who had had a good deal of ale. But the older, wiser warriors held their tongues and pondered.

"You deny it, but it is truth," said the chief. "I could not have dreamed such a thing, but I can see it when it springs. Can we refuse to avenge this raid? Then we would lose heart, and the other tribes would rightly call us cowards. None would follow our lead then. And without our strength against him, Gen-Karn will swiftly gather all the remaining tribes into his hands. Then, even if we did do battle against him, we would be doomed. Not even you, the warriors of Gundoen, could withstand the braves of all the other tribes.

"Yet if we do fight now, what then?" he went on, sadly, relentlessly. "The Korlas will be expecting our attack. We would not catch them unawares as they did us. They will not set foot beyond the log barrier they hide their huts behind now. You can be assured they have ample stores of food and water—enough to last them quite a while. When we attack, the fighting will be hard. There will be Orn warriors among them—perhaps even Gen-Karn himself, though I think not. He is too wily to set himself in our path thus.

"Many of our warriors would die. Many others would be wounded. Perhaps we would succeed—nay, I know it: we would get our women back, and put the Korlas to the sword, and regain the hilt of the sword of Tont-Ornoth. Yet even so we would be weakened. We would have food enough, thanks to the bows of Ara-Karn. Yet the rebuilding of our village will be hard, harder than after the Storm. We would be vulnerable to attacks by Orn warriors. And if we could withstand those attacks, they would press suit against us at the Tribal Assembly."

"No, they would not!" cried the youths. But their hearts were not in that cry.

Gundoen shook his head, still looking down at the wooden table. "He will press suit against us. He will do so in the name of the Korla tribe. He will say, that we hunted bandar on the Korlas' land, that we attacked and slew a band of Korlas in the sacred forests where warfare is prohibited. He will say that the Korlas attacked us only in token of these offenses, and that our raid was simple blood-thirstiness—a violence when we should have gone to the Assembly with whatever grievances we might have claimed. He will call for us to be put forth from the North. He will demand our destruction unless we submit to whatever punishment he decrees.

"Now you might say some of these charges we could refute—that all of them are false lies and slanders. You would speak truth then. But what does that matter? The other tribes will see that we are weak, wounded, and poor, and that Gen-Karn is mightier than ever. They will fear to go against his words lest they suffer what we have. Even those who spurn Gen-Karn and sympathize with us may say that it is a private matter not worth risking their own heads over."

"Yet can we not charge the Korlas for this raid?" suggested one man. "If we do not attack, all the evidence will be upon our side. We could make it a private quarrel, our men against the Korlas. It need not be the final stand regarding Gen-Karn's overlordship on this Assembly, does it?"

"It need not be, but it will be," answered the chief. "I know Gen-Karn. He is tired of waiting. What his plans are I know not; but he wishes to rule all the North, and only we stand in his way. If we do not attack the Korlas, we shall lose more esteem than if we fought them and lost half our warriors. We might attack the Orns directly; I have considered it. But Orn lies too far away, and we would have to travel through several tribes friendly to Gen-Karn. That way, too, lies destruction. Besides, it were a great pity not to kill some Korlas for this affront to us. In the end, I know of only two courses that would leave our tribe alive at the end. But they are courses you would not follow."

"Tell us!"

"We could pack up all our belongings, and our women too. We could make a last raid upon the Korlas, put them to death, and take back our women, gold, and the hilt of Tont-Ornoth's sword. We could travel down the coast to the South, to Arpane on the Sea, before Gen-Karn could strike at us. Then we could become landworkers among the Southrons, or we could fight them for territory. Those civilized men could never stand against the swords of the North."

"And run from Gen-Karn?" they cried, outraged. "Never, never!"

The chief smiled bitterly, sadly. "Perhaps this would appeal to you better," he murmured. "We could send a special embassy to Orn—I myself will go, if you desire. We could reach a secret agreement with Gen-Karn. We will get him to take his protection from the Korlas and let us raid them. In return all we would need to do is swear to serve Gen-Karn."

"Never!" they cried again. "Never, never!"

The chief stood to his feet suddenly, sweepingly. The great carved high seat fell away behind his legs; a fire lighted up his blue eyes. He was suddenly Gundoen again. "Well, then, what do you say to this!" he roared. "We could go to destroy these stinking Korlas and burn their village to the dark earth. And when we had done that, we could set our backs to the sea and Goddess, and march toward the dark horizon—to Orn. Those who stood against us we would fight and slay. And we would attempt the death of crafty Gen-Karn before the last of us lay dead on red soil! What say you to that?"

They were silent a moment, stunned. Then, as with a single, lusty voice, they cheered their chief's wild plan. They slammed their bowls on the boards and stamped the earth with their feet. Gundoen grinned a wild wolf's-grin, and sat back in his high seat. He took a bowl of dark ale and drank it down in tremendous gulps.

Yet, in the seat of honor across from the chief, Ara-Karn was silent.

When all the clamor had died down once more, he began to speak. Gundoen immediately signed for silence.

"O Chief," he said softly, "there is yet another way, if you would hear me."

The chief frowned. "What way is that, my guest?"

"You should attack the Korlas, because you must. But not the Orns. There will be no need. Your warriors will not be weakened or slain. You will still be a powerful tribe and even more honored than before. Did I teach you all for nothing, then?

"O Chief, a man can hunt more things than the beasts of the wood with a bow."

CHAPTER TEN
A Summer's Raid

They crept through the dense forest like passing shadows propelled by the wind. No noise or disturbance marked their passage. They swarmed through the leafy underbrush as if they had no more substance than dusty spirits come to seek a sacred vengeance.

After the council of war, Gundoen had led them up to the Grove of dark God. They had come ceremonially, as was custom; and among them had been the foreigner Ara-Karn, as naked and smeared with ash and pigment as the rest. Gundoen had made the sacrifice, and they had sworn the destruction of the Korlas, promising dark God much death and blood, which is said to please Him. Then they had gone down again to the village and armed themselves for war. The women of the tribe had seen them off solemnly with no weeping. They too had learned to be as hard as the bark from the canthin tree.

They crept up to the village to the Korlas.

The village of the Korlas was large—almost as large as the main village of Gundoen's tribe. But this was the Korlas' only village. On three of its four sides the forest came right up to its walls; on the fourth side were the green fields. As the warriors crept up to the three forested sides, some of them could see some Korla men and women out in the sunshine working on the fields.

The village of the Korlas was enclosed by a high wall of oak logs—tree trunks felled, lopped of branches, sharpened at the top, and lashed upright closely together. Along the top of the walls could be seen the Korla sentinels, walking back and forth, watching the forest for the enemies they did not see.

Gundoen grunted when he saw the wall. The sight never failed to excite his disgust. "That shows what cowards the Korlas are," he murmured to Ara-Karn. "There is no other tribe in all the North that must hide behind walls as if they were no better men than civilized landowners."

He spat to punctuate his words.

The warriors moved into positions on the three forested sides of the village. By silent signals they told Gundoen that all the men were in position and ready. Gundoen grinned. He raised his fist with the thumb set apart from the knuckles. A dozen bowstrings sang, and there were no more sentinels on the walls.

From the inside of the stockade came the sounds of heavy things falling inertly to the earth. Cries of alarm followed.

"Quickly now!" roared Gundoen, leaping forward.

Ropes tied with loops were thrown up the walls; the loops fell over the sharpened ends of the logs and held fast. The warriors began to clamber up the ropes.

First to gain the summit was Ara-Karn, climbing with both hands, his bow between his teeth. When he reached the catwalk he took the bow in his hands and swiftly nocked an arrow.

There was a shout from below, from a tall man with long brown hair. Brandishing his lance, the man leaped upon the ladder to the catwalk. He never reached the top of the ladder: he fell back gurgling to the ground, dead. A long black-feathered arrow protruded from his throat.

Other warriors had climbed the ropes now on all three sides of the village. Ara-Karn could see them along the walks, gesticulating and brandishing their curved bows. The Korlas saw them also, and seeing them appear so suddenly and grimly, with naught but murder in their wild eyes, they cried out for fear. They had trusted in the promises of Gen-Karn and felt secure. They had believed that they could slaughter and burn at will in Gundoen's village and never have the payment of it. Now they saw that they had been wrong, and that the payment required would be their lives.

The women screamed and clutched their children by the arms, dragging them into the sheltered huts. The warriors also ran in, but only to take sword and armor. They returned with their weapons of iron and bronze in their hands and their helms upon their heads.

Gundoen only laughed to see this.

"Greetings, neighbor Korlas!" he shouted down at them. "You thought to burn my village and war upon women and babes. And now you think these walls will keep us out. O eaters-of-dung, they will not keep us out; but they will keep you in!"

Like the king of the bandars the chief shook his massive head and shoulders. He lifted his bow, which was powerful and doubly curved and which no man could draw back but he. And he shot an arrow down at the nearest Korla warrior. So powerful was that bow that the long arrow plunged into the warrior's leather chest plate and passed completely through his body, embedding itself in the ground before the dead man had even fallen. First thin streams of blood spurted out from two neat holes in the man's armor—one in the front, the other behind. Only then did the body fall.

The Korlas never stood a chance.

They milled about in the clearing, charging first this wall, then that; but each charge ended in chaos, breaking under the onslaught of deadly arrows. And the warriors on the walls only laughed and jested, and drew back arrows to their ears. It was not a combat but a slaughter. Quickly the compound filled with the writhing bodies of dead Korlas.

They would have fled screaming long before, save that they were led by two great warriors dressed in armor unlike that of the others. These two bullied and beat the others, ordering them here and there; and the Korlas, cowed and frightened like young lambs bleating over the corpses of their ewes, obeyed. But the look of death was surely in their eyes.

Gundoen pointed out the two large warriors to Ara-Karn. "They are not Korlas," he shouted. "They are Orns, from Gen-Karn's tribe. Did I not say it?" And he laughed horribly, so that his laughter overcame even the screams of the dying, floating like a cloud over the whole of the village.

The sounds of his laughter even came distantly to the central square of the village. There, in a great wooden cage, were imprisoned the women who had been abducted from Gundoen's village—all save one. Here they had been penned for public display. Here the women of the Korlas and their children might spit upon and revile their enemies. And here the men of the Korlas might pass by to inspect their property. The captive women were not quite naked, but their tunics had been torn in the slaughter at Gundoen's village and the mad flight therefrom; therefore the Korla men had much to see when they passed them by.

Later, after a certain amount of time, the captives would be sold in auction to the Korla who lacked a wife, or desired a pleasing concubine, or wanted a serving wench to clean his hall, bake bread in his ovens, and mend his tunics. What a man bought a woman for depended upon the desires of the man and the comeliness of the woman.

Only one of the women was not being held in the wooden cage. Alli, because of her beauty and her dark slanting eyes, had been chosen out by one of the Orn warriors who had led the raid. He had seen her in the hall of Gundoen when he had burst in, swinging his wide bloodstained sword. And even as he was smashing the bones of the foreign champions and stealing the hilt of the sword of Tont-Ornoth, he had lusted for her.

At first they had penned her with the other women, but the Orn could not wait and demanded that she be his come the next sleeping. Nor did the leaders of the Korlas dare deny him, after they had seen him in his battle-madness. So he had taken her to the Korla chief's hut, which he and the other Orn now used. And because Alli did not resist him, but only wept and shuddered and let him have his way with her, moving as he commanded, the Orn did not chain her in his dim place or return her to the wooden cage. Instead he dressed her in gold and fineries and boasted of the envy of the other Orn warriors when he returned to Orn with her.

And when the warriors had appeared on the walls suddenly and the Korla women screamed, Alli poked her head out of the hall of the Korla chief. She looked about in timid curiosity. She saw the Korla women running into their huts, and she saw the men strapping dark helmets over their heads, rushing toward the back walls of the village. Then the streets were empty again.

"Alli!" cried a voice. "Alli, come hither!"

Alli looked over to the large wooden cage. There Turin Tim, the homely daughter of Kuln-Holn, was gesturing to her. Cautiously, Alli stepped to the side of the cage.

"Alli, do you hear the sounds of battle?" Turin Tim asked. "Gundoen has led our men here to avenge the raid and free us!" The plain girl's eyes sparkled at the thought.

Alli could only think of the gossip of the tribe, which pitied Turin Tim for being plain and only the daughter of Kuln-Holn, who was not only a cracked-pate but a poor one to boot. The poor girl had had to fend for herself and support her own father. She had never even learned how to dance.

"Alli," said Turin Tim, "we must help them to rescue us. There are no Korlas here to guard us now. Go you into the hut of the Korla chief and find a sword to cut the ropes that bind shut the door of the cage."

Alli's eyes widened in fear. "What if they should catch me?" she wailed.

"They are all at the walls fighting. And their women are more frightened than we are. They know their men are no match for our warriors. Do you not hear that laughter? Know you not whose voice that is? No one will catch you. But go quickly before any of them return."

"They are returning?" cried Alli. "No, I cannot dare." And she turned and scampered back into the safety of the chief's hall, leaving the other women still penned in the wooden cage.

The sounds of battle grew louder, nearer.

The terror of the Korlas grew until the Orn warriors could no longer command them. In a sudden rush they broke and fled for shelter beyond the nearest huts, where the deadly arrows might no longer reach them.

Gundoen's warriors put up their bows and climbed down into the compound. As he waded through the heaps of dead Korlas, Gundoen laughed merrily.

"Come out, come out!" he called to the hidden Korlas. But no Orn or Korla ventured forth. Only the leader of the two Orn warriors shouted angrily from the shadows.

"Only cowards fight those who cannot strike back!"

Gundoen chuckled. "Is it so? Then what of you, attacking our children when we were gone hunting? Well, then, if you will be shy, we will put away these toys." And he pulled out his great flat sword instead, leading his warriors into the shadows of the Korla huts.

Then was the fighting close and heated. Sword met sword in clangorous strokes, and blood spattered the walls of the silent huts. Gundoen was everywhere, laughing horribly, cursing merrily; and at his side was Ara-Karn, the stranger, matching him death for death.

Under that mad onrush, the terrified Korlas gave back quickly. They sweated and ran and stumbled, rose to give back blows, then, wounded again, ran back further. They fought among their homes in the streets of their own village, and every hut the enemy swarmed about meant women and children lost. And still they dared not hold their ground but retreated, for all the beatings the two Orn warriors gave them.

They fell back to the clearing before their chief's hall in the center of the village. And there, away from the toil of battle for a moment, they paused, and leaned against the wooden cage for rest.

But behind them the captive women laid hands on them, taking their swords and striking them senseless. Turin Tim lifted one of the heavy swords and swung it with her thin strong arms. The blade bit deep into the thick cord binding the cage door. She worked the blade free and struck again. The cord snapped in twain, and the women rushed out into the freedom of the square.

By now the battle had reached the square. Already battle was boiling around the cage. Gundoen went in combat against the tall Orn warrior, the one who had taken Alli to his own dim place. And that battle was a sight to behold. Sparks flew from their hot, blood-drinking swords, and the thunder of those blows was deafening.

Gundoen struck a blow with the full strength of his bull-like shoulders, and the head of the Orn leader flew into the air trailing blood.

Gundoen shook the blood out of his eyes and called to Ara-Karn, "One ahead again!"

"Is it so?" asked the stranger; so he turned suddenly and engaged the other Orn warrior. And in three deft strokes his sword was buried in the man's loins. "We are even again," he said calmly, drawing forth the blade.

The chief of the Korlas went mad with panic when he saw the two Orns dead. He grabbed one of the freed women and held her in front of him. "Cease battling and leave us!" he cried. "Or your women die before you!"

The men paused, uncertain of what to do. They looked to the chief for an answer; but before Gundoen could think, Turin Tim had come up behind the Korla chief.

She tripped him suddenly with her long bare leg, and as he fell she swung the heavy sword, so that the blade buried itself deep into the soft flesh of the exposed throat.

Panting, Turin Tim raised the bloody sword. She said, "Warriors of our tribe, will you let your women do all your fighting for you?"

Garin went up to her and put his strong arm about her waist, for he saw that she was about to fall for weakness. The women had been fed only one meal since they had been captured, except for Alli; and except for Alli they had slept only fitfully in the exposed cage.

With the death of the Orn warriors and the chief, the surviving Korlas broke into an uncontrollable panic and fled from the square. And the hooting, howling warriors of Gundoen's tribe followed after them and killed them to the last man they could find. The last of the Korlas tried to open the gates of the village and flee into the green fields; but Gundoen's warriors reached them before the great wooden bar could be raised, and they slew them screaming on the high walls of their own stockade.

Then the Korla huts were looted of all gold and weapons and ornaments, and the hilt of the sword of Tont-Ornoth was recovered from the Orn warrior's pile and returned to Gundoen. The men found Alli cowering in the Orn's dim place and at first mistook her for a Korla woman because of her garb. But she cried out to them, and they recognized her voice. She emerged from the Korla chief's hall and fell familiarly into the blood-spattered shelter of Gundoen's arms.

The Korla women were dragged out into the streets with their children, there to be reviled by the vindictive freed women. Any boy with second teeth the warriors slew outright, lest he grow to seek vengeance for the slaughter of his father. The other children and most of the women they let be. But if a woman wore a costly tunic with fine bright colors, a warrior would strip it from her back to give to his own wife at home. And if a woman was comely enough, a warrior would take her for his concubine or his serving wench, as the Korlas would have done to the women of Gundoen's tribe.

And Gundoen would have no pity for the last remnants of the Korla tribe. "They struck at us most foully," he declared. "And made war upon our women and children. And they did this thing for no other cause than greed and the urgings of Gen-Karn. No mercy did they show, and none shall they receive. Their destruction will be a sign and a warning to all the tribes of the North of the power of our tribe." And some said that these words were not wholly the chief's, but both they and the plan were of the stranger's devising and instance. But if this were so, Gundoen did not appear sorry to follow the advice.

So they left the gates of the stockade barred, and set their torches to the village, and burned it to the ground. From the cool shade of the forest they could hear the screams of the women and babes, and the beatings upon the too-high walls. But Gundoen's face was like the carved face of dark God as he watched the black, baleful smoke rising from what once had been a village of one of the tribes of the far North.

The warriors set their backs upon the scene and wearily traveled homeward. They fed and clothed the women who had been captives of the Korlas and rejoiced that they were safe and still untouched. Alli rode nestled in the lap of Gundoen, which he allowed even though they had taken all the Korla ponies and had three ponies to every rider.

Alli snuggled against the bloodied armor of that broad chest and kissed the chief, sighing for sheer comfort. And Gundoen smiled down on her gently and patted her soft rump. But later, when they had come to the village again, he put her aside. And things were never the same between them again.

The tribe held a great victory feast upon their return. Hertha-Toll ordered that all be made ready and the boards brought out into the sandy square, stocking them with what meats and breads the Korlas had not found.

With great ceremony Gundoen returned the sacred relics to their places. The warriors paraded all the loot taken from the burned village, and the women laughed and rejoiced in their new fineries. Now that swift and heated vengeance had been taken for their slain loved ones, the people of the tribe felt that their spirits could pass peacefully over to the lands of the dead. They put aside their hatred, for it had been slaked in swift action. And they made merry instead. Even Gundoen put on a cheerful face and danced drunkenly before the clapping onlookers.

But Ara-Karn sat apart.

The chief had offered him the seat of honor, but he had refused it. He drank little and ate nothing at all. He lounged on the sand lazily, yawning now and then, seemingly bored. There were none of the green flecks in his eyes now, so that they seemed dead and empty even in the face of the joy of victory. In the middle of the feast he rose and stalked off into the shadows.

No one noticed his passing save Kuln-Holn. But before the Pious One could rise to follow him, Garin came up.

With Garin was Kul-Dro, walking upright now with hardly any pain in his ribs. Kul-Dro had battled well in the Korla village despite his nagging bruises, though Kuln-Holn knew it not. Kuln-Holn had not gone on the raid.

"Kuln-Holn," said Kul-Dro, sitting cross-legged before him, "I am here on the part of my firstborn son Garin. He wishes you to know that he was with your daughter in the heat of battle and was greatly impressed by her. He wishes you to give her to him in marriage."

Kuln-Holn sat back and blinked. Never before had a marriage offer come for Turin-Tim, and because of her late age he had begun to lose all hope. He nodded eagerly. "Certainly, to such a fine young man as Garin I will give my wholehearted support."

"Nor do you have to worry about a dowry," said Garin impulsively. "Let Turin Tim come and live with us."

"Quiet, boy," growled Kul-Dro.

"No." Kuln-Holn shook his head. "That would not be right. Upon her marriage I will give Turin Tim nothing less than all I possess. My hut was not burned by the Korlas, and my boat, because it was far down the shore, was left alone. I will give these things to her. Also my fishing nets —though I confess that the nets are old and rotted in places."

Garin's face brightened at this unexpected news. They drank a bowl of ale to seal the bargain, passing it around on the right hand; then Kuln-Holn took Garin to Turin Tim. When he told her of the proposal, he was surprised to see Turin Tim blush and stammer; she could hardly have hoped for such a match as this.

But Garin caught her around the waist and chided her. "You showed more spirit in the cage in the village of the Korlas," he chided. "Are you another girl now, or am I so much worse than Korlas?"

So she laughed and kissed him. Kuln-Holn wished to leap in the air. This was all the blessing of Ara-Karn. The thought of the stranger reminded him of the man's seeming sadness at the feast. Immediately he went in search of him.

After searching through the entire village, he found him out on the long arm of the bay. The stranger was standing in the coarse grass above the rocks, idly tossing stones into the white foam.

At Kuln-Holn's approach he turned.

"Lord," said the Pious One, "once I was a common man like many another. I was by trade a fisherman, and I was born to this tribe in that same hut where you stayed, when first you came among us. I would mend nets and trade the fish I caught for whatever else we needed. For I was never a warrior or a good man for the hunt, but at fishing I was your man.

"I had a wife and a daughter. And my wife was growing again with the life I had placed within her. That life was to be my son, the first one granted me by the Most High.

"And I was a simple man and not the poorest man in the village: not half so poor as you have seen. Many fish I caught on the wide sea, and with every catch I threw one fish back in, in sacrifice and thanks to Her. Our hut was grander then than what you have seen, for it is long years now since I fished for my bread.

"And then my name was not Kuln-Holn. They called me by another then: that which my father had given me. But now it is years since I heard that name, so that even I have forgotten it. Long years, since a terrible storm came upon us. We knew that a storm was coming, for there had been signs. And many of the other fishermen would not go out upon the waters for fear of the storm.

"But I said to them, in my youth and ignorant pride— for which may She forgive me!—I said, 'You others are old and feeble like women. There have been no bad storms hereabouts for more years than I can tell you. And what have you to fear if you have sacrificed one fish out of every catch to Her, as you should, and as I have done?' Also I had in mind my pregnant wife and baby daughter, and thought I would need all the fish that I might catch. For the fish bite best when they sense a storm brewing.

"So I went out on the waters in my boat, trusting to my luck. They called me a fool, but I only laughed and shoved my boat into the waves. And that time was the finest fishing I have ever known. I sat out alone in the best spots, and every time I cast my nets they returned brimming with fat fish, so heavy I could scarcely lift the nets. My boat filled with fish so quickly that soon I took to casting out the smaller ones of less tasty variety to make room for the larger, prized ones. And I laughed, and tugged my cap, and thanked Her whose ocean it is. But I did not remember that it is not called the Ocean of the Dead for nothing.

"And before I was yet ready to return, though I could have gone back with a full load long before, the storm came overhead. The winds blew, the seas hove, the rain came sideways in its fury. And Her face was blackened with rage.

"My boat was swamped so that I had to take to bailing. And when that did no good, I was forced to cast out those beautiful fish I had caught—though it tore my heart to do so. I cast them forth one by one, for with each fish I discarded I hoped that the boat would be light enough. Only it was never enough, and I was forced to throw away every single last beautiful fish. Then I was so sorely cast down that I almost begged for death in my disappointment. But that would have been too merciful.

"I bailed and strove to fight the storm; it laughed and thundered, and threw my little boat about. So dark it was that I did not know where Her face lay, and where the dark horizon. Long since had my little mast snapped, and my nets and oars blown headlong into the tempest. And I had nothing but the sodden rags on my back. I cried out for mercy in the boiling darkness.

"Only thunder answered me. And in the depths of that thunder I heard a voice. Like to a woman's voice it was, only such a woman as had never trod this earth. Her voice was like that of some great Queen of the Southlands, and it was husky in its anger. I knew then that it was the voice of the Goddess. It was like an image reflected in a rippling pool, distorted for all its majesty. Nor could I make out Her words, save in the fever of my soul. Then I knew that, for all I had obeyed all the customs and sacrificed in thanks to Her, it had been but a show, and unreflected in my heart. I knew it then, though I had not yet the words to say it. They came later, in all the tortured years since I have had to think upon it.

"Only a miracle kept my little boat afloat. I bailed and rowed with my hands, but all my efforts were as nothing compared with the awesomeness of that tempest. I was certain that the current of the Dead had caught hold of my boat, and that I was being dragged still living over the seas to the shores of death. And there the angry spirits would eat my brains in horrid fashion, and such would be my punishment.

"I resolved myself to it and gave over my efforts. 'O Most High,' I cried into the darkness, 'whatever you give to me, that I will take as my due.'

"Then I lay back in the boat and gave myself up for dead.

"She did not drive me to my death. Soon afterward I heard the sound of breakers, and swam among the rocks to the shore. There I collapsed upon the beach, nearly dead, naked, and bleeding.

"When the storm at last abated I took thought of my location, which was many leagues North of here, in the coarse wilderness where none dwelt. Now a clan of our people has set their huts on a bay there. I drank fresh water from a stream and wove clothing out of the long grasses and made my way back here, fevered, wild, and always near to death.

"They were all amazed to find me alive, for they had long given up all hope for me, and had even said the ceremonial words for me. I asked about my wife, and then received the full measure of my punishment: for she was dead, having died in the terror of the storm giving birth to my son. Only the birth had been too early, and the boy, too, was dead—he never even drew the breath of life.

"I went mad in my grief, and only Hertha-Toll, with her wondrous skill, brought me back to life. Many a man thought to be dead from drowning she has revived with her herbs and skills. When I was again able to walk about, I gathered little Turin Tim in my arms and swore to serve the Goddess in all things, upon the very life's breath of my only surviving kin. I went about thereafter preaching of my lesson to the others of the tribe. That was when they began calling me Pious One, and my birthing-name was forgotten. And that was the last time I had gone out fishing before you came here, though I built another boat to tow the dead forth.

"And never since then have I been sure that She has truly forgiven me. It is this thought that torments me more than any other, and will give me no rest even in my dreams. Yet now I feel almost as if the great tidings I had looked for will come to pass. Are you not Her messenger, lord? Ara-Karn, I have given my daughter for Garin to wed, and let them have my hut. I have no ties here now— she is the last of my kin. Let me be your man, lord, and I will aid you in your divine mission."

Ara-Karn looked down upon the kneeling man. For a long while, neither of them spoke. The sounds of the sea birds and the waves mixed in their ears.

"Whatever I might require of you?" Ara-Karn asked at last, his strange accent stronger than it had been for many weeks. "You will serve me as you would a god?"

Kuln-Holn bowed his head. "Whatever Ara-Karn might command, that Kuln-Holn will do."

"If you ever disobey me it will mean your death in the end. I will have no halfway men."

"Aye, lord."

"Then stand." Kuln-Holn rose. The stranger put his hand on the fisherman's shoulder and gripped it tightly. "Very well, Kuln-Holn, I will accept you as my man. But where it may lead you, and what it may require of you, I think you can little dream."

Kuln-Holn did not hear the last words; his ears were filled with the rush of happiness, for Ara-Karn had accepted him. And now it was as if the Goddess were about to bestow the fullness of Her forgiveness, and dreams he had dreamt so long, of peace and plenty and Her good work, were now to come finally to pass.

CHAPTER ELEVEN

The Message of the Warlord

With the utter destruction of the last of the Korlas came a peace to that far corner of the far North. The fishermen wove new nets, and repaired their boats, and went out on the waters of the bay.

The hunters went into the shadows of the deep woods and cut down long straight trees, hauling the logs down the slopes to the village, and they set about the laborious task of repairing all the huts that had been burned by the Korlas on what had been their final raid. The women went out into the trampled green fields and did what they could to save the crops. Not so many had been destroyed as they had at first feared, and with what grain they would be able to purchase from the other tribes, and with the game the bowmen would be able to bring down, the tribe seemed assured of a hearty winter. And no more raids came. Gundoen had scouts posted to warn of any war-parties coming from the direction of Orn, but no war-parties came.

And soon came the weeks of summer's brightest heat. For twenty passes of dark God overhead, the grasses turned a withered brown and the trees dried crackling in the forests. The streams shrank and were quietened, and the dogs lay about on the earthen floors of the huts and would not go hunting. There were fires in the forests on the bright sides of the hills, but none came close enough to the village to do harm. The men and women put aside all their tasks but those most necessary; some went down to bathe naked in the cool waters of the bay, while others simply lay in the shadows, sweating and dozing.

Then the throne of Golden Fire fell back a bit toward the South, and the heat began to depart. The children began to play in the streets again, and the dogs barked once more. The women returned to the fields, and the men to the deep woods.

Emissaries came to Gundoen from the River's-Bend tribe, and the Archeros, and chief Nam-Rog's Durbar tribe. These were all tribes still independent of Gen-Karn. They came because of the wild rumors flying about the North that Gundoen had completely destroyed the Korlas with no damage at all to himself, and that now even Gen-Karn was afraid of Gundoen. The emissaries saw the newly built halls, the stores of grain and meat, the warriors walking about just as if there had been no war at all. That the tribe should have been able to visit such complete destruction upon their enemies at so little cost to themselves seemed a veritable miracle. Even seeing, the emissaries could scarcely believe it.

Gundoen smiled upon them, inscrutable in his triumph.

He told them of the stranger, Ara-Karn—of how he had come from the lands of the dead and of his greats feats in the Hunt. He even gave the stranger much of the credit for their victory over the Korlas, as if the chief himself had not battled as mightily as a bull bandar.

He even allowed Kuln-Holn to sit at his tables and regale the emissaries at length with his visions and early dreams, and of the great dark mission of Ara-Karn, and of what up to this time he had never before dared tell: of how Ara-Karn had gone to the peak of Kaari-Moldole, the forbidden peak, and commanded storm and sea and returned therefrom unscathed. The men from the tribes listened to the words, and they did not laugh or jest, for clearly there had been some strange doings among the people of Gundoen's tribe. Of Ara-Karn they asked few questions, and he answered them none. And this impressed them even more than all the rest; for what sort of a man was it who could refrain from speaking about his own accomplishments?

Of the bows, the chief spoke not at all. Nor did he show them any. Instead he left them thinking that all had been accomplished with the traditional weapons, so that the emissaries shook their heads in disbelief and went back to their tribes full of the mystery of Gundoen's great victory.

Thus, for the first time, the name of Ara-Karn passed beyond the limits of Gundoen's territory, and it did so shrouded in dark awe. So that when the word of Gundoen's doings sped throughout the tribes, the name of Ara-Karn figured prominently. Never before had the tribe done such things. And with the name went the stories of Kuln-Holn's prophecies; so that, though many shook their heads skeptically, with each new telling the wonder and magic of the name grew, so that the stories began to hold things that Kuln-Holn had never intended, but the chief had. And Gundoen laughed to think of Gen-Karn grinding his teeth away in sullen dismay.

The fruit ripened upon the branch; the stalks matured in the field; the chill of autumn came back on the north winds. The harvesting was done by all the women and men of the tribe—cut, threshed, and stored away against the winter snows. The first frosts fell upon the dark sides of the hills, and then it came time for the warriors and important men of the tribe to make ready for the long trek to the Tribal Assembly at Urnostardil. Few tribes dwelt farther away from the meeting-place than did Gundoen's, so they must be about their preparations and departures earlier than most of the other tribes.

Before these preparations were complete, there came to the chief's hall an embassy from Gen-Karn, mightiest of the chiefs and Warlord of all the far North. They were led by Sol-Dat of the Orn tribe, now Gen-Karn's chief man. With him were two other Orn warriors and Estar Aln of the Korla tribe.

Gundoen received them as he would any embassy—in his long hall and with a goodly feast. But he took extra precautions that they should see little of the strength of men he planned to take to the Assembly and that all the bows of the tribe were hidden. And he kept seated beside him with honor Ara-Karn, bedecked in full war-gear, so that they might be sure to see this stranger and take back the word of him to their master. This, like many of the other ideas concerning their dealings with the other tribes, had been of Ara-Karn's own proposing.

When they had eaten, Sol-Dat rose. "I see you are not a

man to boastfully set before his guests the best of his meat and drink, Gundoen. That is well, for in Orn we have too much good food. We forget its quality for having naught to compare it to."

Gundoen smiled. "I would like myself to taste some of Orn cooking, save that I fear I might soon afterward grow ill, like poor Est-Hal of the Kamskal tribe. Perhaps some year after Gen-Karn is gone."

Sol-Dat curled his lips scornfully. "That might be too long to wait, Gundoen." Again he had referred to the chief as if he were not the leader of his people. Yet Gundoen was too crafty to be drawn into open warfare before he deemed it proper. The matter was too important for him to have given vent to his own hot temper, hard though it was for him to control it.

Sol-Dat then turned his gaze upon Ara-Karn and questioned him about the death-barge he had stolen and how much of its loot he had been able to keep after the chief had taken his share.

Ara-Karn only shrugged lightly. "Once, O Chief," he said, speaking only to Gundoen, "a man told me he had seen a monkey, a wild beast, hairy and shaped like a demented man, trained to speak human tongue. But never have I believed that man's words until now. However, though a monkey may talk at me, I will not speak to a monkey." At which there was laughter throughout the hall.

Sol-Dat reddened to his bronze breastplate. "Gundoen, I will no longer bandy words with you. Words are the knives of women's tongues; warriors have other weapons. Be it known that you have broken the peace of the tribes against all prior agreements, the laws of our people, and the wishes of the great Gen-Karn. You have invaded the lands of another tribe and stolen their game. You have attacked the Korlas and killed them wantonly, slaying warrior, woman, and babe. You have burned their village to the ground. But not all the Korlas were in their village, Gundoen—some fled to the woods before you could massacre them, and others were at Orn, the guests of our Warlord Gen-Karn himself.

"These have come to great Gen-Karn and supplicated him. And since the Korlas are now too few to defend themselves, we of the Orn tribe have agreed to press the suit on their behalf. At the Tribal Assembly you will be called to defend yourselves, or repay the Korlas in kind. Notice has been formally given."

With these words Sol-Dat turned and signed to the others who had come with him. Without waiting for a reply or to feed their ponies, they left the hall and rode out of the village down the path past Outpost Rock.

Gundoen only laughed, and drank his ale deeply at last, and spat it out upon their trail with relish.

When all the preparations were complete, the warriors who were to go to the Assembly were feasted in a final farewell ceremony. Usually this feast was one of the happiest of the year, for the harvests were in and another year had been survived. Yet this year it was not so gay, because all knew that not everyone who was to leave would as surely return.

Hertha-Toll was of all the women most cheerful, at which the other women took some heart. "Look," they said among themselves, "the wise woman is full of cheer; can matters be as bad as we fear then?" And when she spoke before the feast, Hertha-Toll prophesied only good —a great victory for the tribe, first place among all the tribes, and the downfall of Gen-Karn.

But alone with Gundoen in his dim place, Hertha-Toll put aside her smiling face and begged him not to go.

"It is shameful and without honor, I know," she said earnestly. "But why can you not even now gather our tribe and remove to the Southlands? We have food and drink already prepared; the other preparations would take but a little time. Perhaps our luck would be better in the South."

Gundoen was put off by her manner. "What is wrong with our luck now?" he grumbled. "Woman, you trouble me. Have these matters not already been decided? Why do you wish to cast your gloom over me now?"

"It is only," she said, "it is only because I love you. I do, Gundoen, with as much fervor as I did when I was a young girl famed for her beauty. And I have had dreams. But"—she sighed—"I should have known that I could not stop a truth that I had already seen."

"What dreams?" he growled.

She shook her head. "I burst with them but cannot tell you. You made me promise to speak no more, did you not? —to speak no more against him. Yet only this will I say, my chieftain: If you go to this Assembly, you will die.

And you will die horribly, with no friends about you. And your body will never make the final voyage. And you will have been betrayed by him you hold most high."

Gundoen did not answer her in the darkness. He lay on one side facing away from her, and was still for the entire time of the sleep. Yet she could tell by his breathing that he did not sleep.

And later in the outside brightness of the light of Goddess, when all the warriors were upon their ponies ready to depart, Gundoen laughed at his wife's gloomy looks as if she were a child. And he said privately to her, "When I return with Gen-Karn's head hanging at the side of my saddle-blanket, then there will be an end of prophecy for you."

He brought his pony about so suddenly that Hertha-Toll had not a chance to reply, and he rode to the head of the long columns by Outpost Rock.

He spat upon his hand and stretched it forth. He wiped the spittle gleaming upon the sharp stone.

"Departing I use my own spit," he declared. "But when I return I'll cover the spot with my enemies' blood!"

A cheer sounded from the warriors astride their ponies, from the women standing on the edges of the sere brown fields, and from the children behind them. Gundoen grinned, his sharp teeth gleaming in the light of Goddess. The warriors started forward and slowly, because of their great numbers, entered into the concealing leaves of the forest. Then the last of them waved fiercely and turned the bend, and only the measured beat of their ponies' hooves could be felt in the soft earth.

Eagerly the women bent their ears to the ground. By the rhythms of the beat, much could be omened concerning the success of the expedition, and none was better at this than Hertha-Toll the Wise.

Yet when the vibrations finally fell to naught, and the middle-aged woman lifted up her squat brown frame and turned slowly back toward the village, she said not a word, no matter how many and eager were the questions showered upon her.

CHAPTER TWELVE

To the Dark Horizon

The long columns journeyed through the forests, the hills, and the vales of the far North. Many were the warriors, many more than of any other expedition ever sent out by the tribe—more than twice the numbers of the previous year's expedition to the Assembly. Not only from the main village, where stood the ancient chief's hall, had they come, but also from the outlying clans who dwelt farther up the coastline. All had come in response to Gundoen's call, the standard passed from clan to clan. They had smeared good fish oil on their blades and cleaned the dirt from their armor. Swords, axes, spears had been sharpened; new bows had been passed about and practiced upon. The huts had been emptied at their going, and it had taken much of the winter's stores to victualize them. Yet each man and woman in the tribe had known that, if they all did not depart, there would be no tribe left to face the winter. Gen-Karn had sued them in payment in kind—for the destruction of the Korla tribe, they would themselves be destroyed. They could not submit to Gen-Karn; they would conquer, therefore, or die.

Slung on the side of every man's pony, within easy reach, were their bows and the thick bundles of slender death-birds. Yet more bundles of arrows were wrapped carefully in waterproof pelts on the pack-ponies. These were the tribe's only hope—Ara-Karn's boon—and more than one man found his hand often straying to the bow and arrows to fondle them and gain comfort thereby.

They traveled southward, past the skirt of Kaari-Moldole toward the distant blue mountains of the Spine of Civilization growing above the horizon. This was not their usual path; they feared to travel as they were used, for fear of facing Orn ambushes in every ravine. There were easy valleys by clear-welled streams that all the tribes knew and used in common. They knew these trails; Gen-Karn knew them also. If he had not attacked them after the destruction of the Korlas, it could only have been with some other, greater treachery in mind.

They rode up into the foothills of the Spine, where few tribes went. Above them towered the peaks of the Spine, ever bluely snowbound, cushioning their heads against the clouds. Beyond these mountains lay the soft verdant lands of the lush Southlands, where the streets had golden fountains. But there was no way to cross the Spine, save through the Pass at Gerso.

Even here in the foothills the air was stiff and thin compared to the soft air by the sea. The warriors urged their ponies up the rocky trails, among steep lands where trees were scarce and stunted. Then they turned their faces to the dark horizon and began the long and arduous journey.

Along the way Ara-Karn asked the chief about the Assembly, its history, and of the place whither they were bound.

"It's the Assembly," responded Gundoen simply. "Once a year, at the end of the growing season yet before winter has set his teeth into the earth, all the tribes journey from their home-fires and go beyond the dusky border that separates Her world from His. There, with his head towering out of the darkness, stands Urnostardil, the Table—a great mountain like to one of the higher of those there"—he gestured with his gloved hand—"yet with his peak lopped off. His sides are steep and rough, assailable from but a single face, and there only up a narrow, back-and-forth trail fit more for the nimble beasts than mounted men.

"Upon the top of that Table meet the tribes. Each year we all gather, for there is room there even for all of us, if you can imagine it so great. And the tribes choose the Warlord, he who is by name the leader of all the tribes. In the past several years, because none has dared to go against him, Gen-Karn has been the undisputed Warlord."

"How is he chosen?"

Gundoen shrugged the massive shoulders encased in iron. "How else but by combat?" he asked. "Some years the Warlord is a powerful man indeed, and other years not so powerful, depending upon the man and his circumstances. For a man may be a great fighter, but an indifferent leader of men and not crafty enough in all. Or the Warlord may be the chief of his own tribe or not; and his tribe may not be a powerful one. Now, Gen-Karn has become one of the most powerful of the Warlords ever, for he is the chief of the Orns, one of the most wealthy tribes with great warriors—mountain and lake folk, and great fighters. It has the greatest number of clans, and, since Gen-Karn returned to lead them, they have become very wealthy dealing with the Southron merchants. Moreover Gen-Karn is clever as a wounded fulsar beast and half again as ferocious. Of those who went against him in the first years of his rule, not one lasted for more than it would have taken you to count two score—and not a one did he leave alive, except Elrikal of the Forun tribe. Him he left living, if you care to call it so: missing both legs, one eye, and his right hand. He was a broken man after that, without even the courage to cut his own throat, which any man with honor should have done. And since then no man has dared to face Gen-Karn."

Gundoen fell silent awhile, looking down to where his own gloved thick hands cradled the reins of his pony. For a time there was only the creaking of leather on leather and the clinking of the iron fastenings. Then the wind turned and came from the horizon, bringing with it the bitter chill of the snow-chained peaks. They had left autumn behind in the low golden forests; here in the hills it was winter already.

A low chant arose from the rear of the long columns, hollowly sounded in the throats of metal-clad men—a battle-chant, the chant of the last survivors on the Table—Tont-Ornoth, El-Sabak, Born-Karn, Vel-Star, and the others whose names were legend—and Sil-Sa-Pal, the woman with the hair of gold, who wore her dead husband's armor fighting the man who would become a god, until Elna's men threw her down the side of the peak to her death. It was the Awaiting Chant, of the time when the battle had come to a last long lull, and the final charge was being planned by the civilized men who were led in person by Elna, soon to make himself the first Emperor in Tarendahardil, the City Over the World. It was a chant as desolate as these wolf-spurned hills, as mournful as the last cries of a wounded falcon calling for his dead mate. The stranger seemed to like it.

Gundoen shook his massive frame, rumbled the phlegm in his throat, and spat.

"I could have challenged Gen-Karn," he said. "To be a challenger a man must only be a member of one of the tribes, a good hunter, and have accomplished some great deed. And all of those things are mine. Yet I have seen Gen-Karn fight, and though I know his tricks and weaknesses, I also know my own. And I am not the man to beat him. He is clever with a sword, and fast—and only greater cleverness and speed will best him. Now if it were only wrestling, ah!" The chief's great chest swelled. "Then you'd see a sight. I'd crack him like a rotten nut between these arms of mine. But with a sword I was never your man. You saw me, back among the Korlas—sometimes I fight as if I were wrestling."

He turned back on his pony and "Ho there!" he called. "Have you nothing pleasanter to sing than that old dirge? Do you trust my leadership so little as that?"

Laughter answered him, and the men changed their tune to a simple marching chant, picked up from the happier peoples of the fat Southlands.

Gradually the sky fell darker before the traveling columns. Goddess sank low in the sky, four fists high, then three, then two. And at last She was but one fist above the far, undulating horizon, a great copper ball in a yellowed corner of the blooded sky. Above them the sky was a deep darkness, more green than blue; and ahead, where the ponies' heads were turned, the sky was almost black.

Only once did they cross the tracks of other men. That was when they were crossing the wide smooth trails leading down to rich Gerso at the Pass of Gerso. Then they could not help but meet other travelers, for it was only in the very deeps of icy winter that these paths were still. Yet the men they encountered were no more than a few traders with their ponies returning with pelts and gold to Gerso— no threat to Gundoen's strong warriors. Ara-Karn looked

to the South curiously, as if he wished to leave the warriors
and go that way.

After they had crossed the paths leading to the city of
merchants, they headed more toward the North. Gundoen
led them down out of the rocky hills for the softer forested
lands. Here they made much faster progress without wor-
rying about treachery. For it was doubtful that Gen-Karn
could have guessed they would be coming at Urnostardil
from so far to the South. And by now he would have
drawn in whatever spies and ambuscades he had set to gall
them, for the time of the Assembly was very near. By now,
Gundoen said, the man would be concentrating on the politics of the tribes, for he had ever been the first among
chieftains to lead his warriors up the Goat's-Track.

When they had come down into the lowlands they found
that here, too, winter had beset the land. The trees were
nearly naked, and chill winds blew the thick leaves about.
Here, where She was weaker upon the border of His lands,
the air was darker, colder, and more bleak; summer was
none so intense, spring came later, and winter lay upon
this land many passes more than upon the lands on the
ocean's edge.

And now they were come to the great dusky border, between the lands where men may dwell in Her light and
those forever dark beneath His sleepless Eye, where none
but Madpriests dwell. Here the valleys were dark like shut
dim places, and only stunted, distorted things grew therein.
And whenever the warriors rode down the back of some
great hill, flaming Goddess would fall away beyond the
earth, and Darkness, chill and implacable, would swallow
them. Their breaths would come steaming from their
mouths, and they must guide their ponies more slowly, lest
they stumble and fall.

And when they would rise once more to the Goddess-
swathed gold of another ridge, then they would breathe
more easily, a bond seemingly loosed from their chests and
the prickling gone from their armpits. Nor would they
hasten their pace, now they could see the path clearly; but
rather they paused and milled about. They gloried even in
this faint warmth of Her gaze, looking to see Her, faint,
pale, and shrunken upon the lip of the far horizon.

They came over the crest of a spiny-backed hill with
more of rocks than shrubs. And when they passed away
over it they said a final prayer to Her who looks down

upon us all with warmth. They prayed for their women
and children and the fate of their village. They prayed for
victory in the coming struggles. This was no ritual prayer
beset with high formulae, led by arcane initiates, priestesses, and kings, but a simple sincere thing, spoken in the
silence of every man's heart. But whether the stranger
prayed or not, none could say.

The chief then tried to cheer them, and they laughed
with him. But the darkness echoed back their hollow
laughter, and the eyes of the men were wide and dark. Not
even the chief's voice sounded as heartily as it was used.

Then they kicked the flanks of their unwilling ponies
and passed from the lands of living men. For now they
had gone beyond the utmost reaches of the dusky border
and were in the lands on which only His Eye looked down
from blackened skies.

And they knew that somewhere beyond the last hills,
not far along, the land fell sloping down to the dark chill
seas of darkness, broken only by rare jagged peaks of bare
sweatful stone, where nothing lived but monstrous reptilian
fishes with jagged sharp teeth and no eyes bulging in the
darkness of those sunless seas. And above it all, darker
than the darkness, hung the citadel of black rock, of Him
who loves men not.

They rode on in silence for some time.

Only the beat of hooves and the hiss of pine torches interrupted each warrior's solemn reflections, and not even
Gundoen broke that silence. They had come this way
many times, but before they had always known they would
return.

The ponies started in the darkness. Wide flared the nostrils of the ponies. Even the men could smell that clammy,
reptilian smell that fills the stomach with revulsion. The
ponies tried to break away—they were held in line only by
the strong fists of the riders.

"Where is it?" called Gundoen, forcing his pony back
along the lines. "Can anyone see it?"

"I cannot see it," shouted one man in terror. "But it's
there to the right of us! *Listen!*"

They fell silent.

A noise came to their ears—a noise of horror. A sham-
bling, brutish slithering, a rustling, a slime-filled crawling
sound. Softly it parted earth and the stunted branches,

softly—yet such was the bulk of that monstrous thing that even in stealth it made the noise of a troop of men.

The sound grew steadily for several moments, then stopped, pausing uncertainly. It came again, louder, and the frightened ponies bucked and neighed. Yet there was no cause for such alarm, for the noise was receding.

"Come on now," called Gundoen, when the dank dark woods had been silent for several moments. "No need for worry now. The Assembly and Gen-Karn are more than enough concern for us."

Gradually the warriors started forward again—yet more slowly, more cautiously, than ever before.

"A Darkbeast," replied Gundoen to Ara-Karn's question. "They are the only large things that can live in the darkness. They exist off ponies and such animals as get lost in the darkness. They can swallow a colt whole, in a single gulp! The scent of so many of us must have been what frightened it away. What a deed it is to hunt one! It takes more than a score of trained warriors just to kill one; but those men can wear the teeth of a Darkbeast and be honored above all other hunters. In my hall there is such a tooth, from a Darkbeast slain by Oro-Born, one of the great chiefs of my tribe. If we return aright, I'll show it you."

The men moved forward at hardly a walking pace. They traveled in a silence broken only by the curses of a man whose pony had made a misstep or been lamed. Twice they ate in the darkness, but did not lie down to sleep. It would not have been necessary to cover themselves with the small tent-dim-place here; but to lie in the snow in that defenseless land, under the moveful, malevolent Eye of God, was too eerie to let any man find rest.

They came to a long, tall slope and followed it up to the weird, star-pointed sky; and when they had reached the peak of the ridge, they spread themselves out in the frozen darkness. There they fed themselves and their ponies one more time and stooped to examine their weapons in the flickering torchlight.

Before them, glowing like a crown of flames, stood the flattened peak of a great mountain, standing far above them. This mountain had no root nor head, but only the slanting middle, suspended under the vault of heaven, glowing as if alive. Along its edge tiny figures worked their way up the slopes—antlike things, which were men mounted on horseback.

Gundoen swept his massive, ironclad arm out in an expansive gesture before Ara-Karn.

"Behold Urnostardil the Table, site of the Last Stand, and ever since the spot of the Assembly of all the tribes of the far North," he said.

In the lambent darkness among the few scattered fires, Kuln-Holn regarded his master. This was the first time he had ever journeyed far away from the sea and the place of his home village. The mountains he had disliked, for they were cold and foreboding; nor did he like being among the warriors of the tribe, who could speak of nothing but the men they had killed and their chances of survival when they went against the Orns. This kind of talk was chilling to Kuln-Holn. Mostly he had ridden in silence, nursing his unfamiliar pony along and concentrating on his dreams. He had looked to his master often, in the long and wearisome journey. It was upon him that he depended for comfort and secureness.

The warriors about him spoke and jested in low tones, eating dried meats, fish pasties, and hard dark bread. They had found some pools of sour water nearby; in addition to this they drank ale out of the stoppered clay jugs. They drank until their throats burned and hearts beat faster, then they wiped their beards with their gloved hands and threw the jugs away. This was to be the last meal before the ascent to Table, and Kuln-Holn heard their murmured questions about what they might encounter on that golden summit.

Kuln-Holn ate somewhat with them and took a bit of ale as well. When they drew forth their weapons to care for them, he searched about in his packs. He had only a long knife, more fit to the task of skinning fish than slaying men. He had never been in battle or even killed a man and did not know what it would be like. He feared it. Yet if battle did come, he knew it must be with Her consent, a part of Her plan—for was not Ara-Karn Her messenger, and had he not counseled it? So, dutifully copying the motions of his fellows, Kuln-Holn the Pious One began sharpening the long blade in the firelight and the cold light of ever-moving God.

He was still drawing it across the whetstone when Ara-

Karn approached him. The shadow of his master blocked off the nearest fire, plunging Kuln-Holn's hands into darkness.

"Assemble your gear and bring our ponies."

Kuln-Holn scrambled to his feet. "But, lord, there will be time for that. The others have not yet—" he began, but stopped. His master had turned and strode away, hearing none of Kuln-Holn's words.

Quickly, Kuln-Holn sheathed the fish-knife and tossed the whetstone in his wallet. He took the ponies from their feed, threw their bags over the backs, and tightened the straps. He followed his master, leading the ponies carefully through the bunched masses of men and horses.

He found Ara-Karn standing before the chief, awaiting him. When Kuln-Holn had brought the ponies to him, Ara-Karn turned back to the chief.

"I do not know how to answer you," Gundoen said hopelessly, in tones that surprised Kuln-Holn.

"I have known you well, Chief," said the stranger, "and liked you even better. Yet I am not one of you. Ask your men—they know it well. I have profited much from living amongst you, and you have also gained much from me. We are quits, then: you saved me from the sea, and I helped you destroy the Korlas."

"They are not all gone," pleaded the chief in harsh tones. "Some are even now on Table, above us. But we'll slay them, you and I. I killed one more than you, remember."

Kuln-Holn saw his master smile. "God grant you will. Yet to my mind we were even. At any rate, that is no longer my quarrel. I will leave you now, taking my servant with me."

The chief looked down at the ground, up to the golden crown of Urnostardil, and suddenly back to Ara-Karn. "I cannot stop you, then?"

"No." The master's head shook, gently yet firmly. "I would have gone earlier than this—back when we crossed the paths to the South. But I wanted to see this Table of which you have spoken so much. Do not fear; what is the loss of one man among so many warriors? I have shown you the ways of the bow, which none there"—he gestured to the mass of the Table above—"will know aught of. Believe me, your cause is not now so hopeless as you fear. You need me no longer."

"We do need you!" protested Gundoen.

"You underestimate your own powers, O Chief," said the stranger, smiling, "and overestimate my own. My fate does not lie on yonder peak, but to the South. Farewell."

"You I had thought were better than most Southrons," the chief said hotly. His voice sounded in Kuln-Holn's ears as it had in the boat, when the voyagings of those massacred by the Korlas were done. "I thought you were almost one of us. But of course a civilized man has little to do with filthy barbarians. He must seek his own kind, among the thieves at Gerso."

The chief took off his heavy gloves and threw them down to the earth. "But for all that, let us part as friends," he said impulsively. He gripped the stranger's hands, embraced his chest, yet not so hard now as when they had wrestled. "You were the only man ever to best me, and I love you for it. I shall not soon forget you, Ara-Karn. I cannot blame you for not wishing to share our fate. Fare you well wherever you may go."

Ara-Karn swung himself up onto his pony. "Come, Kuln-Holn," he ordered.

The Pious One looked back and forth between the two of them, his chief and his lord. He hardly realized what was happening. His look was dumbfounded.

"Go, Kuln-Holn," Gundoen commanded. "You were never a warrior; we shall not miss you, at least. You need not come with us."

The chief turned his back and gathered his heavy gloves. He went back among the others. He threw himself down by a cook-fire and tore savagely into a bit of dried meat. He did not look back.

Kuln-Holn turned to Ara-Karn, sitting his pony above him, looking down expectantly. Clearly he wished that Kuln-Holn would only hasten and mount.

"Lord," began Kuln-Holn stumblingly. "Lord, why do you leave the tribe? These men worship you. Gundoen loves you as he has loved no other. How can you leave them all to die? We must stay—you must lead them to victory over Gen-Karn. Else what can be your mission?"

Ara-Karn smiled.

Still smiling, he lifted a green length of branch in his gloved hand and brought it down. It vanished in the darkness. A sudden pain fell cuttingly across Kuln-Holn's face. The force of the blow knocked him to the ground.

Above, the master was still smiling. "Now," he said softly. "Will you obey me?"

Numbly, Kuln-Holn got to his feet. His face burned in the frozen darkness. He touched his cheek, felt the warm sticky liquid on his fingers. He did not wipe the wound clean. Rather he let it bleed freely.

"You swore to be my man," said Ara-Karn, "to follow me no matter where I led. Am I not a god to you?"

Kuln-Holn bowed in silence.

He gathered the leads of the pack-ponies and climbed upon his own. Upon the pack-ponies were five choice bandar-pelts—enough to bring them wealth in the civilized cities. Kuln-Holn did not look at the face of his master. He felt no sadness, no anger, and no fear. He did not know what he felt.

Ara-Karn touched the flank of his pony with the bloodied branch. He started down the hill, back toward the dusky border. He chose a path that led them around the men of the tribe, where he would not have to face Gundoen or the others whose lives depended upon him. Kuln-Holn did not blame him in this; he knew that his own sleeps would for some time be haunted by the visions of how these men died in battle upon the golden crown of Urno-stardil.

He followed behind his master, looking down at the ground.

Slowly, the rim of golden fire that was the peak of Urnostardil fell down into the swallowing darkness. Then the small twinkling torchfires also winked from sight. The two riders followed a slow path in the darkness. The slanting, cold light of the hostile Eye of God fell on their backs, shivering like a blade newly thrown. The hooves of the ponies crunched in the snow. Kuln-Holn shivered and looked back to his master, a darkly moving form ascending a new slope, blotting out the gray-blue sky of the bright horizon. This sight, too, gave Kuln-Holn no comfort.

He wondered with some fear what lives they would lead in the Southlands and what new people his master would betray.

CHAPTER THIRTEEN

The Dusky Border

The golden cliffs of the Table shone brightly in their eyes as the warriors of Gundoen's tribe trudged up the narrow winding trails to the summit. So many generations of the tribes had ascended here, along these very trails, that the stone was worn hollow and smooth. There was not room enough for two men to ride abreast, so the warriors ascended singly. And so many were they that the last warriors had only just worked their way into the light when Gundoen and the leading men had gained the summit. There they paused, waiting for all the warriors to form together before they ascended the last short slopes to where the Assembly was held.

Far, far off in the distance shone the throne of Golden Fire—pale now and little darker than saffron. From this distance a man might even behold Her a moment unblinking. Her rays were wan and weak, but still they held comfort after the clammy darkness of His world.

They gathered together and led their ponies up the short slope. Before them stretched the campgrounds of the Assembly—a great field shaped like a slightly hollowed plate, the far side in light but the near side mostly shadow. A man standing on the entrance side might behold his own shadow falling vaguely across the field almost to the far lip of the mountaintop.

Scattered over the plate were all the camps of the tribes, the short tents pitched in the plains with cook-fires before and ponies behind them. Here and there were piles of snow, cleared away from the rock before the many tents. Many men went to and fro, setting up their tents, selling beer or linens or weapons in their stalls. The tribes who dwelt near the dusky border always made good trade off the things they could bring to Assembly. There a crowd gathered about an old man telling tales of the shadowed past, here a group followed a chieftain about as he went to the tents of other chiefs seeking support for his tribe's suits.

In the center of the great field was a broad shallow pond formed by the frequent rains. Into the pond, through the cracks in the thin skin of ice, several men were dipping their wooden buckets. And beyond the pond, on the far side of the wide plain, stood a tremendous pile of brushwood. There were sticks, branches, and logs there from every forest in the far North.

Gundoen led his men around the edge of the Table to this pile of wood. As he went he could see the men from the other tribes pointing at him in surprise, as if they had not expected to see him here this year. Many dashed off to the tents of their chiefs to tell them the news; a rare few waved and smiled greetings.

When Gundoen's people reached the pile, they unburdened two ponies whose backs were loaded with cut wood from the forests around their home village. These faggots they threw upon the pile. Every tribe brought their own loads of wood from home. By the size of the pile, Gundoen could see that his was the last tribe to arrive. The pile symbolized the unity and common brotherhood of all the tribes. It would be kept burning throughout the Assembly, to make up in light and warmth what Goddess lacked. It was also a symbol of the resolve of those who had made the Last Stand, the founders of the tribes led by Tont-Ornoth and Born-Karn. And again, it was a sacrifice to God for His favor, for He was said to love destruction of all sort and particularly delighted in burning. After the Speaker of the Law had called the roll of the tribes, then it would be the duty and honor of the current Warlord to light the branches and so begin the Assembly.

Afterward would come the time for any challenges to Gen-Karn's authority. Yet Gundoen knew that there would be no challenges this year. No champions had yet arisen who could hope to best Gen-Karn, who was still in his prime. Once again he wondered whether it might not be best for him to challenge the Warlord. But he shook his head. Were it only himself, he would take even so slight a chance to slay his enemy. But he had also his people to consider.

Gundoen swept Urnostardil with his sharp eye, searching for the best place to pitch his tents. These things were neither done at random nor in a traditional pattern. Instead tribes who were friendly camped next to each other, to guard each other's tender rumps, as the saying went, so that each year the camping-patterns changed as tribes fell in and out of friendship with one another.

Now this year on one side of the pond there were many, many tents pitched, many tribes crowded against one another. And in the center of those masses was a single great tent, above which hung the orange banner of Gen-Karn. Banners were rare in the North: Gen-Karn had taken this standard after the fashion of the civilized races of the faraway South, which he had visited in his youth.

On the other side of the pool there were a few lonely tents pitched, with much space between them. These were the tents of the last few independent tribes who yet withstood Gen-Karn's absolute rule. And between the two groups were some other tents, belonging to the tribes who did not side with Gen-Karn or against him. Some of these were of the lower tribes, whose men were poor warriors at best; others were waiting to see which way the last winds would blow before making their choice.

Gundoen looked about. Hanging about the pile of wood were several men from opposite tribes, waiting to hear what he would choose.

"Well, now," he said in a loud voice. "There seems to be little room on the northern side of the Table this year. I can tell it with my eyes closed, whenever the wind blows from the north. Let us camp on the southern side, where we may have the room to stretch out without kicking each other in the groin."

The men of his tribe chuckled at his words. The others scurried off toward the tent under the orange banner, doubtless to tell Gen-Karn the news and thereby worm themselves into his favor. Rump lickers all, thought Gundoen contemptuously.

So they pitched their tents among the independent tribes, who were glad enough to see them. Gundoen had been the greatest of the independent chiefs ever since Gen-Karn had brutally mutilated Elrikal years before. That had been late in the Warlord's rise to power, and few of all the tribes had forgotten it. It was not indeed for love of him or for wealth that the small tribes had flocked to Gen-Karn, but simply out of fear. If only something would happen to make them believe Gen-Karn's power and luck were done, Gundoen thought, they would desert him like flies from a kicked dog-turd.

The other chiefs came to him as soon as he had set up his tents. Gundoen greeted them as they sat cross-legged in their pelt breeks on the soft cured skins he had strewn on the floor of his tent. He had one of his men serve them beer in plain wooden bowls, and he looked them over man by man.

There were Bur-Knap of the River's-Bend tribe, a stout fellow who loved food and ale too much but had a sturdy heart for all that; Ring-Sol of the Archeros, a hot-blooded youth who hated Gen-Karn because the Warlord had taken his prettiest concubine in a raid over a year before; Ven-Vin-Van of the Borsos, whose good green eyes twinkled in the dimness. Also had come Nam-Rog, the chief second in importance here only to Gundoen, and Gundoen's firmest friend among the other chiefs. Behind them sat Kepa-Trim of the Karghil tribe, who did not object very much to Gen-Karn or his rule, but opposed him because the Buzrahs had been among the first to support Gen-Karn. Between Buzrah and Karghil there had been bitter hatred since the beginning of time. And beside Kepa-Trim sat Ren-Tionan, who led the remnants of Elrikal's once-mighty tribe and who would have cut out his own liver with a rusty knife, if he could only have bought Gen-Karn's death thereby.

According to custom, they did not at first speak of what had brought them all together. First they sipped at their ale and discussed the health of the women left at home, and how harsh they guessed the winter would be this year, and how many babes would die of the cold. And finally they complimented Gundoen on his victory over the wretched Korlas, Ring-Sol voicing the wish that a similar fate might shortly overtake Gen-Karn.

Then they came at last to the politics of the Assembly.

The more important of the cases were discussed, with guesses at the probable voting. Each tribe would receive one vote, and then additional votes depending on how many warriors the tribe boasted.

And upon every case where the verdict was not clear-cut one way or the other, the voting seemed to stand one party against the other: Gen-Karn and his tribes voting one way, Gundoen and the independents voting the other. Among these cases was the suit by the surviving Korlas. And in every case, as things stood now, Gen-Karn's men would gain the victory.

"Things are foul indeed," said Nam-Rog, shaking his bristling gray beard. "If only you had come sooner, Gundoen, some of the smaller tribes would not have sided with Gen-Karn. As it was, there was talk you might never arrive. It is an open secret that Gen-Karn set ambushing war-parties along the major paths to your village."

"I thought as much," grunted Gundoen. "That's why I went down along the Spine, avoiding the most-used trails. The journey took me longer than I had thought. Still, I am here on time, am I not?"

"Too late, too late," moaned Ven-Vin-Van, closing his green eyes. "The small tribes have already chosen. They have despaired; now our cause is lost."

"It is not so bad as that, my friend," chuckled Nam-Rog. "There are still several neutral tribes who could come over to us. And I have been in contact with several chiefs who are now camped on the northern side. Now that you have come, Gundoen, they may still join us. All they await is a sign."

"Yes, a sign!" exclaimed Ring-Sol. "We looked for him among your party, but saw only familiar faces. But among so many, who can pick out a one? You have brought enough warriors for a war, chief Gundoen—and well will we need them. Yet most of all we need the one. Where is he?"

"Yes, where?" demanded Ren-Tionan.

"Yes, Gundoen," added Nam-Rog. "Old friend, I expected you to display him by your side, as crafty as you can be. Where is Ara-Karn?"

"Ara-Karn!" demanded all the others. "Where is he? His fame has spread before him. Show us this man they speak of as if he were half a god!"

Gundoen bowed his massive head for a moment.

"His fame was spread by me," he said softly. "I had hoped his legend would give Gen-Karn pause. Yet now he is gone. Before we came to Urnostardil, he left us and traveled back toward Gerso."

"Foolish man!" cried Ren-Tionan in anguish. "We needed him!"

"Tionan, hold your tongue," Gundoen ordered, looking at him sternly. "Could I stop him from going, him who was as dear to me as my own son might have been? He would go; I could not but let him."

He looked around at their crestfallen faces and saw that the only hope that had held them together was now departed. They were defeated already, he thought. Gen-Karn will have his victory.

"Still he has left us something," he said with cheer in his voice. "Something of which not one of you has heard. The fame of this thing I would not spread. It will be the key to the door of our success, as the Southrons say. He gave it to us and showed us many of its uses—though still I do not know all of its uses in warfare. Yet this thing, and only this thing, gave my tribe our great victory over the Korlas."

He set down his bowl and reached behind him. From his opened pack he drew it forth.

"Behold before you, fellow-chiefs, the weapon called the bow."

Carefully he laid it before them. Black it was and doubly curved—the great bow none but Gundoen's strong arms could bend. They touched it gingerly, questioningly. They handed it between themselves. They turned it this way and that, frowning, chattering among themselves.

"Is it magic?" they asked. And: "It looks like something for music. Yet it has but one string." And: "Surely you are jesting, Gundoen. Where is the rest of it?"

Gundoen smiled. "The melody this plays brings death. Try to draw back the string."

They tried—hesitantly at first, then with determination. None could draw it back more than a finger's length.

"It was made too powerful for your arms," he explained. "Yet they can be fashioned in any strength by him who knows their secrets. Only a fist of men in my tribe know those secrets yet: he himself taught them. With only one of these, and one death-bird"—and he showed them a long black arrow—"a man can bring a fully grown bull bandar to the earth."

They looked their disbelief.

He laughed. "Very well, then—follow and behold the proof."

They went out of the tent to the rear, out of sight of the orange banner. There Gundoen had a heavy sack of meal placed on end upon a rock, covered with a leathern breast-plate. A hundred paces away he stood and drew the shaft swiftly to his ear. A hum sounded; down the field the sack fell into the snow with a crunch.

Meal was pouring from it like blood from a dying man.

Gundoen grinned at their amazement. They flocked down to the sack, examining the protruding arrow. Gundoen brandished the bow before them. "For every man of mine there is a bow; for every bow two score arrows. And every arrow has the death of one of our foes upon its sharp tongue. You said I brought many men, Ring-Sol. But you did not know how many men." He laughed at their consternation, a confidence he did not truly feel in the center of his laughter. "For every hundred of my men, two score hundred of my enemies will surely die. Now let the tale of *that* circulate about the camps, Nam-Rog, and see how many of the tribes remain with Gen-Karn!"

And it was even as Gundoen had foretold. Like rain-water on slick rock, the tale of this magic spread over the Table. The tents of the tribes buzzed with it; with every telling the weapon became more deadly and fantastic. Other chiefs came to Gundoen—neutral chiefs as well as chiefs who had pitched on the northern side. And to all of them he showed the bow, though he did not again demonstrate it.

"Gundoen does not lie," he said simply. "As for proofs, I do not wish to waste another sack of hard-packed grain. One of you stand forth, then, and I will show the others how this works upon a man." They wondered and shook their heads doubtfully. But not a one of them would volunteer.

Soon many tents were pulled down on the northern side and repitched on the southern. And when the tallies were told again, though Gen-Karn still had the edge, it was by not nearly so large a margin.

And Gundoen sat alone in the dimness of his tent. Wherever he may be, he thought, Ara-Karn must have known it would be thus. And he was right again. He listened for a while to the sounds of tent pegs being pounded into the rock without and smiled sadly.

A warrior stuck his head into the tent.

"Chief Gundoen," he said excitedly, "there is a man come to see you from the Orn tribe claiming to be a messenger from Gen-Karn. He says to tell you that the Warlord would meet with you in the privacy of some neutral place to talk about the suits."

The ancient and most respected Bar-East had been born of the Vorisal tribe. But that had been many years ago, and since then Bar-East had spent most of his winters among other tribes. He was by nature a wandering man, and it was said that he had traveled to lands so far North that the ground was covered with snow and ice even during the summer's heat. Not even the burden of his many years could give a pause to his restless feet; he traveled and traveled regardless. All tribes knew him; all men respected him for his wisdom. These were the reasons he had been chosen the Speaker of the Law, many years ago. Bar-East had no prejudices and would prefer no one tribe to another. So was it unsurprising that it was the tent of Bar-East that was finally chosen to be the meeting place of Gundoen and Gen-Karn.

The tent of Bar-East stood in the center of the Table, between the pond and the pile of wood. There were no other tents nearby. It was a simple tent, aged and much weathered but still of good use, like the man who lived within. It was a tent made for traveling. This tent had seen more sights of the far North, from the Sea of Goddess to the Darklands, from the Spine of Civilization to the lonely desolated lands, than most of the men who lived in those lands.

And now the tent looked down upon two groups of warriors, clad in leather, mail, and plate, helmets gleaming, fists never far from their weapons. These men eyed each other sharply, suspiciously. The men of Gundoen's tribe stood upon the darkling side, and the Orns upon the light.

Within, Bar-East served beer to the two chieftains in plain wooden bowls without designs.

Bar-East kneeled above them, the crags of his ancient, weather-beaten face looking darkly down. He spoke few words and took no part in the negotiations. Yet his eyes were bright with wisdom.

Below him sat the chiefs, legs crossed on luxuriant bandar-skins, drinking their beer slowly, each trying to gain in words a good hold upon the other.

Gen-Karn was a giant of a man. Standing by Gundoen he would have towered above; yet since most of his height was in his legs, sitting he was only a little taller. His face was dark and darkly handsome; black ringlets of glossy hair hung about the long rectangular face. The great black beard was spread over the chest plate like a kerchief. The eyes of Gen-Karn were dark, like raisins dried in the sun; the nose of Gen-Karn was a great hook, with full and flaring nostrils. The lips of him were thick and sensual, curling around the rim of his bowl with relish. Many were the women who had succumbed to the charms of that dark beauty—to their later regret, if any of the tales Gundoen had heard were true.

Gen-Karn was dressed in full, beautifully made armor from the metalworkers of the Southlands. He had gained this armor—or so the story went—when he had slain a great noble of one of the civilized lands in single combat. That had been during Gen-Karn's wanderings as a youth through the South. There, many had been his adventures; and he had learned the tongue of the Southrons, and how to set words down as symbols upon hides—his proudest feat and one he had taught to his highest men.

"Ah, there is such wealth there," Gen-Karn said, holding the large ale bowl in one bronzed and callused hand, "as you could never dream. More of gold and silver and rubies and other gems than could ever be held within your imaginings, or mine, or of all the men in the tribes put together. And their greatest treasure, Gundoen, is land. Their land is not rocky and hard, giving over its fruits only with reluctance, as is the land of our North. No, their land is soft and yielding like a woman's full breast; and the milk of that breast spurts forth almost before you put your teeth to it. There are lands there where the people do not even need to plow the earth—they merely cast their seeds about and return in a month's time to see the land blossoming and pluck its fruit. The winters there are so tame and mild that the snow rarely mounts up—not even in the shadows of great hills. And those winters are so short that they have as many as three separate planting-seasons in a single year! I tell you, life in those lowlands would be a garden evergreen compared with what we poor fools are forced to accept here."

Gundoen grunted. Would the man never get down to business? He had heard other tales of the softness of life beyond the barrier of the Spine, and these new ones did not impress him much. "If life is so nice there, why did you return?" he asked rather sourly.

Gen-Karn slammed his bowl down savagely. In the background Bar-East calmly refilled it with the syrupy brown ale.

"Because I did not belong there," growled the black-haired man. "Because I was an outcast, looked down upon and despised. Because I was nothing but a barbarian worth less than even a good slave to them. My beard was not so neatly combed, nor set with ribands, as those of the delicate lords. And my hair was not perfumed, and I did not go arunning to the baths every time my flesh became sweatful. Their women laughed at me behind their flimsy veils and put their painted fans before their eyes whenever I would look upon them with the hot lust they inspired in me—as they would, and did, inspire it in every man, being no better than harlots in their hearts. Even the highest of them are naught but whores. And yet, for all that, such is the beauty of their forms, and such the sweet passion in their loins for the man who knows how to pluck it forth, that they make our Northern women look like beasts of the earth, fit only for burden and toiling in the fields."

"I have heard of Southron women too," Gundoen growled.

"But you have not seen them," insisted Gen-Karn. So absorbed was he in these private imaginings that he grew not angry at anything Gundoen said. Gundoen sighed.

"Nor have you felt the unthinkable softness of their thighs," Gen-Karn went on. "Even their lowliest whores are a loveliness upon the earth. Think, then, what it would be like to possess a queen of them!" He sighed, drinking down ale thirstily. "Yet such is not for us, because we are only barbarians. They think of us as less than human, because of what their Elna did to our ancestors. And we deserve to be treated as such, so long as we take it without fighting.

"And Gundoen, as much as their women are softer than ours, so are their men softer than we. Why, save for a few sea dogs and brigands who would not fight anyway, if a Southron were put in a bed in your dim place, and you cuddled up to him, he'd feel like any woman to you. They do not work, they do not hunt, they do not fight. They are all soft and fleshy as the fatted lamb. They are not even ashamed of this, but if a man takes to manly things they ridicule him! Slaves do all their tasks—and slaves do not know how to fight. And these are the greatnesses who dare to look down their pale long noses at us!"

With great gulpings, Gen-Karn finished the beer in his bowl and poured the dregs upon the ground. He set it forth for Bar-East to refill again and drank once more. With a harsh belch of satisfaction, he wiped his mouth and began again:

"Gundoen, we have had our quarrels here, our bickerings and troubles. Strong men and great will have such. But do not these fall away to shadow compared with the hatred we should bear toward those of the South? Listen, Gundoen, and hear of what I learned during my wanderings. Much of it you know, but some is only shadow to those of us in the North. And yet, there they even dare to boast of it!

"Long, long ago there were no tribes or men in the far North. This land of ours was empty and wild, a place where none but spirits and gods might dwell. And those ancestors of ours did not shiver in snow and ice here. Instead they rode as conquerors throughout all the lands of the South. They went wherever they wished; whatever they desired they took. They lived off the fat of the land and drank sweet heady wine, which is far better than this brown ale we swill. And they each of them had as many women as the tree does leaves in early summertime. The land quavered at the tread of their ponies and grew dark beneath their long shadows.

"And then they grew careless, or soft, or luckless—why they lost their hardness no man can tell. But the civilized lands they ravaged banded together, under the leadership of a single man—one warrior with a vision even as mine."

"Great Elna," said Gundoen.

"Yes! Elna! And he broke our ancestors in a battle whose blood was like the water of a sea, and he scattered them before him. He chased the last few survivors, a pitiful ragged band of a few score men and women not worth

bothering over. But he bothered, because Elna had sworn
terrible oaths to dark God, oaths that could never be
broken or gone back on, to destroy our ancestors utterly or
forever lose the war, no matter how long it took for its
eventual end.

"He chased them over leagues of the earth, ever north-
ward, until at last the backs of our ancestors came up
against the mountains of the Spine. They went through the
Pass at Gerso, which up until that time no man had ever
dared cross save only a few madmen, and those had never
returned. For it was said that the Spirit ate their brains
until they went berserk with lust for blood and slew all,
including themselves. Yet even there Elna followed.

"Our ancestors were mighty men, giants of the earth,
but they were broken, wearied, and few against many.
They could not win. Had they been less, they would have
surrendered themselves, as many of the others had, to be
sold as slaves for Elna's people. Yet our ancestors—Born-
Karn, Tont-Ornoth, Allik-Ran-Fay, and all the others—
did not give up. They retreated, battling every step of the
way, until they came to the dusky border. Then they broke
once again, and fled into the depths of the Darklands. And
even *there* did Elna follow them. He chased them here, to
the Table, and here the Last Stand took place."

"The Last Stand," breathed old Bar-East reverently. "Tell
us of the Last Stand."

Gen-Karn swallowed a big mouthful of ale.

"They ascended here onto the crown of Urnostardil and
put their backs against the darkness. Elna's great horde
had to camp below in darkness, ever guarding against the
serpentine Darkbeasts. Yet there they camped, besieging
the Table. Long was that siege—months it lasted, and yet
more months. Ever would the Southrons come up the trail,
which was the sole means of gaining the summit; and ever
would our ancestors beat them back.

"Oh, but those must have been glorious battles! These
hills have not seen their like since. Our women battled like
strong warriors, our men like madmen. And the Southrons
never took Urnostardil. Our ancestors drank the rainwater
of that pond without; they trapped the birds that land
here; and they ate their ponies, one by one. And even so
our waists grew leaner and our children wailed for more
food. The Southrons, for all that they must camp in darkness, still could send men to cut wood for fires and to

hunt the many beasts for food. Almost as many of our people died of hunger as were slain by the foe.

"And still, still, we stayed and fought. And in the end of all ends, Elna was forced to break camp and travel out of the North, giving over his strong heart's desire to slay the last of us, though he broke his terrible oaths thereby. Even in the shadow of their defeat, our ancestors had triumphed over Elna—cursed Elna!

"They sent out their scouts, one by one, and each report was the same. The Southrons were gone. Elna was behind Gerso. They came down off Urnostardil and built new homes in the wilderness. But they did not soon forget the glory that had once been theirs. Nor did they lose the lust for vengeance, to return some pass to the South and overthrow Elna's empire and give Elna's body to the dogs.

"Yet they were too few. So they waited, holding patience firmly between their hands. They knew that sometime all would be theirs again. And that they might never forget, and that they would not fall out amongst themselves and slay each other rather than the enemy, they agreed to the Assembly. Once every year when the harvests were done, they agreed to meet here and settle all their disputes peacefully until the time came when they might be strong enough to break out of this prison and ride in red glory through the green lands of the South.

"O Gundoen, that time has come. We are great enough, many and strong enough—and the Southrons are like women! When they laughed at me and held their painted fans before their eyes and soft breasts—when the nobles cursed me and had me whipped like a slave's dog—then I swore I would return and king it over them. That is why I came back here. That is why I became chieftain at Orn. That is why I have become Warlord. And that is why I have reorganized the tribes below me. We can fight; we can win. Under my rule, we *will* win. O Gundoen, is this not more important than our petty differences? What are the Korlas to you, or to me either? It is the South we should burn with lust for! Yet she can never be ours while we bicker among ourselves.

"Gundoen, you are a powerful leader. I am a powerful king. I had resolved to crush you—this I admit freely. Yet such may not be without a war that, though I would surely win it, would only destroy the very warriors I shall need. Apart, we stand like the Darklands and the Desert, holding

no life in either of us. Together we would hold all the
realms of men between us. I offer you not service under
me, but an equal footing. I am sick of waiting. My gray
hairs sprout, and the women of the South beckon. Have
you ever heard of the Empress Allissál, whose golden hair
is spoken of with rapture by all the Southrons?—And she
is the direct descendant of Elna himself! Let us agree,
then, to join. Come springtime we could be knocking on
Gerso's door—and in ten years' time, who knows—we
could be kings of all the world! What say you, Gundoen?
—shall you choose wisdom and wealth or foolishness and
death?"

Gundoen did not answer for several moments.

He had listened to the words, enraptured by their power.
Gen-Karn could be persuasive—there was no denying
that. The visions of the flight before Elna and the glories
that had preceded it swam dizzyingly before his eyes. The
thought that they might conquer some rich land of the
South was as tantalizing as the horizon of the Goddess—
and as blinding.

"What you have said," he murmured at last, "is a new
thing to me. In truth, I had not dreamed of it before. Equal
standing, did you say? It is worth considering, truly. Yet,
Gen-Karn, I am not the absolute ruler you are. My war-
iors and friend-chiefs must be consulted in this. Were it
up to me, I would give you a firm answer now. Yet first,
before I speak, I must discuss these things with them."

"Why, that is all I ask," said Gen-Karn, rising to his
feet and gathering his cloak about him. His black curls
swept against the roof of Bar-East's humble tent. "Speak to
them by all means. I have no fear or doubt of what they
will desire. And do not forget to mention the cold gold
and the warm breasts of Southron women."

Gundoen nodded, and rose also. He thanked Bar-East
for the hospitality of his tent. After Gen-Karn had gone,
he asked the old wanderer what he thought of the plan.

Bar-East shook his craglike head. "There is no doubt of
the charm of our Warlord's words," he said. "Vengeance
on those who wronged us, lovely women and wealth besides? Such would tempt even a holy man. I too have wandered in the South, though not so far as Gen-Karn. Those
men are soft indeed, and their wealth is as great as he
says. Yet I will not take sides and counsel you to join
him. He is a strong man, our Warlord, who little likes to

be denied in anything. And this is a dream he has long cherished.

"Only this will I say to you, Gundoen of the broad chest—that he who spills enough blood will one pass surely choke upon it."

Gundoen bowed and left the tent. His men formed about him, asking him questions, but he returned to his tents in silence. And there in silence he sat upon the pelts in the dimness, pondering, allowing none to enter or speak with him. And he thought long and deeply on those things that Gen-Karn had said. He thought so much, he wrinkled his brow on it.

One thought only returned to him, and that was of Ara-Karn. Where was he now? Had he come to the trails that lead to Gerso yet? Gundoen wished that the stranger might sit now before him and counsel him. Already he missed the man's wisdom. If he were here now, what might he say?

The chief envisioned the stranger's face, and in that image his decision came to him. He sent word to summon his warriors and the other chiefs allied with him.

While he waited he poured out some warm ale into his bowl, and in the darkness he drank a bowl to the spirit of Ara-Karn. Through the opening in the tent-wall he could see the snow falling, fragile and lovely as the curling fingers of a newborn babe.

And he thought, He was right to leave us. He is not of our blood, and these quarrels are not his. Why then should he wish to die with us?

CHAPTER FOURTEEN
The Darkbeast's Head

The flaps of his tent drawn up so that he could look out at all of them, Gundoen addressed his men. These were the warriors and the fellow-chiefs who were all dependent upon him; these were the men whose lives were in his hands. And these were the men he had condemned by his own decision to die.

Yet he would not doom them unknowingly. To them all he gave the choice, telling them what Gen-Karn had told him, though in words of his own choosing. And when he spoke to them of the flight before Elna and the Last Stand, he could see that their eyes shone as brightly as his own must have done. Their teeth flashed at the thought of vengeance upon those who had done their ancestors wrong. They yearned for the masses of gold, lusted for the soft loins of Southron women, and longed to be free of their hard, rocky lives in the frozen North. And finally they burned with resentment, thinking of the only Southrons most of them had ever known, the thief-merchants from Gerso—soft, pampered men with the smell of women.

When he had finished, Gundoen gave them their choice. "Nor will I tell you of my own mind until you have given me yours," he told them. "Yet this only would I add: that though Gen-Karn has offered to lead jointly with us, that is but a word that has flown from his tongue. And words

once uttered are free as the birds, as they say. Gen-Karn
will not be content to let any other man gainsay him. He
alone will rule this thing, and we will be no more than
any of the other tribes below him. And if at any time we
went to him to claim an equal share of any of the loot,
he would put us off with soft sweet words, and then—well,
you all know how cunning is our Warlord."

"Treacherously cunning," swore Ren-Tionan.

"So what would you have me do?" asked Gundoen.
"Shall we stand up to this man or shall we go and kiss his
curling toes?"

Bur-Knap of the River's-Bend tribe rose to speak. He
stroked his bristling beard for a moment, then began.
"For the war against the Southrons, well. It is time indeed
we paid back those dung-sniffers and avenged those whose
blood still stains these rocks." A rippling murmur of assent
rose to echo his sentiments.

"But as for Gen-Karn," he added, "there can be but a
single answer. To join in peace with that man is to invite
the Darkbeast to share your tent. I will go on no war-
parties where he might be standing at my back."

"Never," swore Ren-Tionan.

And "Never so long as I taste the air," added Ring-Sol
of the Archeros. And "No, never," said all the rest of them,
down to the last man.

Gundoen nodded. "It is well," he said. "That was my
own mind also. Then leave to me how we shall answer
Gen-Karn. And keep your blades sharpened; they will be
drawn for blood soon enough."

"Have we not the bow?" cried Ven-Vin-Van suddenly.
"And how shall they stand against it?"

"The bow, the bow," they chanted; and the chant became a cheer. And they laughed, as Gundoen smiled sadly
on them, to think of Gen-Karn with an arrow protruding
from his mouth. They laughed and cheered so hard that
the men in Gen-Karn's camp heard only the joy in their
throats and none of the desperate doom. And Gen-Karn
nodded in his luxuriant tents, smiling at the happy sounds
of assent and dreaming of the golden women of the South.

The horns blared, the great wooden drums beat. It was
the signal for the opening of the Assembly of all the tribes
of the far North. The warriors of the tribes came out of
their tents, forming a large ring around the dark pond in

the center of Urnostardil. They grouped according to their tribes, each chieftain bearing the color or totem of his tribe. Foremost in honor were those who represented the original eighteen tribes who had survived Elna's assaults on the Table. After them were the more numerous lesser tribes, whose ancestors had split off from the original tribes when the numbers of a tribe had grown too great for the area it claimed. Some of these later tribes were now larger and more powerful than the tribes they had once been part of.

In the center of it all, near the dark pond, stood Bar-East, his oaken staff in hand. So long had he leaned upon that staff, over the hills of so many lands, that by now it seemed a part of him. Where he was used to hold it was worn slick and white. To have seen Bar-East standing without his staff would have been almost to behold him in his nakedness.

Bar-East rapped the staff loudly upon the rock, and the horns and wooden drums fell silent. The murmurings of gossip and politics that were upon the lips of many men were stilled. A silence swept across the gently curving summit of Urnostardil the Table.

Bar-East spoke.

"Are all the tribes of the North assembled?" he called out. "If there are any tribes not yet present or who are not yet ready to meet here in peace, let their names be called out." He waited, but there was no response.

"Let us be gathered then in peace. Begin the roll, chieftains, and call out your tribes in order with the numbers."

Nam-Rog then stepped forward, for this year his tribe was gathered in the first position.

"I am Nam-Rog, chief of the Durbars. And we are seven score times a score and more warriors strong. Our tribe is ready." As Nam-Rog stepped back, the warriors who had accompanied him yelled, stamped, and rattled their swords on their shields.

The next to step toward the pond was Kepa-Trim. "I be Kepa-Trim of the Karghils!" he shouted fiercely, scowling across the Table to where the Buzrah tribe was massed. "We number five score times a score and more warriors and we are ready! So let the dung-sniffing Buzrahs beware!"

The Karghil men shouted and cheered, but they were

almost shouted down by the curses and jeers volleyed at them by the Buzrahs.

"Silence!" shouted Bar-East, pounding his staff upon the rock. "Let all tribes wait their turn!"

So it went from tribe to tribe, each chieftain identifying himself, his tribe, and his strength. The full rounds would take some time, for every tribe would cheer upon hearing its name, and each tribe tried to shout louder and longer than the tribe that had gone before. And there were many tribes to go through.

In the midst of the proceedings, after he had identified his own tribe, Gundoen felt a man plucking at his wrist. He turned around. It was a man of the Orn tribe called Ful-Dar-Drin.

"I have been sent by the Warlord, great Gen-Karn," the man shouted over the din. "He wishes to know why you have not yet come to him with your answer. Also he wishes to know your answer now. And he bids me to remind you that if your answer is no, he still has the power to take what he wishes."

Gundoen looked across the pond and saw before the massed warriors of the Orn tribe Gen-Karn, resplendent in his shining stolen armor of the Southlands. The Warlord was looking intently back at him. Gundoen smiled, and nodded his head, like one friend to another. Gen-Karn's grim face brightened, and he nodded back pleased, as if all were agreed upon.

The din of noise quieted somewhat. A minor chief on the other side of the pond was identifying himself. "You may tell your master these words from me," Gundoen said over his shoulder, still keeping his eyes upon Gen-Karn. "That the reason I have not gone to him is that Gundoen does not go to babes or women or weaklings, but they must come to me. Also you may say that I was reluctant to sit with him again, because after he has had too much beer Gen-Karn belches, and the stink of it is enough to offend any man not born in filth as all Orns are. As to his proposal, tell him that I agree we should war upon the Southrons and that I will be glad to lead Gen-Karn in battle, provided he first come to me and kiss each of my curling toes in all humility and swear to serve me well. Can you remember all of that, Ful-Dar-Drin?"

The Orn spluttered. "I cannot say that to Gen-Karn!"

"Why not?" Gundoen shrugged cheerfully. "Are you not

a free man? Those are the words I give you. Now give them back to Gen-Karn."

Cursing beneath his breath, the Orn left to make the wide circle back to the Orn position. Gundoen smiled broadly across the pond and nodded again. Gen-Karn nodded eagerly back and held up ten fingers, as if to say, "In less than ten years' time."

The messenger worked his way among the massed Orns. He reached Gen-Karn. Gundoen could see him speaking softly into the ear of the Warlord. Gundoen caught the eyes of Nam-Rog and Ren-Tionan and pointed across to Gen-Karn as if to say, "Watch, and you shall see a thing."

Gen-Karn's face turned first white, then red, and finally a deep blossoming purple. His curling beard parted to show his animal teeth. With one metal-clad arm he lifted Ful-Dar-Drin up and threw him to the earth.

Gundoen broke into laughter. Behind him he could hear his warriors also laughing. "By the Goddess, what a sight!" he exclaimed to them. "Now even if we die to the last man, it will all have been worth it, thrice over!"

The cheerings of the Buzrah tribe came to an end. It was time for the Orn chieftain to stand forward.

Gen-Karn came forth in silence, his gigantic frame quivering with rage. Scarcely could he speak—twice he opened his mouth before the words came forth. The warriors of the tribes of the far North looked upon him with dismay. It had suddenly struck them as a real thing that this year the Assembly would end in civil war.

Gen-Karn cried out, in a voice as cold as the eye of God, these words: "I am Gen-Karn of the Orn tribe and Warlord of you all! We number fifteen score times a score and more warriors, and it is we who are the greatest fighters of the North! And if Gundoen will have war, then let every man of you decide in his heart whether he desires to stand with me or die with him!"

The tumult that followed must have carried all the way to the lands where men dwell. Not a single tribe refrained—it had come to that last choice, when every tribe must be judged either for Gen-Karn or against him. The followers of Gen-Karn beat their shields, their drums, their booted feet against the rocks and snow. And their opponents jeered and hooted and stamped their own feet. The hollowed surface of Urnostardil became like some primitive drum of the immortal gods, its deafening heartbeat echoing off the massy clouds of the dark heavens. Had any wanderer come so far into the Darklands beyond the dusky border, he would have seen the golden cliffs of fire and heard those savage, demonic cries, and he would have fled the scene in terror for his very sanity.

Gundoen cheered and jeered with all the others. One of his followers shouted, with all the might of his lungs, into the chief's ear: "Worry not, Chief—have we not the bow? We'll slay these doglets yet!"

Then Gundoen gave off his cheering and looked away. Several of the tribes that had joined him after the word of the bow went round now seemed to have taken affright at the Warlord's terrible visage and changed sides again. No more than a quarter of all the warriors on Urnostardil would dare to oppose Gen-Karn with blood. The bows had been of great help against the wretched Korlas, penned in their little village, but here, on an open field against Orn warriors, Gundoen had sad doubts.

The shouting went on for longer than a man would have cared to count. Passions grew strained in it, and, except for the fear of being the first to break the peace of the Assembly, many of the tribes might have leapt upon each other there and then. Yet their chieftains quietened the braves, and gradually the tumult subsided. Many men were hoarse from it; they fell down to the dark icy waters of the central pond and sucked up drink like so many wild beasts. And the last few tribes identified themselves in a strange silence. There were no more cries: the warriors heaved their broad, gleaming chests in convulsive pants, their hair wild and streaming, staring at one another with wide and awful eyes. Through the scene crackled a mixture of lust and fear—a lust for combat and mad blood, a fear of what might be the result.

Finally it was done. The roll of the tribes was now complete. The circle had come around again. Every man seemed to draw back a pace within himself and take firm hold of his soul. Several swords were sheathed, followed by many more.

Bar-East, the ancient wanderer of the far North, stepped out into the center once again.

"It is done," he said wearily. He rapped the staff upon the rock again. Its sound was like a brittle tapping after the roar that had before resounded in the darkness. Bar-East faced Gen-Karn. The chieftain of the Orns, of all

warriors, was the only one still raging. He had not taken
his eye off Gundoen since Ful-Dar-Drin had spoken the
message in his ear. Still his shoulders worked back and
forth, still his chest plate rose and fell, still his fist-bones
shone as they tightened upon the handle of his great heavy
sword.

Bar-East faced him and spoke. "Now it is time, chieftain.
Now let him who is our Warlord step forward and take the
torch."

Something of the quality of a man came back to Gen-
Karn. He sighed, and took his gaze off Gundoen. He
seemed to realize now where he was and what there was
for him to do.

Bar-East stood at the edge of the dark pond. In his hand
he held a bundle of long dry twigs bound by two gut
strings. Below, at his feet in the melted snow, a small
cook-fire was faintly crackling. Gen-Karn came and took
the twigs from Bar-East.

In one hand he held the twigs and in the other his still-
naked sword. He stooped suddenly and thrust the bundle
of twigs into the cook-fire. He twirled it about a bit, a
spume of smoke arose, then the twigs lighted in a burst.

A subdued cheer sounded. This was the beginning of
the solemn rites of Assembly.

Gen-Karn swung the flaming brand triumphantly about
his head, the flames running in circles in the air. He gave
a single, horrible glance at Gundoen; then he stepped
toward the huge pile of twigs and logs, assembled from all
the forests of the far North and representing the unity of
all the tribes and the memory of their ancient call of vengeance. As soon as Gen-Karn should ignite the pile, Bar-
East would recite the litany of the Law, from beginning to
end; and then the suits would begin. Now that the time
of the suits had come, the warriors broke into buzzing
groups, trying to gain in the final moments whatever support they had failed so far to gain, or else make sure of
those promises they had already acquired. The buzzings
slowly grew in intensity. For his own part Gundoen stayed
apart from them, letting Nam-Rog argue for their inter-
ests. A strange sadness had suddenly come over the chief—
ever since he had laughed at Gen-Karn's purpled face. He
knew it would be red war and was resolved to it, but he
hated to admit that Hertha-Toll's prophecy would prove its
power over him.

A sudden cry sounded from the Table's far side.

Gen-Karn never got to light the pile of wood.

He stood but a pace away, ready to thrust the brand into the dried wood—ready to initiate the Assembly, which would finally deliver all the tribes into his hands, which would at last begin the work that would see him revenged upon the civilized lords and their laughing ladies, no matter what the cost. He took that last step and lifted the torch above his head. Then the cry of startled alarm sounded.

And an arc of living flame shot through the darkened air. It moved like God, yet shone like Goddess, through the darkened, frozen air. It passed like a bird of prey arching for the kill; and it lighted in the midst of the great pile of wood. The flame lighted softly beneath its thin coat of snow, yet it spread with speed through the dried, dead wood, bringing it alive in the process of consuming it. Branch, twig, and log ignited. In moments it was all ablaze, a great fire roaring upon the golden crown of Urnostardil like the jewel of Overlordship in the darkness beyond Her, where only Darkbeasts and Madpriests might live. So intense were those sudden flames that Gen-Karn could not stand them even in his fine Southron armor. He tossed his little brand to the ground, turned his back, and stepped away.

With astonied rage he looked about to see who had done this thing, robbing him of his right. At the other end of the Table, over where the wandering Goat's-Track finally reached the summit, he saw through the masses of warriors a single man step forward, clad only lightly despite the cold in a simple skin hunting-tunic.

He seemed a tall man, though, of course, not so tall as Gen-Karn; a strong man, though, again, not so strong as Gen-Karn; and his square black beard was not so dark as Gen-Karn's. And in his hand he held a strange instrument of curved wood, such as Gen-Karn had briefly seen a few of Gundoen's warriors wearing. And he was a stranger—not of any of the tribes of the far North. And even across so great a distance, Gen-Karn could see his dark eyes greenly glittering.

Behind the stranger another man appeared: Kuln-Holn, the cracked-pate of Gundoen's tribe. He, with the help of two others who had been standing nearby, was dragging a large, heavy burden from a weary pony. When they had got it down, they cut away the ropes binding it and tore off the concealing pelts, and a cry of wonderment rose from the crowds. For beneath the pelts was an enormous head still stained with flowing black blood.

It was the severed head of an enormous Darkbeast.

"Alone he hunted it!" cried Kuln-Holn above the hubbub. "And alone slew it! Only I watched, and I did no more than help him bear it up the cliffs. With fire he blinded it, with fire slew it! Three score strokes it took to sever it from the body!

"Men of the far North, behold the man who has done it, the man sent us from the gods—behold Ara-Karn!"

In the awed silence that followed, the stranger spoke. And his low tones somehow were heard even above the roar of the flames.

He said, "Wherever he is, let Gen-Karn step forward. I challenge him the right to lead the tribes."

CHAPTER FIFTEEN

Warlord of the Far North

Gen-Karn stepped farther away from the roaring pyre, shielding his face from its terrific heat. "Who is this foreigner?" he demanded angrily. "And what has he to do with us? He has defied the laws of our people. Let him be hurled from the cliffs, along with any who might aid him."

"He is Ara-Karn, as Kuln-Holn has said," called Gundoen. "He has challenged you to combat, Gen-Karn. Are you afraid?"

Gen-Karn did not even look at the chief. He argued to the tribes at large, "The time for challenges has not yet come. This foreigner has no right to challenge me at all. He is not of the tribes. Bar-East, tell them if I lie."

The wanderer stepped forward. He looked upon the stranger with wonder, as if gazing upon some new land he had never explored before. "Gen-Karn speaks truth," he said, nodding.

Gen-Karn laughed. The terrific heat of the fire combined with his own rage to make him sweat within the iron plates. Carelessly he stripped the armor from his body, dropping it to the ground for another to pick up. He flexed his great limbs; the flames gleamed off the sweat standing on his shoulders, from the steam issuing from his lips. He scratched the curls of his glossy black beard and laughed again. Gundoen must be desperately afraid to attempt such a trick as this.

"After we throw the stranger down from the edge of Urnostardil, you will be next, Gundoen. For you have brought an outsider up the cliffs of Table."

"This is no stranger, but a man of the tribes by right," shouted Gundoen. "He has lived among us since the end of last winter. Many of you know him. He is no foreigner."

Gen-Karn laughed scornfully. For the first time since he had seen Gundoen unexpectedly arriving upon the peak, he felt himself in control of the situation. His great dream of vengeance was at hand. The other chiefs were shaking their heads doubtfully at Gundoen's words. They looked from Gen-Karn to Gundoen to Ara-Karn in silence and back again. But those around him looked only on the stranger, with wonder and awe in their glances. They exchanged questioning glances among themselves. Was this truly the man who had come naked from the sea, the one about whom there were already such extravagant legends? The way he held his head, proud as the highest of chiefs, the way his light hands casually gripped the strange weapon fascinated the tribesmen. Surely he alone could not have brought death to a monstrous Darkbeast! Yet there were the head before them and the flies still buzzing on the wet blood.

"Know you all that before we left our village," Gundoen exclaimed, "we conducted the ceremony to bring this man into our tribe. I have adopted him as my own son."

"It makes no difference," said Gen-Karn. Now the heads turned back to him. "Still he has no right to challenge me. And still he has broken our law."

Ara-Karn and Kuln-Holn had now come to where the men of Gundoen's tribe were massed. Gundoen greeted him with joy on his broad face. "I thank the gods that you have come back to us. Yet still we will be lucky to emerge with whole skins from this." Ara-Karn nodded.

Among the warriors there were many murmurings. Many took Gundoen's position, and as many sided with Gen-Karn. But by far the most of them only shook their heads. "It is not for us to decide," they said. "Let the Speaker of the Law determine it."

Bar-East shook his head. "There are difficulties. Such a case has never come before me. It is a matter that should only be decided by the entire Assembly."

"I ask you, where are the difficulties?" asked Gundoen. "The man is of the tribes and has done a great deed. What man of you could hunt a Darkbeast? He has challenged Gen-Karn. And if the chief of the Orn tribe fears this man, then he should be our Warlord no longer."

Gen-Karn only sneered. "No, Gundoen, I am not so foolish as to fall for such a trick. Yet, to set any of your minds at rest, I will agree to fight this man, if Gundoen will agree to one condition."

"What condition?"

"That if this man falls before me, as he will, you will swear allegiance to me and be utterly obedient to my will."

"Do not agree," urged Nam-Rog. "Look at Gen-Karn! His arms are longer and more powerful than your friend's. This is a foolish thing, Gundoen."

But Gundoen looked at the strange green fires in the eyes of Ara-Karn. He remembered when he had last seen them thus—in the square of his village when they had met to wrestle. Despite himself, he felt himself falling under the godlike power, the spell of inhuman calm of Ara-Karn.

"It is agreed," he said, not looking at Gen-Karn.

"You will swear your tribe's fealty?"

"Yes."

"You will obey me, no matter what I demand of you?"

Gundoen looked back at Gen-Karn. He saw the evil in those eyes that were as dark as dull black pebbles. He would never while he lived forget the insult Gundoen had given him. If Ara-Karn lost this battle, Gundoen would suffer things far worse than falling in combat.

"Yes," he said. "I agree to it all. If you win."

Gen-Karn laughed. "Do not worry, little chieftain, I will win!"

"Then let the duel be fought," cried Bar-East.

The Speaker of the Law brought down his oaken staff with all the finality of death.

"Beware his shield-arm, my son," warned Gundoen in low tones, as they prepared Ara-Karn for the combat. "I have seen Gen-Karn fight in past Assemblies. He plays tricks with his shield-arm to distract his opponents, and once I saw him throw his shield at a man's legs in order to trip him up."

Above him, Ara-Karn stood as if he did not hear. He was looking across the area that had been cleared of snow and ice to where Gen-Karn stood with his attendants, arming himself. The strange eyes of Ara-Karn were like the black pits in the wild firelights of the blazing pyre. His naked chest rose and fell with a rhythmic, hypnotic regularity. To Gundoen he seemed almost like a living statue, still yet alive with potential motion and menace.

Truly, I know not, thought the chief. He has bravery and shows no fear, but it is still madness—he has not half Gen-Karn's size or weight. Does he have some device in mind, some special trickery to rely on? Or does he know in the depths of his unreadable heart that he is about to die?

"Gundoen," Ara-Karn breathed, and the chief was startled at the metallic power in that flat whisper. "Gundoen, in the heat of battle, all eyes will be upon us who fight. Choose thirty of the best bowmen and position them while all else concentrate on the battle. You will know what to do then, and when to do it."

He knows then, decided the chief. He knows he is about to die. Aloud he said, "Ara-Karn, my son . . . you know that this is unnecessary. You are not truly of the tribes. It will be no dishonor to you to withdraw even now."

The living statue did not turn its head. Slowly, with a liquidly metallic motion, it stepped forward, advancing into the center of the broad clearing as if it had not heard the chief's words. Gundoen followed behind, his broad shoulders low, resignation on his face.

Gen-Karn and Ara-Karn met together in the center of the clearing. They wore not sandals, tunics, mail, or helms —just rags knotted about their loins and cord fillets to bind back their hair. This was an ancient ritual, not to be altered with the passing of years: as the tribal contenders had battled centuries before, before the fire in darkness beyond the dusky borders, so too would these two contest each other's strengths. The firelight played over their naked bodies, the long heavy swords, the small round iron shields. Between them stood old Bar-East, the Speaker of the Law, his long smooth staff in hand. Behind Ara-Karn stood Gundoen and Nam-Rog as his seconds. Sol-Dat, Gen-Karn's chief man of the Orn tribe, and Estar Aln, the last chief of the Korlas, were behind Gen-Karn.

Gundoen looked across to them and saw how Sol-Dat was puffed with boast-ready pride and how Estar Aln's yellowed teeth gleamed in an ugly grin. If he should win, thought Gundoen—if Ara-Karn could only win—O how these swell-bellies would be deflated! O, what a sight that would be! He muttered a prayer in his heart to God that it should be so, though he knew in his head that his adoptive son stood no chance.

Bar-East raised his long bony hands, in one of which was held the oaken staff, and the murmuring crowd fell into a hushed, expectant silence. And Bar-East began to speak in a piercing, high-pitched voice, the ancient words of ritual:

"Let all know that there will be a battle shortly to test the fitness of our chief and decide if perhaps another be more worthy to lead us. There will be no replacements of weapons, no rests, and no quarter. Who loses this combat will die; the other will be Warlord of all the tribes of the North!"

The crowd gave a raucous roar of approval. Gundoen looked about at the assembled warriors, men stark in black-and-red relief in the firelight. Beers were in abundance and bets were being bickered heatedly. They enjoy the excitement, thought Gundoen—even the tribes who have the most to lose when Ara-Karn is slain. He suddenly realized the lucklessness of his words and spat over his shoulder to appease it.

He returned with Nam-Rog to their places at the frosty edge of the arena. Heavily he squatted down on the thick mats and took a bowl of beer in his massive horned hand. He signaled to Esra, the best man with a bow outside of himself and Ara-Karn. He spoke to him in low tones, gesturing to various positions about the crowd. "Take thirty of the best," he told him. "More would attract suspicion. . . . When I give you the signal, you will know what to do?"

The young man's eyes glittered his answer. Curtly he nodded and moved off among the tribesmen.

From the arena came the high-pitched tones of the Speaker of the Law. "Lords, you know the rules," he called to the two armed men. He began to walk to the edge of the cleared area. "Now begin!" he shouted suddenly.

The crowds quieted immediately. All heads were turned now to the two men in the center, who slowly began to circle each other, shields and longswords held in readiness. The great fire roared, and the melting snow around it hissed softly.

They feinted probingly at each other, testing guards and deceits, each learning how the other moved. Their swords touched each other, slipped, and licked at the small round shields flashing in the firelight. These were tentative blows of little consequence. The roar of the flames of the great pyre drowned them out completely. The two men fought as if under water, slowly, delicately, and silently. In the warmth of the great fire, and with the dark beer filling his belly, Gundoen felt suddenly drowsy and bemused. The battle seemed unreal, like some vague dream being played out. The others felt it also; all bets had ceased, all voices stilled. There was only the throbbing roar of the fire and the two silent men moving. The great bulk of Gen-Karn made Ara-Karn look like a child, an untried youth whose beard was still downy soft.

Gundoen shook his broad head angrily. This was no dream, he growled to himself. He looked around the Table, checking to see that all the bowmen were in position. He slipped his bow in closer to his thigh, ready to be strung in moments. With his other hand he felt for his arrows. After Ara-Karn fell, Gen-Karn would be the first to die, he thought. And by my own hand.

Suddenly the Warlord rushed in, yelling horribly, waking all the crowd, swinging his great sword like a scythe. Ara-Karn stepped swiftly to one side and raised his shield. The metal shot sparks in a loud clang.

"Gen-Karn! Gen-Karn!" shouted the supporters of the orange standard of Orn.

Again the Warlord moved. Ara-Karn stooped, easily catching the blow on his shield again, darting a counter-stroke with unbelievable speed. The long blade shot forward, opening a long nasty gash over Gen-Karn's ribs.

"Ara-Karn!" shouted Gundoen. "Ara-Karn!" Beyond his own voice he could hear the cries of others also cheering the stroke.

"A good blow, that, craftily delivered," commented Nam-Rog. "Yet it will take more than skill to best Gen-Karn."

"Do I not know this?" growled the chief. "But whatever it takes, he will give it. Have you not heard that he is of the gods?" He gulped down the dark beer, almost believing the words in his elation of the moment.

Across the circle Sol-Dat heard the words. "Yes," he cried out to the battlers, "show us your godhead, O Ara-

Karn! Vanquish him with a thunderbolt from your terrible eyes!"

Gen-Karn rumbled with laughter at the jest. He spat upon the wet earth. "Enough of this playing," he growled. "Prepare to die, little one."

There came a flurry of swordplay. The Warlord swung terrific blows, but Ara-Karn ducked them, parried them, caught them on his shield. He fell back easily, moving little, tiring not at all; but the big-bodied Gen-Karn was sweating and panting at the exertion of his blows. He growled, angered that he should not be able to land a good blow where he wished and end the battle with one stroke. His efforts began to grow wild.

He feinted, then drove straight in, a murderous blow impossible to dodge. Ara-Karn parried with his own sword and held. Their swords locked together, hilt to hilt, and shield and shield banged together. For a long moment they strove against each other, main strength against main strength. Their feet clawed for grip against the sand and slick stone of the ground, their thighs strained, their backs and shoulders bulged with effort, hard muscles cracking. For a long moment, Gundoen saw them straining, and it seemed to him that in this contest of sheer strength and bulk Gen-Karn must needs be the victor. He saw the Warlord prevailing; he was leaning over Ara-Karn, the weight and strength of his great body applied with grunting, ferocious power. Gundoen picked up the long black bow and gripped it with readiness in his hands.

The two combatants looked up.

Gen-Karn gazed into the eyes of Ara-Karn.

A rasping clash of steel and they were apart again, not circling now, but standing warily a few paces apart, panting with exhaustion, considering each other. The cheering from the crowds died down, the calls for Gen-Karn falling first. And it occurred to Gundoen that the shouts for Ara-Karn were hopeful and boisterous; but many of the shouts for Gen-Karn seemed forced and artificial, save for those coming from the group of Orn warriors. And Gundoen realized that, after all, Gen-Karn was not really a popular man, but gained his sway through fear and power alone. And even those who had followed him from the first had done so not out of any love or worship for the man, but only because they saw they had something to gain thereby —an enemy to be destroyed or gold to be raised—or because Gen-Karn had threatened them, and they had not wished to become like poor Elrikal of the Forun tribe. And Gundoen knew that, if by some miracle Ara-Karn should slay Gen-Karn, the tribes would acclaim him unanimously.

In the arena, the two naked men came at each other once again. And looking at Gen-Karn Gundoen could see something new in the Warlord's expression. It was a look of hatred, of doubt, almost of fear. Gen-Karn moved slowly, as if unsure of himself and of what he should do next.

"Now is the moment," breathed Nam-Rog in Gundoen's ear. "By the darkness of God, do you see the look on our Warlord's face? He has seen something not to his liking, that is sure. If Ara-Karn strikes now, he will have the clear edge."

"Yes," said Gundoen, raising his voice. "Strike now, my son! Strike to kill!"

The two combatants turned and faced him for a moment. Gen-Karn could sense the truth in Gundoen's words and made a visible effort to pull himself together before all should be lost. Ara-Karn looked into the eyes of Gundoen, and the chief saw again the statue and heard again those weird and alien words on the beach after the eclipse. The look in those shadowed eyes struck deeply into his soul, and though he loved him, he cringed suddenly. For the second time he was struck by the strangeness of the man who had washed upon his shores. And the first time had been when he had looked out of his stupor into that face the first and only time he had ever been beaten wrestling. Are the stories and dreams of Kuln-Holn really true then? he wondered.

Ara-Karn turned that merciless gaze back upon Gen-Karn, and everyone in the assembled multitude could see the Warlord start under it. Slowly, and with the greatest of contempt, Ara-Karn unbuckled the leather strap of his small iron shield and dropped it to the ground. He pushed it with his heel several paces from him. He took his sword in both his hands and swung it, easily, gracefully, powerfully.

"The fool!" hissed Nam-Rog in despair. "Does he not know that this is a combat to the death, without pause? Now he is defenseless!"

"Be silent, can you not?" Gundoen spat, a chill entering his lungs.

Gen-Karn saw the shield drop and seemed to take some comfort from it. He limbered his great shoulders and forced a barking laugh from out his throat. Perhaps it had been the contempt with which Ara-Karn had moved that now served to light the Warlord's rage.

"Why, you miserable piece of filth!" he began. "You'll not—"

Ara-Karn attacked. The chief of the Orns never had a chance to complete his words.

The longsword leaped everywhere, swinging right and left, back and forth, in and out, up and down in those capable hands. It performed strange feats—tricks and feints and movements unknown in all the North. Gen-Karn was sorely pressed to defend himself; even with all his efforts, a dozen wounds appeared suddenly on his limbs, his chest, his shoulders. There was never any question of a counterstroke—the man had difficulty even holding on to his blade.

Back Ara-Karn forced him, and back again. The combat weaved first to one side of the arena and then to the other. Suddenly they burst from one edge, flying into the opposite side of the crowd from Gundoen into the snow and spectators. They battled beneath the orange standard of Orn and over the rolling bodies of the crowds. Shouts and curses rose around them; Ara-Karn gave no heed, but held to that ferocious assault. Men scrambled cursing out of their way, snow and ice flying in the scuffle, tents upset and pans sent clattering.

Gundoen and the others around him rose to their feet, straining their eyes to see the fighters.

"Truly," murmured Nam-Rog in awe, "he fights like one possessed. His wrath is of something much less or more than mortal."

Gundoen had known that fury, that mindlessly destructive rage, in Ara-Karn before, so he was silent. He had felt its power; some wakings his bones still ached from it.

The two battlers passed from sight in the shadows of the crowds around the tents. Gundoen could only hear the clangor of the blades ringing over the dull roar of the fire.

"Come along," he ordered, setting out across the arena, forgetting in his eagerness the black bow. Others followed, murmuring to one another, leaping up at times to see over the heads of those before them. They forced themselves a way through the crowd, past the fallen tents to the very edge of the precipice; and there they paused.

Still the two were battling, the very edge of stone and ice crumbling beneath their heels. Once Ara-Karn in his wild eagerness stepped too far to one side; nothing met his foot and he almost fell. But he recovered somehow and went on as if nothing had happened, attacking Gen-Karn still.

"What does he do?" muttered Nam-Rog in the roar of the crowd. "He fights as if he is immortal! Does he truly wish to die?"

Gen-Karn's shield was but a battered rag of metal now, his sword notched and blunted where it had met the bite of Ara-Karn's edge. He was sweating profusely, his mouth open with fear, exhaling acrid steam, wavering with exertion. His body bled from a score of brutal wounds, and his right leg was deeply cut above the knee. He fought desperately, ferociously, as Gundoen had never seen him fight before. Yet his best was not enough; for all he could do, he was being driven into defeat. He was stronger than the stranger, his weapons just as good, and his reach longer. But there was this difference between them: Gen-Karn fought to hold on to his life, and Ara-Karn fought as if he did not care whether he lived or died. And that difference was a fatal one.

The crowds of warriors saw the Warlord's condition and guessed what Gen-Karn now knew—that Ara-Karn was to be the victor. Fewer and weaker came the cries for Gen-Karn; louder, longer, and more tumultuous arose the shout,

"Ara-Karn! Ara-Karn! Ara-Karn!"

Blindingly, Ara-Karn moved in response to that cry.

He struck with such power and suddenness that the Warlord was almost hurled over the icy edge of Urnostardil. Wildly scrambling, Gen-Karn threw away his sword and clutched for the rocks. But it was clearly too late; already his body was toppling over the darkness of the abyss.

The victory-cry was halfway up Gundoen's throat when Ara-Karn struck again.

Double handed, he swung his blade with glittering speed. The edge smashed into the side of Gen-Karn's head with superhuman force. But because the Warlord was falling and his head twisting to see where to reach out, the blade struck only a glancing blow. No one ever knew for certain whether the blow had fallen where it had been aimed or whether it was but an accident, a freak of the God's will.

The stranger, Ara-Karn, never would say. But what they all saw was the spattering of blood and flesh from the force of the blow, and the bone ripped clean, and the flesh torn, half from Gen-Karn's right ear, most from his cheek, and the great clump of hair torn from his head.

With such force did that blow strike that it actually *lifted up* the great bulk of the Warlord in midair, twisting him about and hurling him with a massive crash to the ground, a full pace away from the edge of the golden crown of Urnostardil.

And instead of victory-shouts there was only silence.

Men stood with still tongues looking down on that writhing, bloodied form. In those cuts and gashes, in the sweat and steaming dirt, it was hard to recognize what had once been the Warlord of the far North. And there was nothing left at all of the dark handsomeness in that ripped-open mess of a face.

From the moaning body on the bloodstained ice, the crowd turned its eyes to the conqueror, standing not exultantly but calmly on the edge of the abyss, the sword leaning casually against one bloodstained hand, the blood smoking, the chest rising and falling rhythmically, but the eyes still ablaze with the madness of combat. The feet were blued by the frozen cold and bleeding between the toes. From a dozen cuts the blood also gelidly flowed. The cord fillet had broken asunder, leaving the clotted hair to hang free about those wild eyes. And those savage men of the hard, far North saw in the victor not a man, not an outlander barge-robber, nor yet a god or messenger of gods, but a wild beast, whose desperate, destructive fury outdid anything that they in their supposed savagery could match. And there was not a man among them—not even those who loved him best, not Gundoen or Kuln-Holn himself—who did not at that moment feel the fearful awe of him who stood alone amongst them.

Ara-Karn straightened, and those of the Orn tribe nearest him stepped back a pace, as the gentle animals will do near a predator even when his hunger for blood has been sated. And Gundoen knew that there would be no need for bowmen now. With Gen-Karn dead, none would dare oppose the victor's will. Cautiously he approached and placed a fur mantle about the naked shoulders of his adopted son.

The man with the sword seemed not to notice. He

glanced down and pointed with his sword at the writhing body and spoke.

"Take it away," he said. His shoulders sagged a little with a great onrushing weariness.

"Lord, not yet!"

Bar-East spoke these words. The Speaker of the Law forced a way between the crowds and confronted the stranger.

"Lord, I have seen the battle; we all have seen it. You have conquered and are the Warlord of the North. Yet one final duty remains before the title is fully yours. Your enemy still lives."

"What of that?"

Bar-East blinked his old eyes, as if he had not understood. "His death lies upon your hands," he answered simply. He pointed to the sword, blood still oozing down to its point. "Slay him."

But Ara-Karn asked, "Why should I?"

"Because it is our custom."

Ara-Karn shook his head. "No. That is not my way."

"Because he is an evil man who has pressed our necks beneath his toes for too long!" cried another of the crowd, a Durbar.

"No."

"Slay him," said Bar-East slowly, "because if you do not, he will only hate you all the more, and strive and scheme and never give off scheming to murder you for this defeat."

But Ara-Karn only smiled, wan as the icy crystals round his ankles. "No. That, too, is not my way."

"Lord, what softness is this? Your mercy is to no avail with this man. He is a chief, and he was the Warlord of the tribes." Below them, the great sprawling figure of Gen-Karn writhed and groaned in pain.

And Ara-Karn looked at the Speaker of the Law with eyes like pebbles washed upon a lonely shore, and he said in tones of pitiless hardness, "Old man, you know more of mercy now than I am ever likely to."

At this there was only silence from that mass of blood-aroused men—looks of confusion and disbelief and one or two of anger. They had turned upon their former king and now would see his death—or, if not his, another's. Their lusts demanded to be sated to the full.

Gundoen, at his side, spoke in low swift tones: "My son, he is right. It is customary. If you let Gen-Karn live and he survives, then he will never forget this defeat. I know his nature, lord: ever will he seek a way to destroy you henceforth. Kill him now and have done. It is your right— and your duty."

"And who are *you* to speak of *my* duty?" Ara-Karn asked, contempt heavy in his voice. He turned and let his gaze fall on all the warriors assembled closely around him. He raised his voice. "And why should I wish to rule over you anyway? What are you but unwashed savages?" And he started to walk away, his feet leaving little red flowers in the snow. He headed over to where the path came up to the summit of the Table, where the pack-ponies still waited by the huge severed head.

But the tribes followed after him, dismay in their simple hearts. Already they had fallen under his spell. Not a one of them would have believed he could by any luck defeat Gen-Karn; now they had seen him do so with great ease, scarcely being wounded in the feat. Many remembered the tales that had spread of this man, of his magical powers and his influence with the gods. And now they would have him for their king. They followed after him, leaving the writhing body of Gen-Karn behind. A few of the Orn men picked up their chief and carried him to the great tent by the fallen orange standard; but after that they too followed after the stranger.

"Be our Warlord, Ara-Karn!" they cried after him. "Lead us in battle and protect us with your powers!"

But he turned and spat upon the ground before their feet. "I will not lead you," he cried aloud. "Why should I wish to rule such mangy dogs as you?" He turned and walked away again.

At this insult, there were grumblings among the warriors. There were many men of great pride among them. They had followed this man like beggars, and he had spat at them. Now their dismay turned to anger in their breasts. "Who dares to call us dogs?" they grumbled.

"Many enough of the pampered soft men of the South, I am sure," said Ara-Karn over his shoulder. "Dogs and worse than dogs they call you."

"Let them come *here* and call us that!" they shouted.

"They have done so!" shouted Ara-Karn in turn. Again he turned and faced them down. "Listen to a tale: A rebellious hound once growled at his master's table, and the master's ladies were afraid. So the master took the dog out to the sheds and whipped it a skin's distance from death and banished the dog from his lands. Yet this dog was a servile dog, a lackey of a dog—for though he was stronger than the master and could have slain him and had his pick of all the rich foods of the table, he went away. And even then he came arunning at the master's every whistle, hunting many things for the master who had whipped him. And what are you, the tribes of the far North, if not this very dog?"

"We are not dogs!" they shouted. And now their anger was very great, so that Gundoen was afraid they might fall upon Ara-Karn and throw him from the cliffs. "We are not dogs! We have no masters! Who will tell us that we have masters?"

"Do you deny it?"

"Aye!" they shouted. They bustled even closer now, teeth gleaming in rage in the firelight. "We deny it!"

Ara-Karn only laughed at them. "Then answer me this, if you can: How much do the merchants get for a single bandar skin at the bazaars in Tarendahardil, the City Over the World?"

This stopped them, and they considered. But none of them could say. And their confusion grew, though their anger did not cool.

"You see, you cannot tell me! Yet you give them these pelts whenever they demand them of you. Your hunters strive and risk all, and many of them die—all so that the Emperor's lackeys may get their pretty cloaks!"

"We are paid for them!"

Ana-Karn shrugged. "A lackey's wages—or rather, the table leavings for the master's dog. And your master— what is he but a pompous swine surfeited with wine and gluttony, sprawling on his bandar rug? And still you serve him!"

The warriors surged in confusion. No longer were they angry at Ara-Karn; instead their anger was turned toward the soft men of the lush Southlands, who had cheated them on the price of skins.

"Generations and generations ago, or so I am told," continued Ara-Karn, "the civilized lands beat you into this North. Many were the dead, but you found this Table and held your ground, though there were few tribes and of them many were women, children, and men wounded near to death. And even so they held off all the fierce attacks of a thousand thousand Southron warriors fresh and well fed and clad in expensive armor. They wanted to destroy the tribes utterly, but you laughed and spat in their faces, and in the end they were forced to leave—aye, even so many of them, and so much better men in those times than they are in these!

"And so, it would appear, were the tribesmen of those times better! Those men—ah, they were giants and ravishers in those times! They went where they pleased, striding red-handed over the soft belly of the Southlands; *they* would not have hid quavering behind the Spines. They grew so great that the Southlands trembled and combined together in numbers beyond imagining, and even then they were victorious only by a slight chance of luck!

"You are not even worthy of their names. That dog I fought"—he gestured over at the great tent beside the fallen standard—"he was the best among you, yet he would be a fearful weakling beside the likes of Tont-Ornoth. You have offered me your lordship. Well, I spit upon it and scorn it utterly! Pick out a blind man or some golden-haired woman to lead you. Perhaps you would make better weavers and bakers than you do warriors!"

Now there were no grumblings when he had done, no angry gnashings or gestures. They remembered the old tales of their ancestors, and they recalled how the old dream had ever been to be revenged upon the Southlands. And they knew they had forgotten that dream and fallen into content, trading with the perfumed merchants rather than slaying them outright. They could not be angry with Ara-Karn, for the insults he spoke were truth.

"What would you have us do?" asked one among them.

"Are you children—to be told? I know not, nor care. Do as you will—the choice is yours."

"Nay, we know what we want!" shouted Gundoen suddenly. "We know! To war upon the Southlands and redeem the heritage of our ancestors! And to have none other for our king than Ara-Karn!"

And the others cried in echo, "Ara-Karn! Ara-Karn! Ara-Karn!" The chant rose to the heavens in its volume, quickening like some excited heart's beat, going on and on and on. "Ara-Karn! Ara-Karn!"

"Perhaps I misjudged you!" he shouted, and they laughed to hear him. "Perhaps you are not dogs after all, but free warriors! Well, then, if you demand it, then I shall lead you."

The chanting rose again. The firelight gleamed off their sweating skins, their avid eyes, their sharp yellowed teeth. They drew their swords and banged them on their shields; they stamped the ground with their feet. The rattle and roil of their mail and armor was like the withdrawing of God's fatal jade sword, which is drawn only for blood and may not be denied.

And finally, after the raucous din had died down somewhat, Ringla of the Eldar tribe cried out, "O Ara-Karn! O Warlord, I have a question for you!"

"Yes?"

"How much *do* the merchants gets for a single bandar skin at the bazaar in Tarendahardil?"

Ara-Karn shrugged. "I do not know," he said simply. He swung his great blooded sword suddenly, sweepingly, so that it flashed against the black blue skies. The mantle about his shoulders fell to the snow, so that he stood before them almost naked, the frost steaming from his nostrils, his flesh blue here, dark red there with cold and blood. The light of the blazing pyre shone off his skin; behind him, the wan disc of Goddess was obscured in the far, far distance. He pointed with the dripping sword to the South. "Let us go find out!"

A thunderous roar acclaimed him.

CHAPTER SIXTEEN
The Road to Gerso

The broad, dusty path ran unturning through the age-old woods, beckoning the riders on. Great tree trunks, a horse's length broad and more, reared like guardian towers on either hand and, with their fiery-green young leaves, scattered the road with a thousand eyes of Goddess, sparkling, swirling, and dancing as the overhead breezes swelled and sighed. So had the pathway the likeness of a great tunnel through the ancient forest—or else of some half-glimpsed, half-dreamt Hall of legend, arched upon the twenty-fathom pillars of the old brown trunks. For much of its length, too, a brightly rushing stream followed alongside, with its gladsome melodies, clear fresh water, and bounding fish providing wearied travelers with heart and sustenance enough to go on another thousand or two before they halted in their journeys. From time to time a light rain might fall, pattering upon the leaf-roof so far above before descending into the earth in plum-drops of the size and gentleness they called in the far North the Milk of Goddess. It was very pleasant here, thought Kuln-Holn happily—pleasant and peaceful and merciful, riding down the Road to Gerso.

He looked before him and behind at the long columns of warriors upon their shaggy ponies. The risen dust obscured the most distant of them from Kuln-Holn's sight, so that it seemed to him that there was no end to them or beginning. The sight swelled his heart. All the tribes were represented, from the smallest to the greatest—all the warriors and hunters of the far North, side by side, sharing out of packs and kills. It was a wonderful sight. Ahead of Kuln-Holn rode the Karghil warriors, behind him Buzrahs, and not a foulness or a murder passed between. Yet Kuln-Holn could recall tales of the Stand at Urnostardil—of how a Buzrah chief had thrown a Karghil warrior off the cliffside and, when the food was gone, the Karghil women had feasted on the corpses of two Buzrah men. And Kuln-Holn thought, it was but the will and the power of one man, riding far ahead at the front of the columns, that held them now in peace and brought them even to the point where they bore the semblance of comrades. And if this were done already, how much longer might it be before all the prophecies were fulfilled and the happy years of peace and no want were upon them?

Had it been magic, he wondered, or mere skilled wisdom that had enabled his master thus to tame them? While Gen-Karn lay yet abed, moaning near death in the madness of his wounds, the tribes had been roused to the coming war. Bows had been passed out among all the tribes, and Ara-Karn had instructed men of every tribe how to fashion them: how to pick the best wood, how to clean the guts to make the strongest strings, and what birds' feathers were best on the long-shafted arrows.

"Mostly I have known only hunting-bows," he had told them once. "But are men any better than beasts to be hunted down?" None had spoken against him.

The rest of the Assembly had been spent making plans. Long hours Ara-Karn spent making the rounds of the chiefs, learning what numbers of warriors they could lead into battle, what arms they had, and what they wanted. From the wealthy tribes he took gold and sent men to purchase weapons in the South with which to arm the poorer tribes.

For buyers he chose only trustworthy men who had been to the South before. And he counseled them before they left to act as they were wont and give the Southrons no cause for suspicion. "Do not buy the weapons all at once or all from the same dealer. Send them north in small bundles, making sure you drop no hint of our plans. Surprise shall be our greatest weapon. Do not act but humbly before the arrogance of the civilized men. Let them be secure and smug, smoking costly herbs and sucking on the teats of expensive women. We shall sweep over them with the speed of the black arrow, and their throats will weep blood before their lungs can cry alarm." The messengers nodded, grinning at the thought, and all was done as Ara-Karn had commanded.

After the Assembly, when the warriors had returned to their villages, Kuln-Holn happened to be nearby Gundoen the chief when they rode into the streets up to the hall of Tont-Ornoth. The air was cold now that they stood on the threshold of winter, but not so cold as it had been on Urnostardil. On the shadowsides of some hills there was now snow, and ice in the small streams.

Gundoen leaped from his pony and embraced his wife warmly. He laughed at her care-worn face. "Is this the hug of a ghost?" he asked. "I am well, as you see—and what news I have for you!"

"You are alive," responded Hertha-Toll mysteriously. "But my prophecy said nothing of time. Still I say, husband, beware."

Kuln-Holn wondered what it was the wise woman had spoken of. He felt that he should leave and listen no more, but something held him close by.

"A woman's fears," scoffed Gundoen. "I never yet heard of a prophet who spoke aught but ill words. All will be well with me, now that I have a grown son." He told Hertha-Toll how he had named Ara-Karn his adoptive son before the Assembly. "And we must have the formal ceremonies before he goes to visit the other tribes, so that our relation will be lawful."

Hertha-Toll bowed her head. "As you will, husband. I know you want only good words now, but I have none to give you. My fears are as strong as ever—but you frown. Perhaps it is only foolishness, as you have said. Still, this I know and must say: That man is even more dangerous than I feared. He breathes death like the steam from your pony's nostrils."

Gundoen the chief only laughed harshly at these words, which put a chill in Kuln-Holn's heart, and took his wife into the chief's hall.

Kuln-Holn remained without, angry at the chief's wife. Why should she so hate his master? It was only her witch-craft, and it was probably against her that Goddess had sent the curse on the chief's children. Yet Kuln-Holn's anger could not hide the fear in his heart, for Hertha-Toll was the wisest woman in all the far North.

Before the ceremonies of adoption, Gundoen came to Ara-Karn in the guest hall. "Truly, when I named you it was but a jest, and an ill one at that," he said. "Forgive me. I repent of it now. It was a luckless thing and an ill-omened name. Now you are a former king no longer, but a true king in your own right, king of the North! Let me give you a new name in the ceremony."

This seemed a good thought to Kuln-Holn, but Ara-Karn only shook his head.

"What for?" he asked, scratching at his beard. "Call you this a kingdom? Let the name stand. I will tell you when you may call me a king again."

At these words his eyes focused as if on a far dim place, and he was lost to his dark thoughts. Gundoen tried to persuade him, and Kuln-Holn also tried; but it was as if he did not hear their words. Somewhat he woke, though, when the chief gave him his naming-gift, and that was a great sword. It had been forged onto the hilt of Tont-Ornoth and worked on in secret so that even Kuln-Holn had heard no word of it till now. Ara-Karn took it into his hands and felt of its heaviness and its bite, and he smiled. But still would he have no other name. So in the end Gundoen left sighing. And Ara-Karn was the Warlord's name still, after the rites.

From tribe to tribe Ara-Karn traveled, even when the snow and ice lay like a shaggy cloak over the lands; and ever at his side rode Kuln-Holn, in the place that seemed ever would be his. Every tribe made them welcome—even the Orn tribe, whose chief was still Gen-Karn. While he was still sickly from his terrible wounds, Gen-Karn's chief man Sol-Dat ruled the tribe in his chieftain's name. Sol-Dat treated Ara-Karn with smiles and as many gifts as if their former enmity had never been; and even later, when Gen-Karn was well, the Orn tribe showed no signs of rebellion.

"Still I trust him not," Gundoen later said. "I have known Gen-Karn of old. He is full of craft. For now you give him what he wants, so he will not challenge you. Yet if ever you falter or make a mistake, then make sure Gen-Karn is not at your backsides."

"I fear him not," Ara-Karn replied, and there the matter lay.

Each time they came to a new tribe, the welcome was grander than the last. At the Assembly Kuln-Holn had spoken of Ara-Karn as the son of God and Goddess, engendered at the eclipse that had swept the North at the beginning of the past spring. The word had spread quickly throughout the warriors at Urnostardil. And when they had come home from Assembly, the warriors also spread the legends of their strange new lord. They told of the great deed, when Ara-Karn alone had hunted Darkbeast; they told of the duel, when he had mutilated the powerful Gen-Karn; and they told of his speech, when he had vowed to lead them down into the fat lands of the South, where their ancestors had been before them. These new tales were added to the older ones about him and grew with each retelling. The people of the tribes scoffed at first. But then they saw the game brought in by the bow and the new weapons bought of the merchants of Gerso, and they came to believe. And when the stranger came personally amongst them, their belief was made into worship.

Chiefs bowed on the earth before him; women were awed at his presence; children fled his path. He was given glory and respect greater than had ever been accorded Gen-Karn. Those who had been reluctant to obey Gen-Karn, who was but a mortal man and only an Orn after all, were eager to worship Ara-Karn, who was of the gods. They came to him to bless their new weapons and breathe his spirit into the soft mouths of their babes. They could exalt him above all previous Warlords, because by doing so they did not exalt a man from another tribe over the men of their own. Kuln-Holn could see that his master took no pleasure in the baptisms and ceremonies the people begged him to attend, but Ara-Karn performed them all with seeming eagerness. This was a wonder to Kuln-Holn. But he knew better than to ask reasons of his master.

When they came among the Buzrahs the adulation was the greatest they had yet encountered. Cap-Tillarn, the chief of the Buzrahs, was most eager to please his guests— the more so because he was afraid that Kepa-Trim of the Karghils had poisoned the mind of the new Warlord when the Karghils had been allied with Gundoen against Gen-Karn. He was forever pestering Kuln-Holn about the tastes and desires of Ara-Karn, even though the Warlord had shown no sign of disfavor toward him.

At last he came to offer the Warlord such a gift as no other chief had dared: a woman. She was a sprightly, delicate girl not seventeen winters old. Her features were refined and of a rare beauty; and when she was not prettily smiling, her soft blue eyes reflected a serious intelligence that promised an exceptional ability to please. Her breasts were peaked beauties, mounted with nipples like fresh-sliced peaches strewn on the new-fallen snow. And her best feature was her hair, a soft golden color, very fine, braided about her oval face most becomingly.

"Take her," said Cap-Tillarn, beaming. "She is the loveliest maiden in the far North. She is willing enough, if a bit shy—what maid would not be? Yet you shall see that she is skillful and pure as a fresh snowfall. Give her to child and you shall bless our tribe, O lord."

Ara-Karn said nothing. Immediately, Kuln-Holn could see that something was wrong. His master stood for a long time, looking at the girl as if he could see something in her that no one else could. He went up to her and took her by her slight, ivory-tinted shoulders, and he stared into her eyes with a terrible gaze. The poor young girl grew terrified at this look; she turned away swiftly, coloring.

At this Ara-Karn started, and wrenched his head away. He spun her by her shoulders roughly, so that she fell suddenly upon the straw on the floor. "Nothing," he muttered, angrily yet so softly that none but Kuln-Holn could hear his word; then Kuln-Holn thought he said something else, but either it was an unknown word or else he spoke too low for the Pious One to discern it.

The Warlord turned to the chief, who fell to the ground before the thunderclouds upon his brow. "You surely insult me here," he said, in calmness but with an edge of iron. "Do you think that I would lie with any slut in the North? Or do you think that you can get this girl's child proclaimed as mine, though you've doubtless already filled her with your own seed? Take her for your own—clearly you've got a lust to—and bother me no more with such trifles."

With that he left the hall. A wail of sorrow arose from all the gathered Buzrahs.

"Fool!" shouted Cap-Tillarn's woman. "You have offended him! Do you wish us all to be cursed? O Kuln-Holn, servant of our great Warlord, tell us what we may do to placate the anger of him."

"Do nothing," said Kuln-Holn, who was hardly less upset than the Buzrahs. "Wait here. I will follow and speak to him on your behalf. I know you meant no offense."

He went out into the street, where patches of mud showed between the snow. He saw the tracks of his master and followed them out into the woods. At a small glade there were many tracks leading about in circles, then some others leading back to the village by another trail. When he finally traced the path back to the village guest-hall, he saw that Ara-Karn had shut himself up in his dim place, a sure sign he did not want to be troubled.

Kuln-Holn approached the fastened skin coverings and called softly, "Lord, is there anything you will be wanting?"

There was silence for a space. Then the voice came angrily: "Leave me."

Kuln-Holn went. He left the hall and the village, and went to the glade where all the tracks chased themselves. And he sat on a cold rock above the snow. Above him, three fists above the bright horizon, Goddess shone like a faint smear of saffron over the hills. Kuln-Holn sat and stared at the tracks, but could not riddle the thing through. What could he hope to do to serve his master when he did not even know what the source of the trouble was? For he was certain that when he had approached the fastened skin covering, his master Ara-Karn had been weeping.

At the very end of winter, before yet the spring had come, they returned to the village above the deep-water bay. Gundoen welcomed them as if Ara-Karn were the very seed of his loins, and the celebrations and feastings were tremendous. Kuln-Holn returned to find himself a grandfather: Turin Tim had given birth to a fat little boy during the winter. Garin was pleased as a stud bull over his firstborn and asked Kuln-Holn to be the babe's name-giver.

"It would never have come about if not for him," Kuln-Holn affirmed. "Therefore I call him Bart-Karan, or the Blessing of the King."

Turin Tim smiled, holding the sucking babe to her swollen breast, and said the name was good. Kuln-Holn could see that less than a year of marriage had already made Turin Tim a new woman. Before, she had only had her work, and work was never enough; now she had her own little bundle of dreams, warm against her flesh. He fell in love with little Bart-Karan immediately, of course, and would have wished to spend more time with the infant. But a man came to them to summon him and Garin to the Grove of dark God for the prewar sacrifice.

The Grove was in the shadow of the trees and a tremendous outcropping of rough-hewn rock, on the dark side of one of the nearby hills. No light ever shone there except the faint light of His Eye. There the air was perpetually chill; there no animals ever went by choice. To the Grove no women were permitted. If any woman had had the temerity to spy upon the rites enacted there, she would have been seized and put to an immediate, horrible death, like to the fate of any man who dared to spy upon the women, when they prayed to Goddess in the Vale of Womanhood.

On all sides of the silent grove were pine trees—dense, tall, aloof. They laid a thick carpet of needles on the dry ground. The ash-smeared feet of the warriors rustled as they shuffled through the brown needles.

They were, to a man, naked, save for brief rags twisted about their loins. Their tunics they had discarded on the sunward side of the hill. Their limbs and torsos were blackened with ash and pigments. Their faces were concealed behind masks of bark carved with grotesque expressions. It was the first time ever Kuln-Holn had come here to sacrifice—he was no warrior, no killer of men. The bark mask was uncomfortable on his face: it itched and he could not see well.

In the center of the Grove was an idol, a tremendous tree trunk twice the height of a man carved into the semblance of a horrible man. The roots of the tree still gripped the earth. Sometimes in springtime the idol would sprout fresh green sprouts full of life and promise. It was the duty of the men who guarded the Grove to crop back those young shoots mercilessly, so that only the horrible figure remained.

His features were as grotesque as those on the masks of the naked worshipers. In His fists He held a sword and an axe, both stained a dull brown-red. His grinning lips were of the same dark stain as was the enormous phallus jutting forth.

The chief, recognizable for his enormous stocky frame, led the warriors forward. Beside him stood Ara-Karn, dressed as the others, only more horribly still. Behind them came the sacrifice: the chief's brown mare—one of his most prized possessions. She was a brood mare and had foaled several of the finest ponies in the tribe. The brown mare loved Gundoen: she followed him daintily and docilely, her great liquid eyes brimming with trust and faith.

Kuln-Holn felt his heart go out to the poor horse. He almost felt as one with her in her adoration and her innocence. It tore his heart to watch what happened next.

Gundoen led her up before the idol, beneath the eyes of Ara-Karn. The smells that came from the stained wood alarmed the mare; she whinnied softly, and Gundoen stroked her muzzle unthinkingly.

Before her forelegs they laid the great wooden bowl. She sniffed at it as if expecting to find it full of grain. But the great wooden bowl was empty as yet.

Ara-Karn handed the chief the ancient worn knife of chipped stone. Gundoen took it and thumbed the blade with his broad thumb.

He held the mare's head gently with his left hand and in his right the knife. Behind the grotesque bark mask, the chief's eyes were in shadow, but Ara-Karn's glittered greenly.

With a swift stroke Gundoen severed the veins in her neck.

The hot steaming blood gushed forth in a fluid arc. It hissed as it passed through the gaping wound in the brown flesh. Kuln-Holn felt sickened; the mare whimpered painfully and tried to twist her head away. But Gundoen's broad hands held her firmly. Slowly she sank to her knees. Her tail lashed fitfully, then idly; then it was still.

The broad head flopped onto the rough red earth. The large, liquid eyes were shut fast.

"Thus ever to my enemies," swore Gundoen, his voice terrible through the bark mask. "Thus for the injuries of past lives."

They anointed the idol with the mare's hot blood: the jutting phallus, the edges of sword and axe, the thick grinning lips. Ara-Karn himself anointed the lips. When this was done, there was still a good deal of blood remaining in the great wooden bowl.

They mixed the blood with ale they had brought from the storage-holes of the huts of the village. The red blood was darkened by the thick brown ale. They lifted the bowl onto a pedestal of rock, and each man drank of the blood-mixed ale. Gundoen as chief drank first. After him drank Ara-Karn. When the stranger rose, his lips were stained and smeared with the blood. The carved grinning lips of the mask were stained also.

"Death and fire, destruction and rapine," promised the chief and the Warlord to the freshly stained idol as the other warriors drank of the bloody mixture. "Blood and the screams of the dying. Men cut down, babes trampled underfoot, women raped screaming. Give us these things, great Lord, and we shall be wholly yours. The hands that hold the blades will be yours and so the head that commands. Our loins will be in your service. Love and pleasure we cast aside, with those whom we love, with those who give us pleasure. We will live only for death and vengeance, and will send all others in death to you. This we swear, dread Lord: and may you destroy us utterly if ever we go back upon these oaths."

When it came Kuln-Holn's turn to drink at the blood, he bent dutifully over the bowl. But the stench that rose to his nostrils assailed him and his gorge rose. Beneath the mask he gagged. The fellow behind him prodded; so, closing his eyes and his mind, he dipped suddenly, so that the blood came bubbling about his half-parted lips. Even with the ale it was horrible. It made him so sick afterward that he could eat nothing for several passes.

And now, as he rode among the hordes of warriors up the path into the hills, Kuln-Holn thought on his master and wondered. And Kuln-Holn remembered and could not dispel the horror of that taste of mare's blood from his mouth. And it made him almost fearful of his master, who had gone again to the great wooden bowl, for more.

An angry word tore him from his reveries. Ahead of Kuln-Holn all the riders were bunched together, halted. Kuln-Holn looked at the graveled slopes and the ragged pines rising sparsely like arrow shafts and he thought, How strange a place to camp. And they had rested only shortly before. Yet before he could question the men sitting about him, a word came flying from above that answered him.

The men ahead had it from those beyond, picked it up, and flung it back of them without another word, so that the voices rose around Kuln-Holn and surged past him like a swell upon the Ocean of Death.

"The Gates!" they muttered. "The Gates! The Gates!"

CHAPTER SEVENTEEN

The Gates of Gerso

Massive and ancient, the Gates of the Gerso flung themselves across the narrow Pass forbiddingly, like a part of the mountains themselves. Indeed, from the end of the Pass, the Gates could not be distinguished from the mountain walls.

Two score hundred paces down from the pine-mantled hills, the mountains abruptly lost all vegetation, sweeping steeply up against the sky: grim, gray, forbidding, vast. They narrowed as well, coming so close together that at their closest point a man might throw a stone from mountain to mountain. And here, thousands of feet below the ice-capped peaks, down in the womb of the vertical cleft of stone, the walls of Gerso had been built.

They had been built of gigantic gray blocks of stone, hewn as if by giants out of the unyielding bowels of these very mountains. Block upon enormous block had been fitted, so snugly that not even the thief's-fingers of water could slip between them to crumble and to crack them. So that now, generation upon generation upon generation after the walls had been built, they stood as upright, sheer, and pristine as on the sunlight of their first summer.

And of all the fortresses, keeps, and citadels of all the round world, none was deemed so impregnable as the

Gerso, save perhaps only one, which sat in the very bosom of the distant Empire with no enemies near: the Black Citadel of Elna itself, on the rocky crags above Tarendahardil. Only that could have been deemed more secure than the Gerso. And it was because of the reputation of the hardness of these walls that those of the lush green lowlands beyond thought themselves safe from those they had condemned and imprisoned in the rocky wilderness of the far North so very long ago. And it was because of the reputation of the hardness of these walls that the civilized peoples felt so secure, and had put away their swords and put on fat instead, to slumber their lives away.

And Gerso, too, felt herself secure. And though she posted guards to walk those ancient, crackless walls, there were too few of them, and those not adequately trained. In all obedience to the traditions of their long-voyaged ancestors they walked the peaks of those walls. And their feet fell in the ancient, selfsame spots on the stone worn smooth by the passage of countless feet, all of them also upon the selfsame duty. They walked, changed guards, called out their time-honored calls; watched the traders come and go, saw ponies burdened with worked goods go forth and those laden with bandar pelts return; chatted among themselves, threw carved dice on bets when their commanders weren't around to see. And when their watch was over, they hung up their armor on the ancient stone pegs in the armory, went down the winding, hollowed steps leading to the cityside, and led peaceful lives with their wives and happy fat children. And though all who passed below them commanded their momentary attention, their eyes were more often turned to the shining domes and red stone palaces of the city within than upon the sandy narrow plain without, which formed the floor of the Pass.

Below the guards, built into the body of the walls, were the Gates themselves. Of these there were two sets: the larger gates were of stone, which none living had ever seen open: these were for the passage of great armies into the wilds of the far North, to harass the barbarians and keep them forever few and fearing. Such had been Elna's intention; but it was long centuries since any armies had passed those gates. They were too cumbersome, too difficult to close once opened, for the passage of individual merchants, when trade began between North and South. So the second, smaller gates had been fashioned, at great expense, by the side of the older stone ones. These new gates were of brass, and were just the size to allow a few men and their horses to pass through for the purposes of trade.

The guard had but recently been changed, so that most of the guardsmen were still within the barracks room or the armory when the sound reached the gates.

The guards came out onto the worn ruts upon the summit of the walls and looked above them. It was a frequent enough occurrence that rocks rolled down the steep slopes above them, though that season had passed. Yet the guards saw no rocks falling. And the sound had come not from above but below.

It came from the pine-mantled hills beyond the Pass, and it came from the sand- and gravel-washed floor of the Pass. Then the guards smiled and nodded their heads; now that the sound grew louder, they knew it well. It was the sound of some merchants on their ponies with their bundled metal wares clanking along behind them. Then the guards frowned and looked one another in the eye. It was too early in the year for any merchants to be setting forth, and these sounds were from the northern side.

The guards leaned forward, casting forth their glances to the end of the Pass. The sounds of the riders, rising louder and more distinct, were echoed and reechoed off the sheer hard walls of the cliffs; yet the men themselves could scarcely be made out as yet. The guards upon the walls cast some bets as to how many would be in the party and what their business was. Shortly thereafter the coins changed hands, and one of the men smiled broadly, having won both bets, for the band was of four men above a score, and they wore the garb of barbarians. The victorious gambler leaned over the parapet, unfurled his cloak, and waved it at the men below, as if to thank them for his luck. Something gleamed off the barbarians, but what it was could not be made out. The man with the cloak made a bet as to what it might be.

Now the riders had come into the shadow of the Gates. One of them, so small he seemed no more than a mouse to be trod upon, rode out ahead of the others, came up to the gates of brass, and lifted up his tiny sword. Holding it by the blade, he reached forward and pounded with the pommel upon the costly brass three times.

The sound of that pounding raised a distant, hollow tolling, which reached up to the ears of the guardsmen on the summit of the crackless walls. And such were the angles of those precipitous cliffs that the sound of the knocking echoed off the walls and the sides of the mountains and filled the entire vale of the Pass, sounding like the tolling of a tremendous, unceasing bell of mourning of the dead.

The captain of the guard cursed jocularly and buckled on his head his official brass helmet, which he rarely wore because it had not been made quite large enough. And he went down the winding hollow stairs to the Pass side and opened one of the brass doors. He looked out over the armed barbarians with a squinting eye.

Now, barbarians came betimes through these gates, usually to buy their pleasure in the fleshpots of the city. Yet those were only wretched fellows dressed in ragged pelts and soiled worn tunics, and never in numbers greater than ten. The sight of that score of grim, avid warriors in their shining mail the captain liked not at all.

"Let us through," said the barbarian who had pounded upon the gates with his sword.

"Who are you?" countered the captain. He was a big fellow with a large belly and a round face fit more for smiling. But he was not one to be cowed—not even by such an armed warrior on horseback leading other such.

"I am Ara-Karn."

Though the man had spoken calmly, the walls of the cliffs caught up his words, hurling them back and forth, until the winds brought them up to the summit of the walls and back down again, louder than before.

"What do you want?" asked the captain.

"For you to open the larger gates of stone and let my men pass."

The captain looked upon those chests of iron and leather and bronze with a dubious eye. "So you can go thieving in the alleyways of our city?" he asked. "Not likely."

"Kill him," ordered Ara-Karn.

The captain suddenly took alarm at this and tried to slam the door shut in their faces. But Gundoen lifted his great bow and shot an arrow right through the soft bronze armor, and the captain fell dead.

"Kill them all!" cried Ara-Karn, raising his weirdly echoing voice against those crackless walls. "Death to all Southrons!"

He plunged through the open brass door, his pony trampling the captain's corpse. Gundoen and the other picked men quickly followed him. And what remained of the captain, after those ponies had cantered past, was not a pleasant thing to see.

The guards atop the broad walls knew that something was amiss. They shouted down their questions. In return the warriors below who had remained outside the gate lifted high their bows. The guardsmen laughed to see the toylike men below, milling angrily about; they knew no such ragged bandits would ever pierce their Gates.

The darting arrows flew high. Some fell short, rattling harmlessly off the stone below; and others flew too high and soared over the walls altogether, falling down into the city streets beyond. But the rest swept over the walls, wounding several of the guardsmen. The rest of them fell back in consternation as two of the wounded men fell over the edge of the wall. Their bodies plummeted like thunder to the earth. The nearby ponies reared, neighing in terror, but from the savage throats rose a shout of triumph.

The guards were suddenly afraid as they had never been before; their fear was like that of the barbarians when the eclipse of Goddess had come. They fled their posts in terror and scrambled down the winding steps that led to the cityside. The more stouthearted of them went down the steps to the barracks rooms within the huge walls. They went down to defend the brass doors and the ancient mechanisms that controlled the gates of stone.

They found only death and destruction before them, and savages with smoking blades who shouted at the sight of them and leapt up the steps to the attack.

Before that onslaught the guards fell back. They had not been adequately trained, and their training had been long ago, and they none of them had ever killed a man, and their bronze armor was suited more to look pretty in the sun than stop iron blades. And against them went warriors with the hardness of wolves, bearing the scars of a score of deadly combats. And it was not long before the last of the stouthearted of the guardsmen lay weltering in gore upon the hollowed stone steps.

The other guards ran out of the brass doors of the city-side. They had to gain help, inform the Governor-General. The savages who had attacked the gates had been only two dozen in number, but the guards in their fear did not think of that. The undreamt of had come to pass. The old prophecies rose in their minds that the barbarians would rise again. Twenty-four became a hundred in their minds; the piny hills beyond the Pass seemed to have been crawling with innumerable savage foes. Some ran to the quarters of the city watch to rouse the men there; others ran for the towers, there to mount the winding stairs and swing hammers against the bells to alert the city; still others ran for the palace of the Governor-General.

The palace was not far from the Gates. The guards scrambled through the courtyard, looking like wild men. Angrily the house-guards demanded of them their business.

"The Governor-General!" croaked the guards. "The Porekan! Let us through!"

"Imbeciles!" shouted the majordomo, twirling his mustache. "Are you toddlers with wet linens? Away, you cannot see the Porekan now. Don't you know he has a dinner party in progress?"

Even then, at the far side of the palace on the cool, pillared terrace overlooking the city, several gentlemen and ladies reclined on cushions around a low table made of the finest, purest marble.

"More wine, good Telran?"

"Most honored Porekan, as superb as your wine is, I fear I must refuse. I feel as though I have had just the right amount, and any more would spoil the effect, as it were."

The Governor-General of Gerso waved the serving maid back to her place of readiness. Zaristin, the Porekan Delbar's wife, offered the observation that the dinner party had been a fine one.

"Ah! most esteemed lady, I fear such a word could hardly hope to do it justice," said Burdelna Tovis, languidly waving his hand through the air in a gesture of supreme pleasure. "And for that, believe me, you have gained my most implacable animosity."

"You surprise me, Burdelna," said the Porekanin. "Explain yourself, please."

"Why, for this reason: that now I will be more wretched than ever in three weeks' time, when I must sit in the dirt in a hovel that would make a pig abattoir smell like arintha by comparison."

"You men are ever complaining of your trips amongst the savages," said Usaris, who was Telran Welsar's mistress. "Yet if you abhor them so much, why do you not send some of your assistants in your place?"

"Don't even speak of assistants," groaned Burdelna. "Those who know enough to do the job well will steal one deaf, dumb, and blind and use the proceeds to start their own houses; the rest will lose one's goods on the way out, but bargain pelts not good enough to line a public latrine— your pardon, Porekanin—and end by professing only consternation when one chokes upon one's words and threatens to give them the beating they deserve!"

At this apt description by the Tovis, several of the merchants present broke into sympathetic and appreciative laughter. Usaris, with all the delicate, calculated grace of a beautiful stylish woman who knows to exactness her every effect upon her male watchers, rose to her feet and glided over to the railing of the balcony. The Governor-General's palace was set high up in the city, nearby the Gates; and from this balcony, which faced south, almost the whole of the city could be seen. The red roofs fell away and outward, filling the expanding plain of the Gerso. Far and away, the undulating verdant pastures of the lowlands could be seen. Usaris sighed, thrilled to her marrow at the beauty of the sight. Telran Welsar had no such view as this. She turned and regarded the Governor-General with a more professional eye. He, drawing another breath upon the water pipe, happened to catch that look. There was a silent moment, questions and messages exchanged, and a tentative agreement. Usaris turned again over the railing, displaying her best side to the Porekan's apparently disinterested gaze. The Governor-General, well satisfied with himself and the authoritative figure of manhood he must present, drew in another lungful of herb and held it in his lungs until just after the pleasure had begun to transform itself into an exquisite ache.

"Well, but I think there are reasons beyond those," offered Zaristin. "Else why should men of such wealth continue to subject themselves to a yearly trek of such toil and misery? And I have heard it said some of these barbarian women can be quite pretty, in an earthy, crude sort of way."

"You would not say so, reverend lady," said Burdelna Tovis, "if you could but see them squatting down in the fields, legs of a color with the mud, hands like leather gloves, and hair crawling with—yet I need go no further, surely, in distressing the ladies present with even more unappetizing pictures, accurate though they may be. Suffice it to say, dear lady, that in their artlessness and filth they do not even deserve the name of woman, especially when compared to such studied loveliness as yours."

The Porekanin, who was then somewhat beyond the threshold of middle age and had begun to put on weight, blushed gratefully and lowered her eyes in a most lovely way; and Burdelna sipped at his silver wine cup smugly. The Governor-General would regret that he had granted those two licenses-of-trade to Telran Welsar's firm.

"Zelatar Bonvis, I believe, has already begun to assemble his goods," said Leilerick Pasch.

"Tut, he always sets out early," said the Welsar. "Old habits are hard to break, they say, in old beasts."

"I am surprised to hear you say so, Telran," offered Rathimin Coracano. "Especially when it was you, I believe, who was soundly cursing Zelatar for gaining an unfair advantage when his firm won the perpetual right to be the first bandar traders licensed each year." Rathimin said this sweetly, with an air of innocence; whereat Telran Welsar scowled. The Rathimin had taken over her father's firm three years ago and had since built it up to a position of great influence—one of the five wealthiest houses in Gerso. She had a way of using her virginal, lovely face and manner that had been the deception and downfall of more than one male trading adversary. This Telran had learned to his own dismay two years ago, when he had taken pity on the poor girl, so lost in the thickets of the merchants' ways, and had ended being taken for some seven thousand golden Elnics' worth. Now he knew better her ways: and thought he could detect in her innocent remarks concerning Zelatar Bonvis a slight, secret air of pleasure. He wondered if the rumors were true that she and Zelatar had formed an alliance to take away his, Telran Welsar's, preeminence among the merchant houses of the North. He had had several confirmed reports of Mergo Donato paying secret visits to the Rathimin's palace. He noticed that Usaris had taken her place at the table again, somewhat closer to the Governor-General. Let her play her games, Telran thought —he had more important concerns to occupy him now. Usaris' expenses were growing out of hand anyway. The Porekan would doubtless find her a luxury he could ill afford; and if he could be made to feel some twinge of guilt for having taken her away from Telran, perhaps he would be more disposed to grant the extra license Telran had requested.

"Well, certainly so shrewd a judge of men as yourself, Rathimin, with such a memory, must be ceded to," Telran remarked with an equable air. "And I must admit that, when it seemed Zelatar Bonvis would by that unfair right gain first choice of all the pelts, I was not a little distressed at it. Several I know called it favoritism and even hinted that the turning face of some golden Elnas had had not a little to do with it. Of course, I disagreed with them. There are few governments in the North with such spotless histories as our Porekanstar. Yet, when Zelatar chooses to set out so early as this, when the savages have not yet even begun preparations for their Hunt, I cannot but feel relief, and, I may confess it, not a little concern for the state of my good friend and competitor's mental judgment. I am certain that one with such accurate sources of information as yours, dear Rathimin, can hardly be unaware that last season Zelatar lost over three thousand Elnics on his expedition. Poor man, he seems bent upon repeating his error this season."

Telran leaned back upon the pillows, calm in the satisfaction of his last remarks. Rathimin's face had let slip she had not known the extent of Zelatar's losses. Let her have the taste of that dissolving on her tongue, and see what she has to say to Mergo Donato next time!

"You don't mean it!" Leilerick Pasch exclaimed. "Did he really lose three thousand?"

"Sadly I must confirm it," Burdelna Tovis said gravely. "All the more sadly, since my wife's father had invested some ten thousand in Zelatar's firm. Well, but I cannot say I did not warn him—nay, entreat him even—from so rash a course." Burdelna did not seem so grave now.

"And what of these other tales of the savages?" asked

Usaris of the Porekan. "Is it true they have a new—what do you call him—now?"

"Warlord, my dear; and yes, that has been confirmed." The Governor-General laid aside the pipe and summoned one of the slaves with what he hoped was a demanding gesture. "Yet you need have no concern over that; in many ways I am glad to see Gen-Karn replaced. I had some disturbing reports concerning him. He seems to have been a bad one altogether."

"Is there such a thing as a good one?" asked the Porekanin.

"Certainly, madam," said Burdelna Tovis, "when he has been properly trained."

The laughter did not further the air of dangerous gravity the Governor-General had wished to preserve. In a dignified (if somewhat pompous) manner he spoke across the laughter, saying, "It had reached me, that Gen-Karn's ambition was to unite the tribes under his rule and make an assault on the Gates."

"How terrible!" breathed Usaris, looking up at the Porekan from the depths of her lake-blue eyes.

"Never fear it," the Governor-General said courageously. "My men would hold against them."

"Zelatar Bonvis believes that the old prophecy may soon be realized in a dozen or score's space of years," said Leilerick Pasch. "Their numbers have been growing at an alarming rate. He believes the barbarians will rise."

"All the greater cause we should fear for poor Zelatar's reason," said Telran Welsar, shaking his head.

"Yet it was ever taught me, that a wise man considers all possible events, that he might thereby be prepared to deal with them," Rathimin Coracano said.

"Stuff and nonsense!" Burdelna dismissed it with a wave of his hand. "When the savages grow too numerous, they generally solve the problem themselves, by murdering each other. By my mind it is a very convenient arrangement; and, moreover, the price they will pay for arms doubles in times of feuds." Burdelna owned, in part or whole, four armories and had a right to feel smug about it. His profits for this past winter, generally his slowest time, had been tenfold his every expectation. Thankfully, he had managed to keep that news secret, so that none of his competitors might know how far his fortunes had risen.

"They have been most extraordinarily quiet this past winter," remarked Zaristin. "Apparently their new leader is not so ambitious."

"In truth," offered Telran, "we have never had much cause to fear them. They are too fractious ever to support a united effort."

"All the more reason we should continue to offer them arms unrestrictedly," said Burdelna.

"Yet if they did come—if they did, I say," said the Porekan heatedly and stoutly, "then we should have nothing to fear. My men should hold them!"

"What courage and fortitude it must require to be a leader of men!" Usaris sighed.

"Tush, my dear, hardly so great as that," the Governor-General remarked with a sideways glance at his wife. "Friend Telran, at our earlier meeting it slipped my mind entirely—I have had a letter of my cousin, the mayor of Tezmon. Shall I summon one to read it?"

"By all means," said Telran quickly, disturbed that the others should know he had met with the Governor-General. "And what is the state of trade out of Tezmon? My shippers have complained that this past winter's storms went on longer than they had any right to."

"You shall hear all," said the Porekan. "Festor, the letter. It lies on my desk. You will never guess what Armand has purchased," he went on, as the slave vanished into the interior of the palace. "A dancing-troupe! Yes, and that is not all; the girls of this troupe were trained by a master from Vapio itself!"

There were exclamations of surprise and envy at this, which pleased the Governor-General no little. Zaristin, his wife, nodded with the others. "And we have been considering asking Armand," she said, "that he send the troupe here to us on loan this summer."

"That would be the height of culture," said Burdelna Tovis. "You know, I usually spend my winters at Tezmon, enjoying the sea instead of the bitter snows that are our fate here. Yet this year business held me here. How pleased Armand must be!"

"Yes," sighed the Governor-General with a downward, lingering glance at Usaris' long, golden-skinned leg where it emerged gleaming from the black pleated folds of her silken skirts. "We are really no better than the barbarians here, you know. Eh? What's that?"

Firmly but most apologetically, the Porekan's major-domo bowed at the threshold. "My most reverend master," he announced, "a man is here—one of the guardians of the Gate—with some frightening and most urgent news."

"Please allow me the privilege of deciding how urgent it may be," said the Governor-General. "And, as for that word *frightening*, how dare you use it? Can you not see the effect it has had upon my wife and these other ladies?"

"Pardon, your worship; yet it really does demand immediate attention," said the majordomo, angrily twisting at his mustache.

"Oh, very well," said the Governor-General, who despite himself grew nervous at this unaccustomed behavior on the part of his servant. He fixed his eye wrathfully upon the disheveled guard. "Well, fellow, what have you to say for yourself? Where is your captain—and what is your name?"

The poor guard, beside himself with the turmoil he had undergone, cast his eyes about upon the assembled merchants and their companions. If the attack meant what he feared, what should become of his city? If it did not mean what he feared, what should become of him beneath the Porekan's rage? His eyes bulged, his throat worked, but at first nothing would come forth. His knees were quavering. "Your honor," he began, then choked in despair. "Ara-Karn!" he wailed. "*Ara-Karn!*"

Burdelna Tovis, Telran Welsar, and several others who had some inkling of what that name was opened their mouths and paled. Usaris and the Porekanin looked each other in the eye and colored. The Governor-General's scowl deepened. His chest swelled and he began to speak, but what he might have said is no more than a matter for conjecture, for at that very instant the terrace, the palace, the entire city itself, it seemed, was rocked in an enormous, deafening crash. The walls reverberated and the ceiling plaster cracked, dividing faced painted figures; the water pipe and wine bottles shattered; the disheveled guard was thrown to the floor headlong and lay there like one dead. So was it like as if some monstrous, malevolent God had chosen that instant to stamp His foot upon the city of Gerso, thereby to announce his momentous arrival.

For several moments all lay still. Their minds and ears

were blank as walls of slate. The crash lingered on and on in their skulls. Slowly, it faded. And then, in the preternatural stillness that ensued, another sound was faintly heard. The ancient bronze bells were being hammered. Again and again they tolled in the quivering air. The city was under attack.

CHAPTER EIGHTEEN

Gray Priestess

Within the Gates Gundoen shouted his triumph over the bodies of the slain guardsmen, shaking his reddened blade; but Ara-Karn was calm.

"The mechanism," he said.

They found it in the next room in the stone walls, seeming vast and monstrous in the dimness. Great wooden gears, metal plates and rods, and cables of great rope thicker than a woman's hips were everywhere. Ara-Karn lifted a flaring lamp, studying the forms carefully.

Gundoen looked upon it too, but it was only a shadow to him. He took down lamps from the walls and put them this way and that, but still could make nothing of it.

"We can lead them through the brass doors," he shrugged. "It will take longer but is there a hurry?"

"We do not know what forces they can bring to bear upon us here," muttered Ara-Karn. "Nor is there time to open the Gates properly." He pointed at a huge cable, the thickest and strongest of all. "There. Cut that."

The warriors who had entered with them sheathed their swords and took out their war-axes. And they began hacking at the cable, which was thick beyond the imagining of any who had not seen it with his own eyes or felt it with his own hands.

Cutting it took as much sweat as there had been blood

spilt and more time. Beyond the walls they could hear the desperate shouts of the guards who had escaped. Finally there was only as much cable left as a strong man's forearm. Gundoen swept the others aside. He drew his own heavy sword and, with a half-score desperate strokes, severed the tremendous cable.

With a thud it fell to the floor. There was no other movement. The gears did not turn, the ropes did not pull. The Gates without remained shut fast.

"It needs oiling," said Ara-Karn. He pointed. "There and there."

So the men took cups and brass tankards from the barracks room walls and scooped up hot blood from the pools about the guardsmen's dead bodies, and splashed it redly upon the cable where Ara-Karn had pointed.

For a few moments nothing occurred. From without the shouts grew louder, more insistent. Then there was a sudden loud creak, and the cable began to move. Slowly it was drawn back into the mechanism, pulled as if with irresistible force. And with that, the force that had held the Gates shut fast departed.

A tiny crack appeared in those gigantic gates of stone.

At first there seemed to be no sign of any movement, but then the dark line cracked down the middle of those huge stone blocks. Slowly, a finger's-breadth at a time, the crack widened, and the Gates parted. Then, in the depths of that dark crack, another crack appeared—this one of light. And beyond that bright crack could be faintly seen shining domes and palaces of red stone.

Now the Gates fell open not a finger's-breadth at a time, but as fast as a man might walk—and even faster than that. It was as if the very mountains were rising, falling, moving back before the warriors of Ara-Karn. The pull of gravity pulled those mountainous Gates soundlessly on the invisible hinges built into the walls of stone by the master builders of Elna in centuries past. The warriors were silenced by the sight: the Gates swinging, the naked fairness of the city beyond.

Wide, wide the Gates swung, fast as a pony might canter. They swung back against the ancient stone stoppers, built like buttresses against the walls of the Pass. The Gates smashed into the stoppers with a sound of thunder and of solid stone shattering. The tremendous clap reverberated wrathfully from the stone cliffs.

Even outside the Pass they heard it. The war-ponies bucked for the madness of their sudden fear, but strong thighs and fists steadied them. The whole mass of men milled about, stunned and doubtful at the fearsomeness of that sound. Tales were risen in their minds—tales of great Elna, whom the Southrons called a god. Was it not prophesied that one pass he would return? Gerso lay before them like the bride upon the marriage-bed, yet they held back and looked at one another and muttered.

Then one of them, Garin of Gundoen's tribe, rode his pony up to the crest of the ridge. His brown cloak waved out behind him and vanished behind the ridge. A few others went after; still more followed them. The ponies tossed their shaggy heads; swords clanked against thighs; lances raked the skies. The movement restored them; the growing fairness of red-roofed Gerso restored their avarice and their hate. The great, antlike mass surged forward, down into the perpetual shadow of the cliffs. All the valley floor filled with them, from the shattered Gates to the ridge beyond the mountains—and still men waited their turn outside the Pass.

Then Ara-Karn emerged from the small brass doors, and at the sight of him the horde stopped and recoiled, like a great wave running back. And they saw him and were struck dumb, and knew again their vengeance.

And he rode quietly before them, from one side of the Gates to the other. And behind him were Gundoen and the others, bearing aloft reddened bits of soft and pretty bronze armor. But the hands of Ara-Karn were as clean as when he had entered, for he had done no killing yet. He reached the far side of the Gates and rode back, sternly surveying the sea of leather and steed and sword before him. He reached the very threshold of the Gates, where the curving grooves, cut deeply into the sand, began. He brought his pony to a halt.

He raised his sword, which was cold and sharp.

"Remember your oaths!" he called, and his hundred voices were audible to all, like the voices of the dead of Urnostardil that cried aloud for vengeance. "Death to all Southrons!"

He wheeled and plunged ahead. Down beyond the Gates he came again into the light of Goddess, and all his armor and his sword gleamed fiercely, as if it were ablaze.

And the warriors behind him, awed by the sight, rumbled in their throats, "Death! Death! Death!" A thousand voices raised that cry of all the warriors of all the tribes of all the far North.

Through the vast open Gates they poured, like the springtime flood that will not be denied and that washes away all that stands before it.

Down those broad streets they poured, yelling the fierce ululations of their tribes. The sound of their ponies' hooves was like a rocky avalanche. The soldiers of the watch, responding to the incoherent prayers of the fugitive guards, had formed in a body in the opened cobble-stoned avenue just below the Gates. The warriors of the tribes saw them and laughed horribly. They raised swords, axes, lances, and bows. And they passed over the mangled remnants of the soldiery of Gerso with hardly a break in their stride.

Before them reared the many-storied palace of the Governor-General of Gerso. The Porekan's palace quartered a full complement of his personal guards: these now issued forth from the gate, bewildered at what had happened. They saw before them a thousand demons on horseback bearing down on them. That was enough; the soldiers turned and ran screaming back into the courtyard. Five hundred barbarians rode after them, up the steps, burst asunder the palace doors, and rode laughing down the corridors within. In moments the palace was a bedlam. Servants, slaves, and houseguests ran back and forth and into one another in their efforts to escape the invaders—leaped from windows and cowered under beds. The warriors rode on, enjoying well their sport, taking whom they would, killing, maiming whom they would, letting free whom they would. Life and death and fate were theirs alone, sweeter far than the smoothest beer.

Up the stairs they rode: found, at length, the pillared terrace overlooking the city. They found the Governor-General and his guests. They found the merchant princes, who had profited from the bandar pelts. The warriors pulled up their ponies, not knowing what to do. With so much store of riches before them, what should be done first?

"Now mark me, you rabble," proclaimed Porekan Delbar, stepping forward. "Know you not who I am?"

The warriors laughed suddenly, and surged forward. Was it not obvious beyond telling what should be done first?

Some moments later, the stairs resounded again to the

clatter of the ponies' hooves. The warriors joined together in the lower corridors like the branches of a mighty river. Some were covered with silks and gold—the treasures of the Porekan's strongboxes; others bore comely women across their saddles; others still held aloft the priceless best of the Porekan's wine collection; but none of them was without his bloody stains.

Behind them, upon the uppermost story's southern wall, the pillared terrace was still. From some pillars were bound the long silk finger napkins of the guests; these, knotted together, passed over the railing and wrapped around the throats of the merchant princes. Like so many rugs held out to dry, Telran Welsar, Burdelna Tovis, Leilerick Pasch, and others hung above their city and slowly kicked and waved, as the silken napkins strangled them. Above them, Usaris lay motionless and naked, raped many times in rapid succession and left for dead. The Porekanin Zaristin was gone; her screams having been considered an annoyance, she had been tossed over the railing. The Rathimin Coracano sat nearby Usaris' body, but the head of the Rathimin was missing and nowhere to be found. Scattered across the marble table (which was hardly so pure now) were all the remains of the Governor-General, after the warriors had castrated him and gutted him as they would a pig to be slaughtered. Across the prettily tiled floor streams of blood and wine were intermingling. From somewhere in the next chamber, wafts of smoke billowed gently into the terrace. A fire was starting. In the courtyard below, the barbarians rode out to join their fellows.

Far, far ahead, the cries of the city-dwellers rose faintly on the winds. They had been stunned to hear the many bells; and they had been shattered to hear what none living had heard before: the awful thunder of those opening Gates. Now they turned and raised their cries, as if the end of the world had come. And they fled. But they fled too few and too late, impeding one another's progress in their haste; and behind them rode the barbarians, like a black tide.

Up side streets, down alleyways rode the barbarians, killing all who dared stand in their way, until none would stand before them, but all fled. And laughing like demons from God's own darkness, they trampled to death those who did not flee quickly enough.

Swiftly they swept through the vast city.

They entered a palace here, a temple there. Nothing was sacred to them, nothing safe from the savagery of their lust. They no longer resembled the hunters and fishermen who attended tribal councils. Now they were like madmen. They emerged from burning buildings with chests of gold, gowns of saffron silk, the ancient treasures of centuries of profitable trade. They heaped the relics in the middle of the bloodied streets, heedless of damage, and returned for more. Great casks of aged wine they found and swilled wastefully, they who had never tasted better than harsh brown beer. Caps, jeweled slippers, and ceremonial robes of state they took—women and girls, golden chalices, fragile porcelain statuary, tapestries, gold-bound books, necklaces, arm bands, rubies, frontals crusted with gems, diamonds, emeralds, silver, gold. And when the palaces were emptied of all loot, they put them to the torch. In only a short time there were a half-score fires blazing about the city, and black choking smoke waving this way and that with the winds.

Great statues they threw cords about, and pulled down with a crash. Precious works of art, valued at beyond the imaginings of any not born to wealth, were strewn in the dirt, trampled underfoot, burned amidst shouts of glee. Palely delicate frescoes painted on banquet walls by masterful hands long ago were splashed black-red with the drying mess of human entrails, with brains smashed out in ungovernable fury. Then what remained of the paintings were ruined by the smoke of fires consuming the palaces of the once mighty.

All resistance was gone. The city lay fully in the grip of the barbarians. And still they would not pause. They rode their ponies, raped the women, burned the palaces of red stone. Centuries of suppression, of the hard hopeless life eked out on the stony cold ground of the North, where a woman might hope to have one child out of three live to grow his first teeth and where a man might survive only so long as he was ruthless and could kill without a tear— these now blossomed in the brown flower of hatred, and were spent viciously in thoughtless, lustfully cruel acts of destruction. Soon the entire city was ablaze, bathed in heat and roaring red light. It was full of the sounds of the victims crying their last, futile cries for mercy. It was drenched in sweat and blood, and it was pungent with the hideous odors of burning flesh and hair, sweat from blackened armpits, and blood. Everywhere there was blood.

And through it all rode Ara-Karn with Gundoen beside him and, somewhat behind, Kuln-Holn and the bodyguard. Ara-Karn looked about him at the spectacle of the destruction of the works of centuries. His face was stained in sweat, bathed in lambent firelight.

That aristocratic face was raised slightly. The lips were parted, the dark beard glossy; the eyes sparkled with the strange jade fire. His nostrils flared pleasurably in the stench; his elbows swung somewhat by his sides to a certain rhythm. He held his pony in fierce check almost unconsciously, with a mind only for the tumultuous carnage surrounding him. And his cheeks puffed and fell now and then, as if he held a light merry tune upon his tongue.

Kuln-Holn could now behold him only with a shudder.

The former fisherman took no delight in those scenes of pillage. His was a peaceful spirit, and his dreams partook of that spirit. He had dreamed of glory and prosperity, but never of how to get them. In his dreams the rosy times somehow just magically came to pass. Yet was he certain that this was not the only road to them. Surely She would have no need to gain respect through blood and terror, as if She were no better than a petty chief whose people detested him. But then he thought, Perhaps these people have been wicked, and this is how She punishes them. Perhaps Ara-Karn had been sent here as Her scourge. That thought heartened him somewhat, though he did not fully believe it.

They rode past a temple of brown stone, whence issued screams of agony and death. Ara-Karn bent over to Gundoen and murmured something, chuckling softly at his own words. Gundoen frowned and looked down at the stones of the street, saying nothing. Kuln-Holn thought, Even the great hunter is disgusted at these scenes. What sort of man can it be who takes delight in them?

They rode down the firelit street. Kuln-Holn shut his ears to the inhuman screams of the brutalized priestesses of Goddess. All he could think was that they must have been wicked indeed to merit such awful punishment as this. And he repeated this thought to himself thrice over, until the screams of the priestesses were lost in the roar of the burning buildings.

Riders crossed their path: Gen-Karn and a handful of

Orn warriors. Kuln-Holn saw Gundoen's hand tighten on the hilt of his sword, as if the chief expected some trouble. But Gen-Karn did not heed. He rode swaying on the back of his large pony, a bottle of wine in one hand, the other pinioning the hands of a naked wench lying belly-down on the back of his pony, her long golden hair concealing her features.

"Ho, Ara-Karn!" roared the chief of the Orns. "Hail to the Warlord of the North!"

Ara-Karn, to Kuln-Holn's surprise, smiled as good-humoredly as if to the companion of his heart. "Hail to the chief of Orn," he said, touching his brow with two fingers in salute.

Gen-Karn swilled at the bottle, smacked the woman's round rump, and roared his approval. "Here's a fine feast for my eyes! Lead us so, Ara-Karn, and I'll be your man for life!" He waved the arm with the wine bottle at the crumbling ruins, the bodies choking the streets, the burning portals. He drank in the fulfillment of his long-awaited vengeance as eagerly as he had swilled the fine wine.

"Enjoy the sight to its fullest, Gen-Karn," the Warlord said calmly. "This will be the last city we take thus." He seemed gray and drained of a sudden.

Gen-Karn frowned his confusion. Then he laughed roaringly and pinched the poor girl's buttocks until she cried out. "Hail, Ara-Karn!" he shouted.

"May Ara-Karn be damned!" cried a terrible voice. "May his loins wither like dried grapes! May his hair fall with his teeth to the ground. May She curse him and his name forever more!"

From the blackened ruins of a building came a haggard figure. Her hair was gray, loose but clotted with dried blood. Her robes were torn and darkened with filth, exposing pale bent legs. She stepped from the smoking shadows, and her eyes blazed with reflected flames.

"Curse you, Ara-Karn," she cried huskily. "Goddess, hear my prayer! Bring down such shadowed doom upon this man's head that he shall be an example for all the ages yet to come!"

Kuln-Holn shuddered at these terrible curses. For even through the blood and filth he could see that her robes were those of a Priestess of the Goddess, those who dedicated their maidenheads to Her. She had been virgin and inviolate—until now, when black-hated barbarians had stormed the city, sparing not even the temples. And her gray eyes gleamed with a holy flame.

Ara-Karn looked down upon the helpless, abject, pious figure; and it seemed to Kuln-Holn that the enjoyment had returned to his features. "Take her," he said.

Gundoen stared at his Warlord. "Do you not see what she is?" he muttered.

"Take her," shouted Ara-Karn.

The guards laid hands upon the shrieking creature. They dragged her to where two pillars stood together in the remains of a charred building. Only what had been of stone, like the pillars, remained to mark where the house had stood. The broken-off stones jutted against the sky, stained black with the smoke, like two inhuman idols.

The guards bound the priestess by cords to the two pillars. Her arms were stretched apart and the cords cut into the flesh of her thin wrists. They bound her swinging ankles to the pillars at the base. She tried to kick and spit at them while they tied her. Even then she struggled, damning forever the name of Ara-Karn.

"The only way to hang a wench," Gen-Karn approved drunkenly.

Ara-Karn ignored him. He was as calm and as stiff as ice. To the guards he directed, "Now kill her."

But at this the guards hung back. They looked at each other, then dropped their gazes. "She is a priestess," one muttered, still ashen at her curses.

"And I a god," replied Ara-Karn. "Now will you obey me?"

But they said, "Lord, we cannot."

"Gen-Karn, will you do this thing?"

Gen-Karn considered for a moment. He shook his head. "She's your wench," he said drunkenly. But even the Orn chief seemed afraid.

"Lord," pleaded Kuln-Holn, taking some hope, "can this be a part of your mission? Surely she cannot have sinned so—"

But Ara-Karn was not listening to the words of his prophet. He was looking at the swaying holy woman, his face growing hard. He looked round, and for one terrifying moment his gaze rested upon Kuln-Holn. But then the eyes passed on by and sought out Gundoen. "And you, my father," he said harshly. "Can you do it?"

Gundoen looked upon the shrieking woman. "Why?" he grumbled.

"Because it pleases me. Will you do it?"

He turned away. "Not I."

"Well then." He swung from the saddle-blanket and drew his long bright sword. Until then the Warlord had done no fighting; the beautiful blade and the hilt of Tont-Ornoth were still bright and clean. He approached the holy woman at such an angle that she could not spit at him or kick him with her blackened feet.

"May your own God damn you in darkness, Ara-Karn!" she screamed. "May you never know contentment! May you be gorged on the blood you spill! May you fall at the very summit of your conquests!"

He drew back the long bright blade.

"May you be your own enemy! May your own woman be your death!"

Her words ceased suddenly. They became choked, then turned to howls of mortal pain.

The bright blade bit into her torso.

Ara-Karn stood before her, his feet planted wide in a woodsman's stance. He worked the sword as a woodcutter would wield his axe. And he hewed at her thin soft belly. The filthy gray robes became sodden with a darker, greasy liquid.

For some moments he worked. Then the blade snapped through the bones of her spine. Her lower half fell away to the ground. Only the chest and arms and lolling head were left suspended, swinging, from the cords. From the severed, gaping trunk gushed forth a sudden outpouring of blood and organs, emptying in a bright mound on the ground next to the stilled legs.

Ara-Karn stepped back, looked up to heaven, and sighed.

Kuln-Holn, Gundoen, Gen-Karn, and the guards looked on with blank, astounded faces.

Ara-Karn turned and put the blade back. He seemed suddenly old and very weary. He mounted his pony once more. The front of his chest, his legs, face, and beard were bespattered with blood. He did not bother to wipe it off.

"By the jade sword of God!" swore Gundoen, staring at the mound of squirming entrails. Kuln-Holn could not look. He had not even been able to bear to see the first stroke fall. Yet in his ears he could still hear the obscene sounds of the hacking blade, the gusher of blood. He felt dizzy in the saddle, as if about to retch.

Even the hardened Gen-Karn was moved. Without a word he dropped the wine bottle and flung the golden-haired wench to the ground. She whimpered, looking about her fearfully, then fled into the shadows. Gen-Karn did not heed. He turned his pony and rode off, his warriors following him, looking back in horror on the ghastly scene.

Ara-Karn put his heels to his pony and rode on down the firelit street. The others, still staring with horror upon the swinging remains, did not start after him at once. Then they came somewhat to themselves again and followed him in silence. When Kuln-Holn could again summon the courage to look at his master, he saw the darkened outline moving slowly against the red flames. But now the head was no longer lifted, and the elbows did not swing rhythmically, and the cheeks no longer puffed and fell with the merry tune.

Not even Gundoen seemed to wish to come up abreast of the Warlord now; they all rode some two-score paces behind him, still in utter silence.

A desperate cry sounded from ahead.

Kuln-Holn looked up. He saw a black shape leaping from a darkened alleyway, longsword in hand. It leaped upon the other black shape of Ara-Karn, knocking it from horseback. The two shapes rolled and struggled in the broken, bloodstained streets, becoming one in darkness, no longer distinguishable from where Kuln-Holn, Gundoen, and the guards were.

Gundoen spurred his pony forward. He shot to where, ahead, one of the figures was rising above the other slowly, longsword lifted on high. The chief drove his pony crashing against the man, knocking him a dozen paces to the ground. The guards came up and pinioned the attacker viciously. When Kuln-Holn reined up, he saw that the man was young and handsome. His chin was smoothly shaven, and the rags upon his naked limbs had once been fineries. He might have been a prince of this land before Ara-Karn had come.

"I am well," said the Warlord to their eager questions, rising to his feet. "But what have we here?" Kuln-Holn was shocked to hear what seemed like humor in his master's voice.

"A young Gerso nobleman, for the look of him," Gundoen muttered savagely. "We should not have ridden so far behind you, lord. Forgive me. It shall not occur again." He looked at the youth with fury in his light eyes. "Shall we kill him?"

"Let me speak with him first." Of them all, only Ara-Karn seemed calm—as if he had not been the one just attacked in the very shadow of death. He approached the boy, who was still struggling, fiercely but futilely, against the arms of his captors. The hardness upon the Warlord's face melted away as he gazed upon the stranger. He smiled.

"You are rather young to play an assassin's role, are you not? How many winters have you, boy?"

The boy snarled savagely, his eyes slits of hatred.

"From your rags, you appear well born. Was your family wealthy?"

The boy kicked against the guards, but they held him firmly.

"Yes, no doubt wealthy. Titled also," calmly resumed Ara-Karn. "Tell me, were you happy? . . . Still you will not speak? Well, deeds are the finest language. Your home is here in the city? Well, of that place that holds so many happy memories there remains only so much ash and blackened stone. You can never go there again. But if you could—would you ever be happy there again, do you think?"

The boy only grunted in his struggles to be free.

Ara-Karn smiled kindly, sadly. "I will answer for you. You could not. There is no going back to what you were before. So you hate me, boy?"

Still there was no answer. But now a savage gleam of hard humor lighted the slits of his eyes.

"Yes, I see. So you can understand this tongue after all. Will you join me, then, and be my lieutenant?"

"Lord!" protested Gundoen; but the Warlord silenced him with an impatient wave of his hand.

The boy spat at Ara-Karn. The white spittle mixed with the priestess' blood on the glossy dark beard.

Ara-Karn smiled more broadly. "So. And your mother, boy," he said suddenly. "Where is she?"

Then it broke from the exhausted youth—a cry of despair and anguish—"Dead!"

"And your father?"

"Dead!"

"Brothers?"

A sigh. "Dead too."

"Any sisters?"

Anger flared again. "Dead, damn you, or—"

"—Or being raped by my soldiers. She must have been pretty, then. Or perhaps not. My men were never too very particular."

The boy screamed his anguish and tried to bite the arms that held him. "Damn you!" he cried. "Damn you! Damn you!"

"Lord," Kuln-Holn asked, swallowing with difficulty, "is all of this necessary?"

"Yes," broke in Gundoen with heat. "Hasn't the lad suffered enough? Kill him cleanly and have done."

"Kill him?" queried the Warlord, his voice rising. "Be sure I'll not be so kind. What is kindness to me? And when have I ever cried, 'Enough'? Why, I intend to let him go free."

"Free!" cried Kuln-Holn.

"As free as he may ever be now," said Ara-Karn.

"This is madness," groaned Gundoen. "Can you not see the look in his eyes? His hatred for you is greater than any feeling he has had before in his life. It must be greater even than that of his first love affair—that is, if one so young has had a love affair yet. If you free him, he will be your unremitting enemy as long as he lives."

The Warlord of the far North looked his general calmly in the eye and said softly, "Yes?" And such was the look in those dark eyes that the chief was forced to look away, a deep disgust growing in his simple heart.

"Set him on a horse," commanded Ara-Karn in that soft, calm tone that admitted no disobedience. Swiftly it was done. The stupefied youth ceased all his strugglings when he found himself astride one of the guard's ponies.

"See that he has weapons," added the Warlord.

"Weapons!" swore Gundoen to the smoky skies.

"And enough provisions to last several passes' ride," Ara-Karn continued, as if Gundoen had not spoken. "Go on—no need to worry about the young lord. He will not attempt another foolhardy attack. He is growing up now. He knows that vengeance tastes best when cold."

The Warlord mounted his own pony. He brought it next to the boy's, head to tail, so that the two men both sat abreast and faced in opposite directions. They were so close that their knees brushed against each other. In one swift thrust, executed so skillfully that none of the guards could have stopped it, the young Gerso could have whipped out his dagger and stabbed Ara-Karn in the chest, thereby exchanging lives. Or he might have brought up the leather reins in his hands and strangled the older man. But the boy, seemingly bemused by all that was happening, seemed not to think of either of these things.

Ara-Karn leaned back, regarding the boy. His posture was relaxed and insolent, as if he only sat before a mirroring pool and not some deadly enemy.

"Boy," whispered Ara-Karn so softly that only the two of them and Kuln-Holn, who had ridden closer in order to protect his master, could hear it. "Boy—until this pass that is all you have been—a young and foolish boy, who has done nothing but play in the sunlight. Now, however, you are a man, for you have a purpose—something only a few ever attain. Most men live and die frivolously, never knowing the darkness of being a god, of seeing a goal that justifies their lives, that makes their existence real. Only a few know that shadowed joy, and of those few only the rarest handful ever attain the heart's dark desire.

"Now you have such a goal, and I wish you luck sincerely. Feel all of that hatred inside you, savor its acrid sweetness—and then you will know what it is to be fully alive. There will be sleeps when you cannot rest for the hatred of me—when your dreams will be full of the sight of your father dying, of the sound of your sister being raped. Listen to those screams, boy. Perhaps, even now, your sister cries out. When my men—and I have many, many men—have finished with her, if she retains any of her prettiness, she may live as one of their concubines. Then they will cast bones to see which one will claim her. If she is no longer pretty, and few are very pretty after such an ordeal as that, they may keep her as a cook-slave. Or perhaps they will have pity upon her and only cut her throat. Perhaps she is already dead, one more blackened corpse among so many corpses, with dark bloody bruises staining her once-soft thighs."

The boy moaned, shutting his eyes fast, but Ara-Karn gripped his arm with fingers of iron, so that he must open his eyes. And he gazed into those eyes with that gaze so like a Madpriest's that the boy's outcry was stifled for very fear.

"Now you begin to feel it," breathed the Warlord, releasing his grip. "Good! Savor the hatred and the fear, boy. Court them elegantly as some nobly born whore, and take them for your own. Live for them, breathe through them, dine with one, sleep upon the other. Let them be the shadow of your companion, and aways follow whither they may lead. Do you hear, boy?—always. Now go. We shall meet again."

The boy, as if in a dream, lifted the reins. Then he hesitated. His eyes ringed his foes questioningly.

"Go on," growled Ara-Karn irritably. "Do you think that if I'd meant to kill you I'd have wasted so many words? Be off with you!" He swatted the flank of the boy's horse with his jade dagger, hard, and the pony started off.

One more glance back the boy gave them, a glance of terror and despair. Then he set his heels to the pony, urging it to a furious gallop. Soon his figure was lost in the smoke and the glare of the fires. Shortly thereafter even the ring of his hooves on the broken stone streets was gone.

"Lord, I can have two riders after him in a word, both excellent bowmen," Gundoen said. "They can be ordered to slay him before he reaches the outskirts of the city."

"No," replied the Warlord in a voice grown suddenly very old and very tired. "No. He shall have free passage from the lands of his enemies this first time. It is the only thing any of us may hope for. Afterward, if you ever see him again, I give you leave to kill him at your leisure."

The boy rode as fast as he could urge the steed onward. They flew so fast that the walls of smoke billowing around them seemed like only storm clouds driven by the winter winds. Shortly he passed beyond the shattered city walls and descended into the broad green plains south of the city. In the fields he could see the dark masses of the barbarians heaping great mounds of loot from the burning city, savage victory-chants rumbling from their throats.

The boy rode past them, his eyes half closed. He rode up the road to the rolling hills beyond. Everywhere he looked, he saw the streams of refugees, fleeing in terror to the South. He shuddered to see them: to him it now became real that there was no longer any city called Gerso.

He paused on the crest of the hill opposite to the rift in the mountain where the ruins of the city were nestled, and panted, exhausted for the ordeal he had passed through. He wiped at the sweat upon his brow. Streaks of grime smeared on the back of his hand. He gazed back upon the city of his childhood for a long time.

By now almost all of the city was in flames. Great billows of black smoke rose between the mountain peaks that had once seen great Elna build the city. The smoke rose in a curling column drifting slowly to the South, a shadow as of a tremendous army below it. Through the pillar of smoke Goddess could be seen faintly lambent, as if fitfully asleep and dreaming a nightmare of destruction and personal torment. The boy wept.

A voice brought him out of his revery.

"It is not a pretty sight, is it? And I fear that there will be other such sights before too long."

Two men on horseback were behind him. They led several other men and pack-ponies burdened with supplies and goods. The boy recognized the bearded one as the famous merchant, Zelatar Bonvis. The other was the merchant's apprentice, Mergo Donato.

"We were still preparing our train of goods to trade with the barbarians," said Zelatar, his lips evincing a sour humor. "Now it seems that the barbarians have come to us." He too looked sadly on the ruined city.

"What was it you said, Zelatar?" asked the apprentice hurtfully. "Did you not say that when we came back this spring not even the name of that man would be remembered?"

"So I did," sighed the bearded merchant. "Now instead of dying, as he ought, he seems to have infected the entire North with his madness. Well, did I not also say beware if the tribes should mass?" He turned his gaze upon the youth. "Young man, you seem to have been of a good house. I seem to recognize you from somewhere. You are one of the few we have seen who had the foresight and levelheadedness to prepare his bags before he flew. We are traveling South. I know many houses where my father traded there. Perhaps we will even go eventually to Tarendahardil, the seat of the great Empire. Not even the barbarians will follow us so far. Will you travel with us, at least part of the way?"

Dumbly, the young man nodded.

The merchant brought his horse about. "Forget about that city of Gerso," he said over his shoulder. "It may once have been home, but it is no longer. There are many cities scattered about the round world, my boy."

Slowly they wended their way down the far side of the green hill to find the road again. They saw the ruins rise and fall back forever behind the hill; only the smoke remained. They traveled Southward, underneath the shadow of that pillar of black smoke, which still obscured the dreaming Goddess.

CHAPTER NINETEEN

Aftermath

The waves broke steeply against the rocky headlands, but within the bay the waters were calm. Goddess gazed down calmly and beautifully upon the tranquil scene, resting Her cheek occasionally upon the soft pillow of a high, fluffy cloud. Along the sandy, pebbly shore, above the high-water marks, the many fishing boats lay side by side in a long mute line. In the bounding stream among the rocks of the southern arm of land, a few women washed clothes and stretched them on the rocks to dry. Nearby some little children, rejoicing in their nakedness, ran and played. Some carrion birds walked the shore of the bay, hungrily inspecting the masses of wrack and driftage there.

In the sandy square below the chief's hut other women met, and other children hung upon their skirts. A few old, old men, purblind and large-jointed, sat upon stones, dozing in the sun. They were the only men who could be seen in the entire village. It was very calm and restful there. And lonely, too; there seemed to be more huts than was necessary just for the women and the children and the old, old men.

On the broad veranda of the chief's hut, the important women of the tribe were gathered. They mended tunics and repaired implements. Some held babes to their breasts.

"Ah, how quiet it is here now," sighed one of them.

"When, when do you think they will return?" asked another. She was young, and very pretty, and, by her dress, unmarried.

"Not soon," answered Hertha-Toll.

"This I will miss," said another. "The grand preparing for the great Hunt. There was good food then, and dancing. My man would always look so brave! Unless, Hertha, you think they will perhaps be back in time?"

Hertha-Toll shook her head. "No, there will be no Hunt this year," she said. "Nor the next, nor the one after. Perhaps there will never be another. Our men hunt other things than bandar pelts now. All, all is changed."

"Changed to the better, I think," said Turin Tim, setting Bart-Karan again upon her lap. "My Garin will not die. Great will be our fortune, when all our men return."

"I miss them," wailed Alli. Her hair was not so finely looked to as it used to be, and her hips were rounder, softer.

"A dream I had, when the God rose," Hertha-Toll announced. "It seemed to me the sea ran back, and all the earth beneath our village rose up, so that we lived as if on a great mountain and looked down on the peak of Karri-Moldole. Then a beautiful woman dressed in rags came to me and gave me a golden ring, and said it was the gift of her husband, and that he wished that I should have its keeping for a time. Then I heard a dim voice on the wind, and it wailed, 'The Gates! The Gates! The Gates are open!' And that was a merchant's voice."

"What does it mean?" asked the other women eagerly.

Hertha-Toll sighed, and shook her head. "It was true, but I knew not a tenth part of its meaning. Still, this much I gathered: that our men have fought in Gerso and gained a victory upon the cityfolk."

Great were the relief and rejoicing of the other women at this, and they clamored for more knowledge of Hertha-Toll, bidding her tell them whether this man or that had survived the fighting and who had won the greatest honor? But Hertha-Toll would not answer, saying that such details were not a part of her dream.

"Yet what of the riches they will send us?" asked Turin Tim. "Surely you could see what wealth will be ours out of this?"

Hertha-Toll looked deep into the eyes of Turin Tim, so that after a moment the younger woman looked down, much ashamed. Hertha-Toll looked very weary then, and older than her years.

After a time, one of the women remarked that the weather had been mild this year. Then Hertha-Toll brightened and said, "Yes, and I think we will get no more storms this season. Winter for this year has passed. It was not a bad winter this year, I think. Not too many of our children died."

"Then must we clear the fields again and plant the grains and vegetables again, as if nothing had happened and our men had not conquered Gerso?" Turin Tim asked sullenly.

"Of course," answered Hertha-Toll, standing and entering her husband's hall, the hall of Tont-Ornoth. "We still must eat."

In a hollow on the sunward side of the valley below the burning city a dozen of the comeliest enslaved women and a score of the hardiest males were slain amidst grateful prayers to dark God. A man from every tribe was there, and each wielded a knife. They cut the limbs piecemeal and strewed the bits among the stones. The hearts and livers and stomachs and genitals they bore down to the valley's end in a great brazen cauldron. There the green fields of the lowlands had their start, and there the entrails were spilled forth. So might God, scenting the savor and hungering for more, lead His avid followers to where the reek should lead. And the winds blew the smoke asunder, and the curved face of God shone forth directly overhead, sharp as a new-cleaned knife. And that was held the finest of omens. The sacrificers held their gleaming knives aloft and rode their ponies back. The smoke was driven together again, and the lurid flames of the conquered city lighted up the savage, drunken warriors as if they stood again on Urnostardil.

Below the burning city the many thousands of tents, ponies, warriors, and captives ran in a great ragged ring between the jutting mountains' arms. Wild laughter and roars of triumph sang out from that ring, and half-choked screams. In the center of the ring was a hill, and it was all of the looted treasures of the city. Gen-Karn the chief of Orn climbed upon that hill, swearing and singing by turns. By him were some of his men, wiping wine-lees from the blood-clotted tangles of their beards.

Gen-Karn spread out his arms and took in the whole of

the soft-curving green land. "Now behold, and tremble," Gen-Karn roared upon that land. "We are returned! The Gates of Gerso are no more! Will you hide? Where will you hide that we shall not find you? The Tribes ride, and the Spine is shattered!"

Below him, the warriors danced with the enslaved city-women, laughed, and drank more wine, their fists filled with slabs of roasted hams and gherwons and neats. The beat of the great drums took away even their roars of triumph here, even the screams of the captives. Chained, degraded merchants were slain here and there for sport, or for annoyance, or for the example of their fellows; and the fallen bodies were kicked about among the dancers until the other captives caught them up and laid them piteously upon the hill of plunder. Over battered armor costly silks were draped, rent and stained; plumed caps were stretched over the ragged curls of great-maned men. Surely not ever in the cold far North had there been a feast the equal of this!

But when hands were laid upon the treasures, then quarrels broke out among the feasters. Foul oaths arose, and fighting. In but moments the drums were ceased and the dancing women scattered. And the flame-lit warriors— not sated yet on blood and recalling, perhaps, old feuds and jealousies—threw to the earth their meat and wine and drew swords, threatening to fall on one another. The fire glared evilly from their reddened, wine-wrought eyes. Gen-Karn, astride the hill, laughed, and goaded on his Orns.

Old Nam-Rog, pale faced beside the tents, went then with haste to the tent-square of Gundoen's tribe. "Gundoen!" he called out. "Gundoen, the feuds are broken out anew, and where is the Warlord?"

Gundoen burst forth of his tent knotting up his breeches. Through the open flap beyond Nam-Rog saw three naked citywomen decked in jewels, languid and wearied, lying among the furs and cushions. "What is about?" Gundoen asked angrily.

Nam-Rog led him to the ring's center. Already a dozen men lay bleeding and maimed on the ground. Gundoen strode through the crowds and hurled men from his path by the strength of his great arms. He wore no weapons; yet, even so, no man dared raise a blade against the father of Ara-Karn yet.

Gundoen climbed to the top of the treasure. He confronted Gen-Karn. "Chieftain, you sit like some unmuscled old man, taking in your water at one end while you let it out the other. Why? Bring the men to peace!"

Gen-Karn glared and shrugged. "Let them fight," said he. "By God's jade sword, it is good to fight!"

"You are drunk, old fool," growled Gundoen. He took hold of the Orn's necklet, lifted up, and threw him sprawling down the hill. He faced the feuding men below, and for a space puzzlement filled his face, and his great empty hands knotted and let go. He opened his mouth and called down on the heads of men.

"Elna," he called. "Elna, Elna, Elna . . ."

The clamor lessened, and some men looked up as if wakened from some ill sleep. But the rest brawled on. Gundoen frowned. At his feet were the bow and bird pouch of Gen-Karn. He seized them, slung the bow, and aimed an arrow down at the throng.

"By God's Eye, the next to strike a blow dies by my hand," he shouted. He was true to his word: in moments three men lay writhing on the ground amidst the blood and wine, struck through by the long arrows.

Now the fighting slacked. The wine- and death-crazed warriors looked up and saw Gundoen dark against the flames above them. The surged up around the treasure-hill, red blades in hand, glaring at the chief and muttering. But men of Gundoen's tribe leaped upon the lower slopes of the mound, ready to defend their chieftain.

"Put down your weapons," Gundoen commanded them. He stood to his full height, like a massive boulder carved and shaped by lightning blasts, ugly and forbidding against the flame-lit smoky sky. A vile oath he swore, then brought up the bow and broke it into splinters across his knee.

"Warriors," he roared hoarsely, "will you forget all your oaths? Will you slay your comrades and do the Southrons' work for them? Be sure they cannot do this thing alone! Look you there to the South! See how lovely that land lies! Tarendahardil is there, and the descendants of Elna! Is all this treasure not enough for you, that you must bicker over it? Are five women not enough for each of you?—yet what would your wives say to that? And then, if these will not content you, rest yourselves, and clean your spears and swords, and put new points on your arrows —and we will go and get you more!"

There was laughter at his words. The beastlike fury faded from the eyes of men. They looked upon the pile before them, turned, and looked through the tents to the South. Gen-Karn, looking evilly at Gundoen's back, staggered down and went with his men to their tents and women. Some men grew sleepy-drunk with the great amounts of wine sloshing in their bellies; others grew saddened, and wept at the memory of Urnostardil, the Last Stand. They settled themselves to count their gains, orderly now. And at that somewhat of an uneasy peacefulness drifted down upon the great ringed camp.

Gundoen sat down heavily on the hill and scratched some crusted blood from his eyelid. Roughly he shook his head, the way a wet dog will, rousing pain to wake himself. Aways overhead the banks of smoke flowed down from the burning city, down the valley, between the mountains and beyond. Gundoen leaned back his head dizzily, and for a moment it was to him as if the world stood head-over-hands and the smoke were a choked barren river drawing them down between the mountains; only Gundoen, lying on the treasure, was somehow held against it. He thought idly of the citywomen in his tent. They beckoned him and filled him with desire, but he despised them. They were artful and skillful in their ways; they had known wealth and ease and all that that brought. Yet what had they to say to him, or he to them?

The green, lush lands beyond the mountains called him. Rich they were, and fabulous in his mind. He saw towers of gold and alabaster, weapons beautiful as jewels, carpets, tunics woven so fine they hung upon the limbs gently as dale-dew, fields of grapes and herb, warm beaches, great sea-craft, palaces great as villages. The many cities formed a line, like sandbars in the river of ash. So many of them there were, so many . . . so many tens of thousands of foes to overcome. . . . He thought of the sinuous women in his tent and his wearied loins began to ache. Almost he could have wished he might be back again in his own village, where he was a chief, and where he might upon each waking feast his eyes upon the bones of all the champions his strength had overborne.

"O Hertha," he muttered, "Hertha, you too were lovely once. Why did you change?—and why was your belly cursed?"

*   *   *

The city burned on between the mountains. Behind the bulky figure of the chief, Kuln-Holn the Pious One clambered uncertainly up the pile. Darker than shadows were the two of them, soot-stained against the flaring city.

"Gundoen," Kuln-Holn called plaintively. "Gundoen, where is Ara-Karn?"

The chief did not move at first, so Kuln-Holn must repeat his question. Then the chief's head rose and he looked around. Their eyes met, and for the first time in the lives of these men, so different in their ways, a look of fellowship, sympathy—of understanding, even—passed between them. Gundoen's eyes were worried also. He shook his head and reared one massive, sweat- and blood-streaked arm. He pointed behind Kuln-Holn into the center of the flames.

"He is—*there*."

Anxiously Kuln-Holn mounted the ashy slope, fast as his weary legs might bear him. Before him the city blazed. The narrowing rocky cliffs roofed over with smoke reminded him of a dream he once had had, an ill dream of captivity and fruitless sufferings. Great fragile flakes of ash fell over him, burnt bitter raindrops. He came to the limits of the city, where the flames rose; for a moment the very spirit within Kuln-Holn quailed, and he desired greatly to turn back among the tents. But thither had his master gone, and there too must Kuln-Holn be. Kuln-Holn wrapped his cloak over his body to above his mouth and struggled up.

Through his shoes he felt the heat of the stone-paved thoroughfare. He cast his eyes about. There was no movement save for the flames: they rose up all about him, great blinding veils. Hot winds swirled about, clawing him. Dizzily he went forward, choking on the fumes. He ran alongside streams of boiling water. His eyes were burning, baked too dry now to weep. How was it that anything might abide alive in this?

"Master!" he cried, his voice lost in the cloak. "Master!"

Only the flames answered him. Half blinded, he thought he saw a thing ahead of him, dark and tall and steadfast. He made out a rider on horseback. "Master!" Kuln-Holn wailed, but the rider was only an ancient statue of Elna in a square, headless and scarred.

Darkness found the eyes of Kuln-Holn. His woolen cloak was smoldering in his nose. He went on fiercely. So many streets—had he lost his way? Behind him a roof fell crashing into the tempest of flame where once a happy family had dwelt. Kuln-Holn ran at the sound. Now he knew he could not turn back but must win the far side of the city. That or perish here. "Goddess, dear Lady," he groaned, "aid me, please help me!" The Governor-General's palace reared blazing before him. Kuln-Holn staggered by. The fire opened before him, and Kuln-Holn crawled through, his hands blistering on the stones' heat. He fell and, gasping, terror-borne, rose.

Far away overhead it seemed to him he saw a figure—a little upright thing upon the high framing of the Gates, there where it spanned like a bridgeway the gap between the mountains.

In the barracks room it was dark, and Kuln-Holn could at first see little. Wearily he mounted the time-hollowed stone steps, coming at last to a narrow wooden doorway a little open. Kuln-Holn pulled aside the door and ventured forth.

Through the Pass the cool winds streamed soothingly, flowing like the potions of Hertha-Toll upon the tortured body of the Pious One. Swiftly the airs ran, so high above the earth; yet for all that sweet. Upon either hand the deep Pass gaped for him. Dizzily he ventured forth across the narrow stone walkway and neared the upright figure.

"Lord," he said, "all the warriors feast below in the honor you have brought them. They fought, but now make merry. You should behold the treasure they have got! Now surely all the tribes may be wealthy and at peace. We may be content now, Lord, is it not so?"

There was no answer from the other. Slowly and strangely the head came round. The gusting winds tore at the long hair, concealing and unmasking the face of Ara-Karn. That was black with soot. Sparks glowed still in his cloak and tunic; even his beard was singed and smoking. In his hand he lightly held his dagger, and Kuln-Holn thought of the sacrifice they had made below. On the stones beside his master's feet lay the sword, dark still with the priestess' life. He stood with his legs wide-planted, the toes of his boots just over the edge of the stone, his arms held somewhat out. Below him the huge Gates were outflung to embrace the burning city; the fire leapt high in maddened dance. As a man returned from a long fruitless hunt in the snowy gloom of winter, whose eyebrows and beard are thick with rime, will stand over the hearth-fire gratefully and happily and warm his chill hands a little: so stood Ara-Karn, and held his arms out somewhat. The lurid gleams lighted up his frontward half like red gold in a smith's brick-pit: all but his eyes. He looked toward his prophet, but Kuln-Holn knew not if he saw him. His eyes, open as a statue's, were flat and pale, like little cups of greenish milk. There was no joy or anger, hatred or longing in those eyes: only curiosity, and a monstrous wonder, as it were to say, So.

"Lord," said Kuln-Holn haltingly, "now the merchants who have robbed us are punished, and the city of the wicked laid to naught. The tribes are one. Wealth beyond my telling is ours. Is this not all you were bidden to? What is yet to do?"

The face of Ara-Karn returned to the burning city. The flames leapt and danced and roared as though to pay him, their liberator, homage. He said, so faintly Kuln-Holn could scarcely hear him, "And how does it please you, Kuln-Holn, to see what you have wrought?"

"Lord, I will not take Her work away from Her. I was no better than a knot in the handle of Her hammer. Yet surely it cannot be denied Her wrath is no little thing."

The Warlord had no words to that. Then it was, an overbearing weariness came upon Kuln-Holn, and he curled up on the stones away from the edge and slept.

When he woke, there was a stiffness in his back. There was a foulness in his mouth as well, a taste like burning he thought he had forgotten. He looked up the twisting Pass. Just a little of the pine trees could he see from here. The sky looked good to bring out the fish from their catch-holes. He wondered how Turin Tim did, and how much little Bart-Karan had grown. He turned back his head gently. He saw his master standing at the lip of the stone, his legs wide-planted, even as before. Kuln-Holn rose. The ruins of the city below were dark now, and consumed. Only a few embers yet glowed in those rocky ash-fields that had once been Gerso, city of merchants, the northernmost fastness of the old Empire of Elna. Through the pale haze of smoke Kuln-Holn could see the treasure-mound much diminished, and the many tents, and the green valley beyond. A road cut the fields, and Kuln-Holn bethought himself of all those who had fled.

"Lord," he said unthinkingly, "that thing that you did to the boy—was it right?"

Ara-Karn looked back, stooped, and picked up and sheathed his sword. So Kuln-Holn saw his face and was comforted, for it was again the face of a mortal man.

"It is what I have done."

So saying, the Warlord of the far North went across the warm stones toward the dark doorway, down to the army awaiting him.